C.L. Taylor  of *The*
Accident, T.. .., . r books
have sold over a mi ve been
..1 Bristol with

...uer and son.

By the same author:

The Accident
The Lie
The Missing
The Escape

THE
TREATMENT

C. L. TAYLOR

ONE PLACE. MANY STORIES

HQ
An imprint of HarperCollinsPublishers Ltd
1 London Bridge Street
London SE1 9GF

This hardback edition 2017
1
First published in Great Britain by
HQ, an imprint of HarperCollinsPublishers Ltd 2017

ISBN: 978-0-00-824056-1

MIX
Paper from
responsible sources
FSC
www.fsc.org
FSC™ C007454

This book is produced from independently certified FSC™ paper
to ensure responsible forest management.

For more information visit: www.harpercollins.co.uk/green

Printed and bound in Great Britain by
CPI Group (UK) Ltd, Croydon, CR0 4YY

For my niece Sophie Taylor

Chapter One

They're still following me. I can hear their footsteps. They think I can't hear them because I put my headphones on the second I walked through the school gates. But they're not plugged in. I heard every word they said as I walked down Somerset Road.

'Why are you walking so fast, Drew? Don't you want to talk to us?'

'She can't hear us.'

'Yes she can.'

'Oi, Drew. Andrew!'

Lacey and her gang of sheep think it winds me up, calling me Andrew, they think it's funny. I don't. My dad gave me my name because my hazel eyes and chubby cheeks reminded him of the child actress in the film *E.T.* He thought it was a pretty name, unusual too. Drew Finch. My name is all I've got to remember him by other than a folder of digital photographs on my computer.

Mum doesn't talk about Dad any more – she hasn't since she married Tony. Mason, my fifteen-year-old brother, refuses to talk about Dad too. Not that Mason's here to chat to. He's been sent to a school hundreds of miles away, hopefully to learn how to stop being so irritating. It's weird, my brother not being at home. He was never much of a conversationalist but God was he noisy. He'd bang and crash his way into the house, kick his shoes off, stomp up the stairs and then slam his door. Then his music would start up. It's eerie how quiet it is now. I can hear myself breathe. I think the silence unsettles Mum too. She's always tapping on my door, asking if I'm OK. Or maybe she feels guilty about sending Mason away.

I speed up as I reach Jackson Road. It's the quietest street on my walk home and if Lacey and the others have followed me this far it can only be because today's the day they go through with her threat. Lacey's been saying for weeks that they're going to pin me down and pull up my shirt and skirt and take photos of me with their mobile phones. I've tried talking to her. I've tried ignoring her. I've spoken to my Head of Year and we've been to mediation, but she won't leave me alone. She's clever. She never says anything in front of any of the teachers. She hasn't posted anything on social media. She hasn't touched me. But the threat's still there, hanging over me like a noose. Whenever I go into school I wonder if today's the day she'll go through it. It's not about hurting me, or even about humiliating me (although there is a bit of that). It's about fear and control. We were best friends in primary school and I was the one she opened up to when her parents were getting divorced. She's the big 'I am' at school but I know where her vulnerabilities lie. And she hates that.

I slow down as I reach the High Street and my heart stops double thumping in my chest. I'm safe now. The street's full of shoppers, drifting around aimlessly or else speed walking madly like they *must* get an avocado from the grocer's before it closes or the world will end. Someone brushes past me and

I tense, but it's just some random man with a beanie and a swallow tattooed on his neck. I glance behind me, to check that Lacey and the sheep aren't following me any more, then I reach into my pocket for my phone, select my favourite song and plug in my headphones. Just two terms of school left and I'm free. No more Lacey, no more lessons, no more –

My breath catches in my throat as my arms are pinned to my side and I'm half carried, half shoved into the side alley between Costa and WHSmith. A hand closes over my mouth as I'm bundled past a skip and forced to sit on a pile of bin bags. They've got me. They've finally made their move. But it's not Lacey or one of her cronies who forces me to the ground as I thrash and squirm and try to escape.

'It's OK. Don't be afraid.'

The woman keeps her hand tightly pressed to my mouth but her grip on my shoulder loosens, ever so slightly. Her pale blue eyes are wide and frantic and her long brown hair, pulled into a tight ponytail, is damp with sweat at the roots. There's a deep crease between her eyebrows and fine lines on either side of her mouth. She's probably as old as my mum but I'm too shocked to hit out at her. All I can do is stare.

'Drew? It is Drew, isn't it?' She glances at her hand, still covering my mouth. 'Promise me you won't scream if I take it away.'

I nod tightly, but the second she lifts her palm a scream catches in the back of my throat.

'Drew!' She smothers the sound with her hand. 'You mustn't do that. I'm trying to help you. I'm trying to help Mason.'

I tense at the mention of my brother's name. How the hell

does she know who he is? He's over two hundred miles away and we haven't heard from him in over a month.

'My name is Rebecca Cobey. Doctor Cobey,' the woman says, shuffling closer on her knees. We're completely hidden from view behind the skip but she keeps glancing nervously back towards the street as though she's scared that someone will discover us. 'I worked at the Residential Reform Academy. I was Mason's psychologist. He gave me something to give to you.'

She lets go of me and reaches into the pocket of her jeans. There's a loud bang from the street, like a car backfiring, and all the blood seems to drain from her face. I've never seen anyone look so scared. For several seconds she does nothing, she just listens, then she pulls her hand out of her pocket.

'Here,' she says in a low voice, as she thrusts a folded piece of paper at me. 'I've got to go. I can't talk. It was a risk just trying to find you.' She scrabbles to her feet and pushes a stray strand of hair behind her ear. She glances towards the street then back at me. 'I would have got him out if I could. I would have got them all out.' The word catches in her throat and she presses a hand to her mouth. 'I've said too much. I'm sorry.'

She darts out from behind the skip, sprints down the alley towards the street and turns right, disappearing from view.

I sit in stunned silence for one second, maybe two, surrounded by split bin bags and the smell of roasted coffee beans and then I launch myself up and onto my feet.

'Wait!' I shove the piece of paper into my pocket. 'Doctor Cobey, wait!'

**

I can see her long, dark ponytail bobbing above her khaki jacket as she speeds down the street ahead of me, weaving her way through shoppers, briefly stepping into the road when there are too many people to overtake on the pavement.

'Doctor Cobey!' I shout as the distance between us decreases and a stitch gnaws at my side. 'Wait!'

I am vaguely aware of people staring at me, of toddlers in buggies gesturing, of car drivers slowing to gawp, of cold air rushing against my face and my heart thudding in my ears. I don't know why I'm chasing the woman who just grabbed me, smothered me and terrified me. I was lucky she didn't hurt me, but I can't shake the feeling that if I let her get away I'll never see her again. She knows something about Mason. Something she was too afraid to tell me.

I see the car before she does. I hear the engine rev and the black flash of the bonnet as the lights change from green to amber at the crossing and Dr Cobey steps into the road. One second the car is a hundred metres away, the next it's at the crossing. The engine roars and there is a sickening thump as Dr Cobey's body flies into the air.

Chapter Two

'He didn't stop. I can't believe he didn't stop.'

'Did anyone get the registration number?'

'Don't move her! She might have broken her back.'

Within seconds a crowd gathers around Dr Cobey's body and I am shoved and pushed further and further away. I don't push back. I don't shout, cry or explain. Instead I stare at the back of the man standing in front of me. But it's not his black woolly jumper I see. Imprinted on the back of my eyelids is Dr Cobey's broken body; half on the pavement, half on the road, her legs twisted beneath her, her neck lolling to one side, her blue eyes wide and staring, a single line of blood reaching from the corner of her mouth to her jaw.

'She's not breathing.'

'I can't find a pulse.'

'Can anyone do CPR?'

The driver of the car aimed straight for her. He revved the engine. He wanted to hit her.

'She was scared. She thought someone was after her.'

'What was that, love?' A heavy-set woman in her fifties with wiry bleach-blonde hair and bright pink lipstick nudges me.

I glance at her in surprise. Did I just say that out loud?

The woman continues to stare at me but my lips feel as though they have been glued shut. She loses interest when the man on the other side of her starts shouting into his mobile phone.

'The High Street. Near M&S. Road traffic accident. It was bad. I don't know if she's breathing or not. Someone's doing CPR. He said he was a doctor.'

The crowd presses against me on all sides, gawping, commenting and speculating.

'There's still no pulse!' shouts someone near the road. 'Where's that ambulance?'

As I take a step to the side to try to force my way through the crowd someone grabs hold of my left hand. An elderly woman gazes up at me as I twist round. She's so short I can see the pink scalp beneath her fine white hair.

'My boy,' she says, squeezing my hand tightly, 'my boy was killed the same way. She will be OK, won't she?'

I'm torn. I want to check on Dr Cobey but people have started to shout the word 'dead' and the old lady holding my hand is quivering like a leaf. She looks like she's about to faint.

'Are you OK?' I ask.

She doesn't shake her head. She doesn't answer. She just keeps staring hopefully up at me, tears filling her milky eyes.

'Is there someone I could call for you? A relative, or a friend?'

She continues to look at me blankly.

I don't know how to deal with this. I glance to my right,

to where the woman with the bleach-blonde hair and pink lipstick was standing but she's disappeared, replaced by a couple of scary-looking builder types. What do adults do in this situation?

'Would you . . . would you like to sit down somewhere and have a cup of tea?'

The old woman nods. Tea, the magic word.

***

I hear the wail of the ambulance sirens as the owner leads us to a table at the back of the café. The old lady is resting her weight on my elbow, telling me that I'm 'kind, so kind'. I want to tell her that I'm not kind. That I'm selfish and ungrateful and lazy and all the other things Tony and Mum accuse me of being. I want to tell her that someone deliberately ran over Dr Cobey but I can't, not when there's a bit of colour in her cheeks and she's stopped staring at me with that weird freaked-out expression.

I wait for her to drink half a cup of tea, my feet tap-tap-tapping on the wooden flooring, as she sips, rests, sips, rests and then, when she reaches for the slice of carrot cake the café owner brought her and takes the tiniest of nibbles, I excuse myself, saying I need to use the ladies'.

I slip into the single stall toilet at the back of the café. I hold it together long enough to close the door and lock it and then I rest my arms on the wall and burst into tears. I'm still crying when I sit down on the closed toilet lid and reach into my pocket. Tears roll down my cheeks as I pull out the note that Dr Cobey thrust into my hands. They plop onto the paper as

I carefully unfold it. I read the words Mason has scribbled in blue biro. I read them once, twice, three times and the tears dry in my eyes.

I'm not sad and confused any more. I'm terrified.

Chapter Three

Help me, Drew! We're not being reformed, we're being brain-washed. Tell Mum and Tony to get me out of here. It's my turn for the treatment soon and I'm scared. Please. Please help.

My hands shake as I reread the words my brother has written. Two weeks ago he was sent to the Residential Reform Academy in Northumberland after he was excluded from his third school in as many years. My brother is a gobby loudmouth, always out with his mates causing trouble, while I like being on my own with my books and music. He speaks up, I keep my head down. We couldn't be more different. Tony, our stepdad, said the RRA was the best place for him. He said that, as well as lessons and a variety of activities, Mason would be given a course of therapeutic treatments to help him deal with his issues. He didn't mention anything about brainwashing.

As soon as I read the note I rang Mum but the call went straight to voicemail. By the time I'd got myself together enough to leave the toilet cubicle the old lady's friend had turned up at the café to take her home. She tried to offer me a tenner, to thank me for my help, but I said no and hurried out of the café, pressing my nails into my palms to try to stop myself from crying. I ran all the way home, only to find that the house was empty when I let myself in. It always is when I get back from school.

I put the note on my desk and run my hands back and forth over my face to try to wake myself up. I feel fuzzy-headed and tired after everything that's happened but there's no way I can sleep. I need to talk to someone about Mason, but who? There are a couple of girls at school that I sit with at lunch but I wouldn't call them friends. Friends trust each other and share everything. Lacey taught me what a bad idea that is.

I pull my chair closer to my desk and open my laptop. I'll talk to someone on the Internet.

But which 'me' should I be? I've got four different names that I use. There's LoneVoice, the name I chose when I was fourteen. It's a crap name, totally emo, but there was a song in the charts with a similar name and it was going round and round my head. LoneVoice is sociable me. He/she chats on music forums about singers, songs in the charts, that sort of thing. XMsZaraFoxX is feistier. She's the kick-ass main character in my favourite PS4 game *Legend of Zara* and she wades in if someone's being out of order on the gaming site. RichardBrain is serious and academic. I log on as him if I want to talk about psychology. Then there's Jake Stone. I invented him to mess with Lacey's head. She thinks he's nineteen and a model and she's a little bit in love with him.

I never set out to be a catfish. I just wanted to be anonymous, you know? I wanted to be able to chat to people without them making assumptions about me based on how

I look, how old I am, where I live and what my gender and sexuality are. The first time I joined a forum I didn't say anything. I didn't ask any questions or join in with the chat. I lurked and worked out who the funny one was, who was controversial and who was a bit of a knob. I watched how they interacted with each other, just like I watched the kids in the canteen at lunchtime.

It was my dad who got me into people watching. If I got bored in a restaurant or train station he'd gesture towards people on a different table, or standing in a huddle on the platform, and he'd ask me to guess who liked who, who had a secret crush and who felt left out. He taught me about body language, micro expressions and verbal tics. He showed me how much people give away about themselves without realizing it. I didn't realize at the time that was he teaching me psychology. That's what he did for a living. He was . . . is . . . an educational psychologist. He'd probably have a field day if he knew about my different internet 'personalities'.

I log onto the psychology site where I hang out as RichardBrain. If anyone can help me make sense of what just happened with Doctor Cobey it'll be them.

Actually, no. They'll ask me what I know about her which is precisely nothing.

Dr Rebecca Cobey

I type her name into Google and click enter. The first link is to a LinkedIn profile so I click on it and scan the page. She's a psychologist . . . blah, blah, blah . . . she worked at the University of London as a Senior Lecturer . . . responsibilities blah, blah, blah and . . . I frown. It says she left three months ago but there's no mention of where she went. No entry that says she worked at the RRA.

Were you lying to me, Dr Cobey? You had a note from Mason. How could you have got that if you weren't at Norton House too?

I stare at her profile photo. She's smiling into the camera, her brown hair long and glossy, her blue eyes sparkling. She looks so happy. So alive. And then she's not. She's lying crumpled and broken at the side of the road, staring unseeingly at the sky as blood dribbles from her mouth to her chin. I shut down the browser but the image of her lifeless face is burned into my brain. I have to find out if she's still alive.

*** *

I ring the hospitals first, asking if they've admitted anyone by the name of Dr Rebecca Cobey. The first receptionist I speak to tells me she can only release patient information to next of kin. I wait a couple of minutes then I ring back, using a different voice, and say I'm Dr Cobey's daughter. This time the receptionist tells me there's no Rebecca Cobey listed. I try the other hospital in town but they claim they don't have her either. Finally, I ring the police who confirm that there was a motor vehicle accident on the high street but they can't tell me what happened to the victim.

'I was there,' I tell the female police officer. 'The car sped up. It deliberately knocked her over.'

'Can I ask how old you are?'

'Sixteen.'

'OK,' she says and then pauses. This is the bit where she

laughs at me or puts the phone down. But she doesn't. Instead, she says, 'What's your name and address? I'll need a contact number for your parents so I can arrange for someone to come to your home to interview you.'

'Of course. My name is Drew Finch and I live at —'

'Drew,' Mum says from the doorway, making me jump. 'Is everything OK?'

Chapter Four

Mum frowns as she reads Mason's note. Tony, sitting beside her on the sofa, reads over her shoulder.

'Who did you say gave this to you?' Mum says, looking up.

'I told you, a stranger.'

'Did she tell you her name?'

'Well, she . . .' I tail off. I don't like the weird way Tony's looking at me. It's like he's *too* interested in what I'm saying.

Mum glances at Tony. I hate how she does that – deferring to him as though she's incapable of making a decision without his opinion. She was never like that with Dad. She made all the decisions in our house back then. Dad used to joke that, ever since the motorbike accident where he lost his right leg from the knee down, Mum wore the trousers because they didn't look right on him any more.

Tony runs his hands up and down his thighs as though he's trying to iron out invisible creases in his suit trousers. 'Have you spoken to the police about what you saw?'

'I rang them earlier. They said they'd send someone round to take a statement from me.'

'I see.' He glances back at Mum but she's looking at Mason's note again. It quivers in her fingers like a pinned butterfly. She's rereading the bit where Mason says how scared he is. I can just tell.

'Jane.' Tony places his hand over the note, blocking her view. 'We talked about this. Remember? About Mason trying to avoid facing up to his responsibilities. We both know how manipulative he can be.'

'He's not manipulative!' Mum shifts away from him so sharply his hand flops onto the sofa. 'My son might be a lot of things but he's not that.'

'He's a liar, Jane. And a thief. Or have you already forgotten that he stole from you.'

'Tony!' Mum glares at him. 'Not in front of Drew. Please.'

It's not like I don't know all this already. They sent me upstairs when we got home from school but I didn't go into my room. I sat cross-legged on the landing instead and listened to Mum lay into Mason about nicking twenty quid from her bag. She told him how disappointed she was. How Tony was at the end of his tether. How they knew Mason had been smoking weed out of his bedroom window. 'And now you're stealing!' she cried. 'From your own mother. What did I do to deserve that, Mason? What did I do wrong?' She started crying then. I heard Mason try to comfort her but she wasn't having any of it. She told him that he'd pushed her to the edge and she had no choice but to agree with Tony and send him to the Residential Reform Academy.

Mason wasn't the only one who gasped. I did too. When Tony had first mentioned sending Mason away (another conversation I'd eavesdropped) Mum was really against the idea. I wasn't. Mason might be my brother but he can also be a prize dick. He wasn't always a dick. He was pretty cool when we were kids but he changed after Dad disappeared. He stopped watching TV in the living room with me and Mum and holed himself away in his room instead. And if he wasn't in his room he was out with his mates on their bikes or skateboarding in the park. He started finding fault in everything – in me, in Mum, at school. He talked back to his teachers, he started fights and he smashed stuff up if he lost his temper. After he was excluded, I barely saw him. When I did he'd make snidey comments about me being the favourite and accuse me of sucking up to Tony.

'You've got no personality,' he'd shout at me. 'That's why Tony likes you.'

He really bloody hated Tony. He made no secret of that.

'Drew,' Tony says now. 'If this woman told you her name you need to tell us what it is.'

'I know but . . .' I pause. Tony's the National Head of Academies which means he knows the people who run the RRA. If he contacts them, Mason will get into trouble. He's not supposed to have any contact with the outside world while he's away. He wasn't even allowed to take his phone or iPad with him. I shouldn't have said anything about this in front of Tony but I was so freaked out by what had happened it all came spilling out before I knew what I was doing.

'But what?' He sits forward so he's perched on the edge of the sofa. 'Just tell us her name, Drew.'

'I'm going to ring Norton House,' Mum says, before I can reply. She reaches into her handbag for her phone and swipes at the screen.

'Jane.' Tony touches her arm. 'Let me deal with this. If you get in touch, Mason will be getting exactly the reaction he was hoping for when he smuggled the note out. He –'

'Yes, hello.' Mum twists away from Tony. 'I'm calling to enquire about my son, Mason Finch.'

'Mum!' I jump out of my seat. 'Mum, please! Don't tell them about –'

She waves me away.

'Yes, that's right. I just wanted to check that he's OK.' She covers the mouthpiece with her hand and gestures for me to sit back down. 'They're just going to find out how he's doing.'

'Honestly, Jane . . .' Tony gets up from the sofa. He walks over the window and stares out into the street with his arms crossed over his chest. A bead of sweat trickles out of his hairline and runs down the side of his face. He swipes it away sharply, as though brushing away an annoying fly. The toe of his right shoe tap, tap, taps on the carpet as Mum continues to hold. I've never seen him took this unsettled before.

'OK,' Mum says into the phone. 'Right, OK. I understand. No, there's nothing else. Thank you for your time.' She removes the phone from her ear and ends the call. 'He's in pre-treatment and can't be disturbed, but they're going to WhatsApp me some video footage so I can see that he's OK.'

Tony doesn't react. He continues to stare out into the street. A new bead of sweat runs down the side of his face. He doesn't swipe it away.

'Mum,' I say, but I'm interrupted by the sound of her phone pinging.

'Here we go. They've sent the video.' She taps the empty seat next to her, gesturing for me to join her on the sofa. Tony doesn't move a muscle as I cross the living room.

Mum touches the screen as I sit down next to her. An image of Mason, sitting in a beanbag chair with a PS4 controller in his hands, jumps to life. There are two boys sitting either side of my brother, both on beanbags, both holding controllers. All three boys are laughing their heads off. They look like mates, kicking back in one of their bedrooms rather than three kids who've been sent away to overcome their 'behavioural problems'.

'Can I look at that for a second?'

Mum doesn't resist as I take the phone from her hand and click on the video details.

'What are you doing?' she asks.

'Checking the date the video was taken. They might have sent you footage of when he first arrived.'

'And?'

I stare at it in disbelief. 'It was taken today.'

'There you go, then.' Tony swivels around so he's facing us. 'And you still claim your son wasn't trying to manipulate you, Jane?'

Mum sighs heavily and looks at me. 'What do you think, Drew? He looks fine, in the video, doesn't he?'

There's desperation in her eyes. She wants me to tell her there's nothing to worry about.

'No one's being brainwashed,' Tony says. He's not sweating any more and his foot has stopped pounding the carpet. If anything he looks ever so slightly smug. 'All the kids get a couple of weeks to settle in followed by an intensive course of therapeutic treatment to help them overcome their behavioural issues. If Mason passed a note to someone – and I'm of the belief it was written before he left – it was done because he's still resistant to the idea that he needs to make some positive changes in his life.'

Waffle, waffle, waffle. Tony might be convincing Mum with his pseudo psycho-babble but I'm not so sure.

'What kind of therapeutic treatment?' I ask.

'Um.' Tony runs a hand over his thinning hair. 'It's . . . er . . . cognitive behavioural therapy, modelled especially for adolescence.'

He's right. Cognitive behavioural therapy isn't brainwashing. It helps you change the way you think and behave. But if it's all so innocent why has he started sweating again?

Chapter Five

Mum and Tony didn't say a word when I left the living room, claiming I needed to do some homework, but I heard Mum hiss at Tony as I climbed the stairs to my room.

'I won't have you talk about Mason like that in front of Drew. Whatever he's done he's still her brother and, as soon as he's completed his treatment, he'll be coming back home.'

She might have bought Tony's crap about CBT but I haven't. Dr Cobey wouldn't have risked her life to pass me Mason's note if that was what was going on.

I open my laptop lid and type 'RRA' into Google. A bunch of links for architects, relative risk aversion and the Rahanweyn Resistance Army appear on the screen. That's not what I'm after so I try again, entering Residential Reform Academy into the search box. This time, when I click return, a website for the school appears.

I've looked at it before. I checked it out after Mum and Tony told Mason that's where they were sending him. On the first page it says it's, *a therapeutic boarding school for troubled adolescents that provides a safe, secure and structured environment to allow them to overcome their issues. Established four years ago, the RRA has seen a huge leap in student intake over the last twelve months due to strong support from the current Government,* but there's not much more information;

a few photos of the huge mansion-sized building and a bit of history about it being a psychiatric hospital in the Eighties. And that's it. Dr Rothwell is named as the director but there's no staff list. No photos of the inside or the kids. No contact information. No directions. Nothing. *A residential school in the heart of Northumberland*, it says. That could be anywhere.

I try another search.

Residential Reform Academy review.

Nothing. I look on Facebook to see if it's listed there. Nothing. No images on Instagram. No hashtags on Twitter. If the treatment only lasts two months surely some of the kids who'd left would have mentioned it on social media? But there's nothing. Other than the website it's as though it doesn't exist.

I try more searches:

RRA experience
RRA story
RRA nightmare
RRA scared
RRA brainwashed

Nothing. Nothing. Nothing.

I slump back in my chair and stare at the ceiling. Why am I even doing this? Mason looked fine in the video. Tony's probably right. The note was his attempt to guilt trip mum into coming to get him. But even if he was, that doesn't explain the things Dr Cobey said to me. Why all the secrecy and fear about this place? What are they hiding?

I jolt forward in my seat and put my fingers back on the keyboard.

RRA conspiracy

Nothing.

RRA secrecy

Nothing.

RRA truth

Bingo!

On the second page there's a link to a blog on Tumblr. I click on the mouse button and the site loads. But there's barely anything written on the page. Just fourteen words.

If you want to know the truth about RRA message me on Snapchat. ZedGreen.

***

I snatch up my phone and click on the Snapchat icon. As I do the landing floorboards creak loudly. Someone's creeping about outside my bedroom door.

'Mum?' I peer outside but it's Tony's shadow that disappears into the master bedroom. I hear the deep, bassy rumble of his voice then the door clicks closed. He's making a call. Mum must be in the kitchen. I can hear plates and dishes clinking and clanking as though they're being loaded into the dishwasher. I close my bedroom door and return to my desk. I swivel my chair round so I can see the door then I add ZedGreen as a friend on Snapchat. The request is immediately accepted so I tap out a message.

ME

My brother is at RRA and I'm worried about him. Can you help?

I have no idea who ZedGreen is. For all I know he could be someone at the academy, an ex-pupil, or even a teacher.

A message flashes up on the screen:

ZEDGREEN
| Send me a photo.

I type back.

ME
| Of what?

ZEDGREEN
| You, holding a sign with today's date written on it.

ME
| Why?

ZEDGREEN
| So I know you are who you say you are.

ME
| But I don't know who you are.

ZEDGREEN
| You're the one who came knocking on my door, not the
| other way round.

I stare at the screen. I don't share photos. Not in real life and particularly not online.

I type back:

ME
| I can't do that. Sorry.

ZEDGREEN
| Then we can't talk. Goodbye.

ME
| Wait! I need your help.

Thirty seconds pass. ZedGreen doesn't reply. I tap my feet on the carpet. C'mon. C'mon. I put my phone down and do a search on Reddit using all the terms that led me to ZedGreen's blog but there's nothing. He's the only person in the world who can help me and if I don't do what he asks is not going to play ball. But if I show him a photo that means LoneVoice isn't anonymous any more. *I* won't be anonymous any more. If ZedGreen screenshotted my photo and put it online I wouldn't be able to be me. I wouldn't feel safe.

I snatch up my phone again.

ME
| Please,

I tap out.

ME
| My brother sent me a message telling me that he's
| being brainwashed. I need to know if it's true or not.

25

ZedGreen doesn't reply.

ME
| PLEASE!

I feel sick as he continues to ignore me. What if he only gave me one chance to respond and I've blown it? I'll never find out the truth. If Dr Cobey was killed just for trying to help Mason, God knows what kind of danger he's in. Mum and Tony are convinced that he's fine. But what if he's not? I could never forgive myself if something awful happened to him.

'This had better not be a wind-up, Mase,' I mutter, as I rip a page out of my journal and write today's date on it. I hold it under my chin, reach out my arm and snap a scowling selfie.

A couple of seconds later and I've sent it to ZedGreen.

ME
| There,

I type.

ME
| Happy now?

The message is delivered but nothing happens. Zed doesn't respond.

ME
| Hello? Are you still there?

A sick feeling grips my stomach. Some random stranger has got my photo and I'm still no closer to finding out what's going on with my brother.

Ping! My phone vibrates in my hand. A message from ZedGreen:

ZEDGREEN

> If you want to discover the truth about the RRA you need to meet me. Grab a pen. I will send you details in my next message. Do not screengrab it. Do not tell anyone where you're going. Meet me alone. If you break any of these rules I will vanish. Do we understand each other?

ME

> Yes

I type back.

ME

> Tell me where and when and I'll be there.

Chapter Six

I am waiting where Zed told me to meet him, under the horse chestnut tree in Redcatch Park. It's seven o'clock and the park is almost pitch black. The only light is the amber glow from the houses on the edge of the park. It's November and the ground is thick with fallen leaves. The red, orange, yellow leaves look gorgeous in the daytime but, at night, every crunch, every crackle, every skittering leaf makes me jump.

When Zed's message flashed up on my phone.

ZEDGREEN
| Horse chestnut tree, Redcatch Park, 7 p.m.

I actually laughed. Meet a total stranger in a deserted park in near darkness? What kind of idiot did he think I was?

ME
| You need to show me a photo with today's date. So I
| know who I'm meeting.

ZEDGREEN
| You'll find out who I am when we meet. This is as much
| of a risk for me as it is you.

| Why?

| You'll understand when we meet.

| Understand what?

He didn't reply.

In fact, he ignored every single message I sent him afterwards.

At dinner, I told Mum and Tony that I was going to Lucy's to work on an English project. Tony raised an eyebrow – I never go to anyone's house – but he didn't say a word. Mum, on the other hand, couldn't hide her delight.

'Who's Lucy? Is she a new friend? You haven't mentioned her before. Would you like to invite her here? She could come to dinner. What's your favourite food? I'll make it if you like.'

She was so embarrassingly OTT I wanted to slide off my chair, slither across the kitchen floor and out the back door. Hooray, my hermit daughter has a friend. Let's roll out the banners and pump up the balloons!

I'm not a total idiot. I didn't go out in the dark to meet a stranger without telling anyone. I sent messages to three of my online friends – Chapman who lives in London, Isla who lives in Scotland, and Sadie who lives in Birmingham – telling them what had happened and including a photo of Mason's note. Chapman replied straight away. He's nineteen, a tester for a computer games company and he doesn't go anywhere without at least four different gadgets.

You're an idiot, he typed back. It's probably some kind of paedo trap. Give me a sec and I'll see what I can find out about ZedGreen.

A couple of minutes later he sent me another message.

Can't find anything on ZedGreen but I still think you shouldn't go.

He only chilled out when I said I'd give him the password to my 'Track My Phone?' app so he could track me on GPS. I'll change the password when I get back home, not that I'm bothered that Chapman will know where I live. I've known him for over a year now and he's never once said anything remotely sleazy or inappropriate. In fact, a couple of months ago he confided in me that he thinks he's asexual.

Isla and Sadie didn't reply to my message. Isla's a student nurse and works long hours. Sadie's doing her GCSEs like me but she goes to kickboxing classes several times a week and can't chat online until quite late at night.

Now, I tap my pocket to check I've still got my phone then rub my hands up and down my arms. I should have worn a coat, it's bloody freezing. All around me the trees are swaying in the wind, their shadows reaching across the grass like long, bony fingers. I scan the park, looking for signs of movement but, other than leaves tossing and turning as they're blown down the path, I'm all alone.

The sound of twigs snapping makes me turn my head sharply. There's someone about a hundred metres to my left, stepping out from behind a tree. They're dressed all in black, the face shrouded by shadows. Even from this distance I can tell from his height, broad shoulders and the determined way he stalks towards me that it's a man.

I skirt round the tree, my heart thumping in the base of my throat. ZedGreen's huge. What the hell was I thinking? I need to get out of here. Having 'Track My Phone' won't be much help if my phone's knocked out of my hand as he bundles me into a white van.

OK, on a count of three I'm going to make a run for it.

One.

Two.

I freeze as leaves directly behind the tree crackle and snap. He's running! I take a step to my left, primed to sprint, but, as I do, something hard smacks against my lower back. A strangled scream catches in my throat and I spin round, my hands raised in self-defence.

'Bess! Bess come here!' A male voice booms through the darkness as a large, brown dog leaps up at me, almost pinning me to the tree with the weight of his front paws. 'Bess, what are you – Jesus!'

The man stops short, eight or nine metres away from me, and presses a gloved hand to his heart. 'Jesus! Sorry, love. I didn't see you there. You nearly gave me a heart attack.'

I don't say anything. I'm too freaked out to speak.

'Bess!' the man shouts as she jumps up and presses her paws against my stomach, her tail wagging frantically. 'Leave her alone. Come here!'

The dog starts off through the leaves and the man ambles slowly towards the park gates. I slump against the tree as I watch him go. This was a really, really stupid idea. Zed hasn't even shown up.

I glance at my phone: 7.17 p.m. This couldn't be down to Lacey, could it? It's just the sort of stunt she'd pull to try to wind me up. No. I dismiss the thought as soon as it crosses my mind. I'm being paranoid. Even if she knows where Mason is she wouldn't set up a web page hoping I'd get in touch. She's too thick for one thing.

I shove my phone into the back pocket of my jeans, pull my hoody up over my head, shove my hands into my pockets and hurry through the park, kicking at piles of raked-up leaves as I head for the gates. ZedGreen's probably having a right old laugh at me. Not only did I send him a photo, I actually went to the park to meet the invisible man.

As I reach the end of the path, I turn round, just to check that I'm not being followed, but the dog walker and his mutt are long gone. There's no one else here. It's just me and the empty kids play park. Mum used to take me and Mason there after she collected us from primary school. My brother loved the climbing frame, right until he fell off it and broke his arm. I was more of a fan of –

One of the swings is moving back and forth on its own. The chains creak as it arches forwards and back, forwards and back. It's swinging vigorously, as though someone just jumped off. I take off, speeding towards the gate. Someone was sitting on the swings. If they watched me talk to the dog walker they also know I'm alone now.

I speed past the play park, and up the tree-lined path. A cold gust of wind showers me with leaves and takes my breath away as my boots thump on the tarmac. I'm too far away from the houses for anyone to be able to see me. I need to get out of the gate and onto Redcatch Road where there are cars, houses, people. As I round the corner, I sneak a look back at the play park, half expecting to see a figure on the swing, staring at me through the darkness but the swing is still. Whoever was sitting on it is still in the park. I can't see them but I feel them watching me.

My lungs burn and my thighs ache as I run up the small stretch of path to the gate. A car's headlights flash through the bushes as it speeds along the road. I'm nearly there. Nearly at the gate. Just four or five more steps and I'll be out onto the road –

'Aaargh!'

One second I'm standing by the gate. The next I'm being dragged backwards by my hood. I twist and squirm, trying to get free, my right hand clenched into a fist. I'm just about to strike out at my attacker when a soft voice says, 'Hello LoneVoice, I'm Zed.'

Chapter Seven

'You're Zed Green?'

I stared down in surprise at the small, skinny girl standing beside me with her hands raised as though in surrender. She's got short hair, clipped close around the ears and a vivid blue or green streak in her fringe (it's hard to tell in this light). Her eyes are rimmed with black kohl and there is a hoop in her left nostril.

'Yeah.' She drops her hands and crosses her arms over her chest. 'Although that's not my real name, obviously.'

I take a step backwards. Just because she's female, and roughly the same age as me, doesn't mean she's not dangerous.

'Were you on the swing?'

She frowns. 'What swing?'

'The one over there. It was moving all by itself.'

'Jesus.' She clutches my arm. 'You don't think the park's haunted, do you?'

She looks so scared that I immediately doubt myself. Did I actually see the swing moving or was it my overactive imagination going into overdrive?

'Oh my God!' Zed pushes me away and bursts out laughing. 'I'm sorry. I couldn't resist. Of course it was me on the swing.'

OK . . .

This is all one big wind-up. I don't have time for this sort of crap.

'Hey, LV, wait!' She tries to grab me by the elbow as I walk towards the gate but I shrug her off.

'Wait!' she calls, as I weave my way through the gate and step onto the road. 'I'm sorry. I was just dicking about. Please. I can help you.'

I turn back. 'I waited for you for fifteen minutes and you were watching me the whole time.'

'I needed to be sure you were who you said you were. I couldn't see your face in the darkness and when you and that bloke started chatting I thought it was a trap.'

I raise an arm to shield my eyes as a car speeds by, its headlights set to full beam. 'What kind of trap?'

Zed shrugs. 'I thought you were both from the RRA. They've been taking down my blog posts. That's why I needed to meet you in person. I can't share what I know on the Internet, the Government doesn't want anyone to see it.'

Ah. She's a conspiracy theorist. The Internet is full of them. She probably thinks the moon landing was faked too. Or that the US Government staged 9/11 so they could attack al-Qaeda.

'You don't believe me, do you?' Zed says. 'I'm not surprised. I wouldn't have believed it myself six months ago.' She glances round as another car speeds down the road then grabs my wrist as it suddenly slows. 'It's not safe to talk here. Come with me.'

She walks back through the gate into the park without looking back to check if I'm following. Do I go with her? She's got a strange sense of humour and she's definitely a bit unhinged but she seems to know something about the RRA and I need to find out what it is. I take off after her, jogging to catch up. By the time I reach her, she's sitting in the shelter by the large field local schools use as a football pitch. She unzips her jacket, reaches into a pocket and pulls out her phone.

'Look at this,' she says.

A video appears on the screen. It's a guy about our age standing on a skateboard, at the top of a ramp. He is dressed in a long-sleeved T-shirt, a beanie, jeans and trainers. As the camera zooms in on him he flashes the horns symbol with the fingers of his right hand and sticks out his tongue then he pounds the ground with one trainer and he's off! The skateboard zooms down the ramp across a patch of tarmac and up another ramp. As it reaches the top, he stamps on the back of the skateboard and it flips into the air. For a second he's separated from it but then he lands firmly, with both feet and zooms back down the ramp.

'Yeah!' yells a voice that sounds a lot like Zed's and then a female hand makes the horns in front of the camera. Clamped between the thumb and fingers is a fat spliff.

'That's for me, yeah?' Skateboard guy approaches the camera, grinning and whips it out of her fingers. He tokes on the joint and blows a stream of smoke up at the sky.

'How good was I?' he says as he looks into the camera.

'Really good,' Zed says. 'Really bloody good.'

Skateboard boy leans in towards the camera. His face gets blurrier and blurrier the closer he gets and then the clip stops.

'That's when he kissed me,' Zed says now. Her voice has changed. She sounds softer, more pained.

I don't get it. What's that video got to do with the RRA and the Government trying to take down her blog posts. He's obviously her boyfriend but so what?

'Come with me.' She tucks her phone back into her pocket and stands up. 'I've got something else to show you.'

I follow her through the dark park, towards the car park at the far end. The gate is locked so we have to climb over it.

'Where are we going?' I ask for the third time since we set off.

'This is my car.' Zed taps the bonnet of a red Mini Metro. 'Passed my test last month. It's ancient but it runs.'

If she can drive she's older than me then, by at least a year.

'Nice,' I say, then jolt with surprise as I notice the shadowy figure sitting in the passenger seat. Zed sees me jump and rounds the car.

'Charlie.' She taps the passenger side window. 'Come and say hello to my new friend.'

The door opens and I take a step back. I've got no idea who's inside or whether or not I can trust Zed.

Two shiny black shoes appear beneath the open car door as Charlie swings his legs out. He slowly stands up, shuts the door and turns to face Zed. I can tell it's the same guy I saw in the video, even in the half light, but they couldn't look more different. He's wearing neat, beige chinos – the sort Tony wears at the weekend – and a navy V-neck jumper over a white shirt. His hair is closely cropped, short but not Marines short. But it's not his appearance that makes me shiver. It's the strange, vacant look in his eyes as his gaze switches from Zed to me.

'Hello.' The edges of his lips curl up into a smile. It happens so slowly it's like watching a robot attempt a grin. As he steps towards me, his right hand extended, I back away.

'It's OK,' Zed says. 'He's not going to hurt you. Just shake his hand.'

I stiffly raise my right hand and lock palms with Charlie. He squeezes my hand and pumps my arms up and down once, twice, three times.

'Did you go to the RRA?' I ask him when he finally lets go of my hand.

He nods. 'I did some stupid things and made some stupid decisions. Being at Norton House taught me how foolish I was. I have learnt how to be a better person and how to contribute to society.'

'Right, I see.'

'It's a pleasure to meet you. Any friend of Evie's is a friend of mine.'

'Charlie,' Zed hisses, 'I told you not to call me that in public. You're supposed to call me Zed.'

'But that's not your real name. Your real name is Evie Elizabeth Bar—'

'Charlie, get back in the car!' Zed yanks on his arm and gently shoves him in the direction of the red Mini. When he reaches the passenger door he touches the handle then looks back.

'Apologies,' he says, his cold, vacant eyes meeting mine. 'I didn't catch your name.'

'Robin,' I say. 'Robin Redbreast.'

I wait for him to laugh or tell me to sod off. Instead he nods, as though Robin Redbreast is a perfectly normal name, and gets into the car.

'Well?' Zed says as the passenger door clicks shut. 'Do you get it? Do you understand why we had to meet? Why you needed to meet Charlie for yourself?'

I glance back at the car. Charlie is watching us from the passenger seat, still smiling in that strange fixed way. I can't believe he's the guy from the skatepark. They look alike but it's as though they're two completely different people.

'What's wrong with him?' I ask. 'Is he on drugs?'

Zed laughs dryly. 'If only. I could stop him from taking them and he'd go back to being the old Charlie again.'

'So why's he like this? What happened to him?'

'They "treated" him.' She fixes her bright, blue eyes on me. 'That's what did this to him. They turned him into this . . . this . . .' She shakes her head. 'I don't know what he is. He looks like Charlie, he feels like him and smells like him but his personality's gone. The Charlie who went to the RRA was a rebel. He was outspoken. He was lively. He kicked back at authority. He –'

'He sounds a lot like my brother.'

She raises her eyebrows and sighs. 'That's what I was worried about. But he won't be your brother when he gets out. You won't recognize him. Charlie used to smoke weed, a *lot* of weed. That's why he was excluded from three schools. He was caught toking in the school grounds. Now if I ask him if he fancies a smoke he gives me a lecture about the psychotropic effects of marijuana and reels off statistics about heavy users being more prone to schizophrenia, yada yada yada.'

I shrug. 'Well, that is true.'

'But it's not the point. The point is there's no way Charlie would have given me a lecture like that before he went in.

And he definitely wouldn't have announced that he wants to train to become an accountant. Or agree with his dad that the police should have greater stop and search rights, or suggest that internet usage should be monitored nationwide and —'

'You think he's been brainwashed,' I say, glancing back at the car. 'Don't you?' Charlie is still watching us intently. He's starting to seriously freak me out.

'Yeah.' Zed runs her hands through her hair and stares up at the sky. She inhales sharply through her nose and blinks rapidly but there's no stopping the tears that well in her eyes. 'Sorry, sorry.' She swipes at them with her coat sleeve. 'I can't believe I'm crying in front of a complete stranger but you're the first person I've really talked to about this and it's . . . it's just so hard. I'm in love with him. Or at least, I was. I keep waiting to see a glimpse of the old Charlie, for whatever's happened to him to wear off, but it hasn't happened. It's been three months since he left the RRA and . . .' Fresh tears replace the ones she wiped. This time she doesn't try to hide them.

'Hasn't anyone else noticed?' I say. 'His friends or his parents? If Mason came back like Charlie, Mum would be onto the police straight away.'

'Would she?' She laughs dryly. 'Andy and Julie love the new Charlie. His mum's always going on about how polite and helpful he is now and how delighted she is that she's got her little boy back. And Andy can't stop telling people how well Charlie is doing at school.'

'But he's so weird. Sorry.' I pull a face. 'I know he's your boyfriend but he's . . . creepy. How can they not see that?'

Zed rubs the back of her neck. 'I think they see what they want to see – their son doing what he's told for a change.

He doesn't answer them back; he doesn't stay out late. He's perfect, as far as they're concerned. His dad keeps going on about how proud he is that Charlie's got his priorities straight at last and how relieved he is that he's decided on a career instead of claiming he's going to sign on as soon as he leaves school.'

I groan loudly. Make This Country Great. Contribute to Society. A Safe Land for Hardworking People. All buzzwords of the new Government. I hate that our parents voted them in. It's our future they've screwed up and we don't even get a say in it.

'What about Charlie's friends?' I ask. 'Surely they've noticed a difference.'

'Of course. They tried to snap him out of it too but they've given up on him now. They think he's a total killjoy. If he's bothered by the fact they don't call or message him any more he doesn't show it. In fact, he's really sniffy about the whole skate scene now. He acts like he's really superior to everyone. If I remind him what he used to be like he says, "I was a waste of space, Evie. I'm just lucky I was given the opportunity to turn my life around."'

It's doing my head in, everything that Zed is telling me. I feel like my brain is melting. The RRA woman Mum spoke to on the phone told her that Mason had just been moved to pre-treatment. That means he could be 'treated' at any time. For all I know it could be tomorrow. Or he might be there already. I can't let them do to him what they did to Charlie. I just can't.

'Zed,' I say softly, as I angle her away from Charlie's strange, staring gaze. 'I'm going to need your help.'

Chapter Eight

I have to wait until morning break before I can use the school library. I head for the bookshelves first, filling my arms with as many psychology books as I can find that cover brainwashing, mind control, behavioural issues and therapeutic practices. A lot of them look a bit too basic but I haven't got time to go to the library in town. As soon as Mum and Tony find out what I'm planning they won't let me out of their sight. When I've got all the books I need I log onto one of the school computers. We've only got one printer at home and it's in Tony's office. I can connect to it from my laptop but I can't risk him discovering what I'm up to. Last night Zed told me everything she knows about the RRA, including where it is. It's a large Victorian mansion called Norton House, formerly a psychiatric hospital, on the Northumberland coast. The sea is on one side and acres and acres of countryside are on the other. It's remote and you can only reach it by car or boat. Zed reckons it would take at least an hour and a half in a taxi to get there from Newcastle upon Tyne train station.

I found out some interesting things about Norton House when I was Googling last night. Very interesting inde–

'What's this?' A hand snatches my computer printout as I reach for it. Lacey. What the hell is she doing in the library?

She never comes in here, ever. She must've been looking for me. I glance around, looking for her sheep. They can't ambush me here, not when Mrs Wilson the librarian is sitting at her desk and there's at least half a dozen kids milling about. But there's no sign of her little flock. Lacey is totally alone.

'You're not the only one who is allowed to use the library, Drew,' she says as though she's read my thoughts. 'I need to finish my English course work and –' She peers at the printout in her hand. 'What's this? I didn't know you did design and technology.'

I try to snatch it back but she whips it away and holds it high above my head. Mrs Wilson glances over, disturbed by the noise.

'Sorry!' Lacey giggles, as she presses a finger to her lips. 'We'll try and keep it down. Won't we, Andrew?'

Mrs Wilson looks away again, reassured by Lacey's fake smile and her stupid, sing-song voice.

'Lacey,' I say quietly. 'Just give it back to me.'

She shakes her head. 'Not until you tell me what it is.'

'Don't do this. Not now.'

'Why not?'

I take a deep breath in through my nose and exhale heavily. I need to keep calm. I swivel round in my chair and press Control P on the keyboard. If Lacey won't give me my map back I'll print out another one.

'What are you up to, Andrew?' Lacey presses her body up against mine as she peers at the screen. The printer beside me makes a chugging noise and I reach out a hand to grab the second printout. But it's not the paper Lacey's interested in.

Click, click. She grabs the mouse and swaps one tab for the next. The first website I was looking at flashes up on the screen.

'Oh my God,' she breathes. 'It's that reform academy that Aoife and Freya Rotheram were sent to. The one up north. Didn't your brother get sent there too?'

'Lacey, go away.' I grab the printout with one hand and shove her away from me with the other.

'Oh my God!' Her jaw drops as she stares at me. 'I know what you're doing. I know what the printout is. It's a map. It's some kind of tunnel system under the school. You're going to try and help your brother break out. Hey, Mrs Wilson, did you know that —'

'No!' My chair crashes to the floor as I stand up quickly. She can't do this.

'Lacey.' I keep my voice down as I step towards her. 'You don't know what you're talking about.'

'Don't I?' Her blue eyes glitter as she smiles at me. 'Why are you freaking out then?'

The room has fallen completely silent. Everyone is watching us. They're waiting to see how this plays out.

'Lacey,' I say. 'Don't go there.'

'You threatening me, Andrew?' Her top lip tightens into a sneer. I used to think Lacey was beautiful, the prettiest girl in our year with her long, shiny black hair and her bright blue eyes but I've never seen anyone as ugly as the girl standing in front of me now.

'Girls!' Miss Wilson stands up and places her hands on her desk. 'Is everything OK?'

'If you tell her,' I hiss, 'I'll tell Jake Stone to drop you.'

Her eyebrows shoot up in alarm. 'How do you know about Jake?'

'I know about everything.'

'Liar. You've been eavesdropping, you little troll. Anyway, Jake wouldn't listen to you. No one listens to you. Even your own parents think you're a drama queen. What was it your dad said in mediation? *Drew can be a little highly strung.*'

'Tony's not my dad.'

'Girls!' Miss Wilson rams her desk and crosses the library towards us. A couple more strides and she'll be able to hear every word we're saying.

Lacey flicks her hair away from her face. 'My mistake, Drew. Your real dad was a nut job, like you. Maybe you should kill yourself like he did.'

Before I know what I'm doing my clenched fist arcs through the air and smashes against Lacey's cheekbone. There's a terrible crunching sound, of bone on bone, then she stumbles backwards. She falls, as though in slow motion, one hand reaching for me, the other curling towards her face. Smash! The back of her head smacks against library carpet. Her body jolts and then lies still. There's a hand on my shoulder, shoving me out of the way and Mrs Wilson screeches for someone to call the nurse. I stand stock still as she crouches down beside Lacey's crumpled body and touches her hands to the side of her face.

'Lacey!' she calls. 'Lacey? Can you open your eyes?'

But Lacey doesn't open her eyes. She lies completely still. As still as the dead.

Chapter Nine

'We came as soon as we could,' Mum bursts into the headmaster's office with Tony close beside her.

'Drew! Oh my God.' She skirts across the room and drops to her knees beside me. 'Drew!' She gathers me into her arms and repeatedly strokes the back of my head. 'Oh my God, Drew. What happened?' She holds me at arm's length and stares into my face. 'Please tell me it's not true. Please tell me you didn't hit Lacey Mitchell.'

'Jane.' Tony touches her arm and nods his head towards Mr Mooney, sitting across the desk from us. 'Let Layton deal with this.'

'Yes, yes, of course.' Mum runs her fingers through her hair as she sits down in the plastic chair between me and Tony. Her forehead is damp with sweat and her eye make-up is smudged. I feel sick, knowing how much this must be upsetting her and I wish there was something I could do to make her feel better but there's nothing I can say, not with Tony and Mr Mooney sitting so close.

'Mr and Mrs Coleman.' Mr Mooney gives them a sharp nod. 'Thank you so much for getting here so quickly. I know how busy you both are, particularly you, Mr Coleman.'

He gives Tony a deferential smile that makes me cringe.

Big suck up. He's got the National Head of Academies in his office and he's not going to put a foot wrong. We all know Tony could get him sacked in a heartbeat if he wanted to.

'No problem, George,' Tony says, giving him a condescending smile. 'We are as concerned as you are about Drew's behaviour.'

'Indeed.' Mr Mooney puts his elbows on the desk and fixes me with an intense stare. 'Fortunately Lacey is going to be OK. She was only unconscious for a couple of seconds and I've heard back from Ms Wilson who accompanied her to A & E that her cheekbone isn't fractured, although she is still in quite a lot of pain.'

Good. I clench my hands so my fingernails dig into my palms. I'm glad she's in pain. People can say what they like about me but no one gets to talk about my dad like that.

'Now the thing is,' Mr Mooney continues, 'there's obviously been a few issues between Lacey and Drew over the last couple of months and we've done everything we can to try and resolve them.'

'Obviously not enough,' Mum says, 'or my daughter wouldn't have done what she did.'

I shoot her a grateful look. She meets my gaze but her eyes are steely.

'That's not to say I condone her behaviour,' Mum says, looking back at Mr Mooney. 'But something needs to be done.'

'Well, obviously Drew will be excluded for several days as . . .'

Several days? He can't mean that. Surely I should be permanently excluded for punching another student in the face! I didn't plan on hitting Lacey. I was going to shove a load of

PE kits down the toilets and flush the chains to cause a flood, then hit the fire alarm button. And if that wasn't enough to get me permanently excluded I would have done something worse.

'. . . obviously there are extenuating circumstances here,' Mr Mooney drones on. 'Then, when both girls are back in school we will restart mediation and –'

'I'm not going to any more mediation sessions,' I say.

'Drew!' Mum clutches my arm. 'Don't be ridiculous.'

'Don't pander to her, Jane,' Tony says. 'It's what she wants. I've never seen such blatant attention-seeking behaviour.'

My stepdad's knuckles are white from gripping the arms of his chair so tightly. He wants to have a massive go at me but he won't do it here, in front of Mum and Mr Mooney. If there's one thing he can't stand it's being embarrassed in public. That's why he packed Mason off to Norton House because his behaviour didn't reflect well on him.

Mr Mooney takes a sip of water from the glass on his desk, then sets it back down again. He's waiting for them to stop bickering.

'I'm not pandering to her, Tony,' Mum says. 'I'm trying to make her see sense.'

'Look.' Mr Mooney splays his hands wide on the desk. The tip of his little finger nudges the glass of water ever so slightly closer to me. 'No one's going to force you to go to mediation, Drew. Once you and Lacey are back at school we will ensure that any teachers you have for the same lessons are aware of the situation. We will also make sure you're separated at break and lunchtimes. Once you feel ready to start mediation again we can –'

'I told you.' I launch myself out of my chair and stand up. 'I'm NOT GOING TO MEDIATION!'

'Drew!' Tony grips my wrist, his face puce. 'What the hell is wrong with you?'

'Drew!' Mum says. 'Sit down.'

'Drew Finch.' Mr Mooney stands up too. He glares at me from across the desk. 'You need to calm down.'

'No.' I yank my wrist out of Tony's grip and, before anyone can stop me, I grab hold of the glass on the desk and hurl the water straight into my headmaster's shocked face.

Chapter Ten

The train guard reaches for the tickets in Mum's hand, scribbles on them and then hands them back. Mum sighs as she tucks them back into her purse then hugs her handbag to her chest as she stares out of the window. She's barely said a word to me all day and it's breaking my heart, seeing her so upset, but what can I do? I can't tell her that I deliberately threw the water in Mr Mooney's face because I knew it would make Tony go off the deep end. Or explain why I refused to apologize (because I knew it would deepen my stepdad's embarrassment) and didn't put up a fight when he announced that 'maybe a stay at the Residential Reform Academy would teach her how to behave appropriately'. When we got home Mum came into my room and begged me to talk to Tony.

'You have to explain to him, Drew. You need to let him know how much the bullying and Mason being sent away has upset you. I'm sure he will listen once he's calmed down. Mr Mooney was only going to exclude you for three days. You can still put this right, Drew. Please, sweetheart. If you won't do this for me, do it for your dad. He was always so proud of you. It would break his heart to see you like this.'

I started to cry then. Partly because she was talking about my dad in the past tense (he's not dead, he didn't abandon his car at Beachy Head and walk off the cliff. He's alive and he's missing. Why doesn't anyone else believe that?). And partly because I knew it was her heart that was breaking.

'I know,' she said as she put her arms around me, 'that this hard girl stuff is all an act. You're still my baby, Drew. You're still my sweet, sensitive little girl. Let's go down and talk to Tony together. He's not a monster. He just wants what's best for you, what's best for all of us.'

I stopped crying when she said that. Is that why he sent my brother away to be brainwashed, because it was the best for all of us? No. It was best for him.

'Please, darling,' Mum begged as she tried and failed to take hold my hand. 'Please.'

After half an hour pleading and cajoling she eventually gave up.

'You'd better pack your bags then,' she said as she hovered at my bedroom door. 'You're going tomorrow. Tony's been on the phone to the RRA. They've found you a bed.'

I barely slept last night. I stayed up until 1 a.m. reading my psychology books and studying the printout I printed off the Internet. My hands shook as I turned the pages. I had – have – no idea what I'm letting myself in for. What if I'm locked up the second I get there and I'm shackled to a bed and wheeled into some kind of treatment room? What if it's not some kind of psychological brainwashing at all? What if electroshock treatment is involved, or an operation? Charlie certainly acted like he'd had some part of his brain removed. I tried to push the thought out of my head and think logically. This isn't *A Clockwork Orange* or One *Flew Over the Cuckoo's Nest*. It's real life. A real school. An academy for God's sake. There is no way they can get away with performing operations on kids without the parents' consent. If they are brainwashing kids they have to be doing it legally. But how? After I put down my book and turned out my bedside light, I felt a fresh flicker of fear. Who did I think I was – charging in there expecting to be able to save my brother? I wasn't a trained psychologist or an SAS soldier. I was a sixteen-year-old girl. And I was all alone.

'You know you can't bring that in with you, don't you?' Mum says now, gesturing at the book in my hands. 'No books, no mobile phones, no games consoles, no music players. Just toiletries and the items of clothing on the printout I gave you.'

'I know.' I close the book. I need to tell Mum how scared I am. This might be my last chance.

'Mum.' I reach across the table but my hand doesn't quite touch hers. 'I've got a bad feeling about Norton House. Don't shout at me, but the other day I met up with a girl whose boyfriend went –'

'Is this seat free?' A short man in a black suit with greying hair and gold-rimmed glasses gestures at the seat next to me. There's a queue of people standing behind him, filling the aisle. Beyond the window is a platform and a sign saying 'York'. I didn't even realize we'd stopped.

'Yes of course.' Mum gestures for me to move my stuff.

I gather my things onto my lap and give the man a tight smile. I hope he's not one of those spreaders who try to knock your elbow off the armrest.

'Afternoon.' He nods at Mum as he sits down. His eyes flicker towards the third finger of her left hand. There's a flash of disappointment on his face when he sees that she's married. Mum's an attractive woman. She's only forty but everyone thinks she's ten years younger. It's partly her height. Unlike me, tallish at five foot seven, Mum's only five foot tall. I get my height from my dad. He's six foot one. My dark hair and hazel eyes come from him too. If I hadn't seen photos of Mum in a hospital bed with baby me in her arms I wouldn't believe that we're related, we're that different.

'Going somewhere nice?' Suit guy asks Mum as he pops a piece of gum into his mouth.

Mum smiles politely. 'I'm taking my daughter to school.'

'Ah'. He casts a cursory glance at me. 'Tough luck!'

I pretend to laugh and reopen my book. I wish he'd found somewhere else to sit. There's no way I can talk to Mum about anything private now and we're only about an hour away from Newcastle.

'Which school?' he asks Mum.

'Well, it's . . . um . . .' I glance up, hearing the indecision in her voice. She doesn't want the whole carriage to know that her daughter is being sent to a Residential Reform Academy. 'Er . . . it's quite a new school. I doubt you'll have heard of it.'

'I don't know about that!' Suit man laughs. 'I'm an OFSTED inspector.'

Mum raises her eyebrows. I can't tell if she's impressed or appalled. 'Are you inspecting a school this afternoon?'

'Well, I shouldn't really tell you but . . .' He taps the side of his nose and gestures for Mum to lean towards him. 'I'm going somewhere quite groundbreaking by all accounts.'

'Is it the Residential Reform Academy in Northumberland?' I ask.

Suit man looks at me, surprised. 'You know about Norton House?'

'Yes.' I smile sweetly, ignoring Mum who's flashing me an anguished 'don't you tell him!' look. 'My stepdad's the National Head of Academies. He often tells us about his work.'

'Well, well, well.' Suitman sits back in his seat. 'Tony Coleman's stepdaughter, eh? So you must be . . .' He looks at Mum.

'Jane, his wife.'

'Ah right, of course. Well, I don't imagine I'll be breaking the Official Secrets Act if I disclose to you that that's exactly where I'm off to.'

'Gosh,' Mum says, looking at me. 'Isn't that interesting, Drew?'

I smile tightly. I've got no idea why she'd think I'd find that interesting but I still reply, 'Fascinating!'

'Right, well.' Suit Man puts a podgy hand on the armrest and levers himself up and onto his feet. 'I'm going to pay a quick visit to the refreshment trolley. Could I get either of you anything?'

Mum shakes her head. 'We're fine, thank you.'

She watches as OFSTED man sways and bumps his way down the juddering carriage then she taps me on the hand.

'You see? You've got nothing to worry about, Drew. There's no brainwashing going on at Norton House. It's a normal school. If there was anything remotely dodgy going on, OFSTED would be down on them like a ton of bricks.'

I look at the OFSTED inspector's seat and raise my eyebrows. He's left his bag and wallet behind.

'Hmm,' I say.

Chapter Eleven

I gasp as the taxi turns the corner and I get my first glimpse of Norton House. After travelling for hours through the countryside, dotted with the occasional sheep, cow or farmhouse, it's a surprise to see such a massive building looming out of the landscape. I saw photos of it online but I had no idea how imposing it would be up close. The centre of the red-brick building is arched like a church with a huge clock tower to one side. The main body of the school stretches several hundred metres to each side. Tall, narrow windows dot the front, six on the first floor, six on the ground floor. The windows at the top peak into triangles, like red brick witches' hats. The roof is black slate, dotted with red-brick chimneys. It's the kind of building you see in horror movies, where a woman in a white nightshirt is running down a deserted corridor, chased by a dark, shadowy figure. I shiver as the taxi driver pulls up at the iron gates.

'What did you say your name was?' he asks, looking back at Mum.

'Coleman.'

The taxi driver opens his window and presses a button on a silver intercom system on a post. 'I've got two Colemans here for you,' he says in a thick Geordie accent.

One, I think. I'm a Finch.

Nothing happens for several seconds then the iron gates slowly swing open.

'OK?' Mum says, gently touching the back of my hand. I'm holding my book so tightly my knuckles are white. I try to give her a reassuring smile but my heart is beating so violently I feel sick. What am I doing? If I just kept my head down and stayed invisible this wouldn't be happening. I'd be in my room, listening to music and chatting to Isla, Chapman and Sadie. I talked to them all last night and told them what was happening. With the exception of Sadie, they all thought I was mental. Isla wasn't convinced by my story about Zed and Charlie. She said she thought they were probably both on drugs. Chapman thought I was out of my depth. You're sixteen years old, he said. You should have gone to the police with Zed.

Nice idea, if it weren't for the fact that the police rang Mum last night and said they wouldn't need a statement from me because they were treating what happened to Dr Cobey as a tragic accident. Several members of the public had reported seeing her stepping into the road when the traffic lights were green and there was no way the driver could have stopped. I couldn't believe it. The lights were red, I told Mum. And the driver deliberately put his foot down and accelerated. She'd been murdered and the police were covering it up.

'No one's covering anything up,' Mum said. 'I know how traumatic it must have been for you, seeing something like that, but you need to put it out of your mind. Now please, go upstairs and pack.'

'Drew?' Mum says now. 'Come on, we're here. We need to get out.'

I touch a hand to my face, surprised to find a tear rolling down my cheeks. I wipe it away briskly and hand Mum my book. 'Can you return this to the school library, please?'

She takes it then touches me on the shoulder, her face drawn, her eyes clouded with concern. 'It will be OK, Drew.'

'Will it?'

'Of course it will. Just behave yourself, please, and I'll be here to pick you up in eight week's time.'

Pick me up? Or pick up the brainwashed, zombie daughter you no longer recognize? I don't say that to her. Instead, I open the door and step out onto the huge, gravelled driveway of Norton House.

Chapter Twelve

As we yank my suitcase out of the boot of the taxi a tall, slim woman with blonde bobbed hair, wide, thin lips and a long, beaky nose appears from behind the huge wooden front door. She walks down the stone steps and heads for Mum, her hand outstretched.

'You must be Mrs Coleman, so pleased to meet you.'

Mum shakes her hand. 'Jane, please.'

'I'm the housemistress, Evelyn Hatch, but everyone calls me Mrs H.' Her murky green eyes turn to me. 'You must be Drew.'

I stiffen, waiting for the inevitable handshake. Instead, all the breath leaves my body as Mrs H. throws her arms around my shoulders and gives me one of the tightest, most suffocating hugs of my life.

'So lovely to have you here,' she says. She pulls away, keeping her hands on my shoulders as she looks me up and down. 'I know you're feeling nervous and apprehensive, Drew, but I think you'll have a wonderful time here at Norton House. We're one big, happy family and you'll be very well looked after.'

Mum, standing behind her, gives me a smile that isn't reflected in her eyes. Two of her kids have been sent to a reform school for bad behaviour. She must feel so ashamed.

'Is it . . . um . . . Would it be possible to see Mason?' Mum asks Mrs H.

Mrs H.'s thin lips tighten momentarily then she forces a smile. 'I'm afraid not,' she says in a sing-song voice that doesn't match the coldness in her eyes. 'We don't want to undo all the marvellous progress Mason has made since he got here, do we?'

'So he's doing well then?'

'Oh yes, absolutely.' Mrs H. clasps a hand to Mum's shoulder (she's one touchy-feely woman). 'He's doing brilliantly. We're very proud of the progress he's made. He only needs to spend another week in pre-treatment and then he'll be ready to start the final part of his therapy.'

She holds her arms wide and ushers us up the steps, through the large wooden door and into a large, cavernous entrance hall. There are several closed wooden doors to my left and right and a large sweeping staircase at the far end of the room.

'Will I get to see my brother?' I ask.

'I'm afraid not, my dear. You'll be beginning your acclimatization phase which takes place in the West Wing.' She gestures to a door on the left. 'Pre-treatment takes part in the East Wing.' She flicks her hand to the right.

I grip the handle of my suitcase. 'What about the actual treatment?'

'In a separate building.'

'Where is that?'

'You'll find out soon enough. Right!' She claps her hands together. 'Let's take you to see Dr Rothwell. He's the headmaster and head psychologist.' She sets off again, trotting across the entrance hall.

She stops outside a wooden door and knocks twice. There's a brass plaque on it that says, Dr P. Rothwell BSc (Hons): MSc: DClinPsy; CPsychol'. Mum raises her eyebrows as she reads it. She's easily impressed by random strings of letters.

'Come!' bellows a male voice.

Mrs H. turns the handle then pops her head round the door, effectively blocking me and Mum from looking inside.

'Oh, sorry, Phil. You've got company. Don't let me interrupt you. I was just going to introduce you to a new student. We'll come –'

'I'm sorry to bother you –' Mum taps her on the arm '– but the taxi's waiting outside and I need to leave soon. Could I ask you a couple of questions before I go?'

'Of course.' Her hand drops from the door handle. 'Let's talk as we walk. I'll give you a quick glimpse at the rec room and then you can say goodbye to Drew.'

Mum nods gratefully. 'Thank you so much.'

As Mrs H. shepherds Mum back across the entrance hall, I sneak a quick look inside Dr Rothwell's study. Through the gap in the door I can see two men, both dressed in suits, standing beside a large wooden desk. The man in the black suit with gold-rimmed glasses is Mr OFSTED from the train. The other man, taller, with a bald head and a neat, black goatie beard, must be Dr Rothwell. As I watch, they shake hands.

'Before we have lunch,' Dr Rothwell says, 'I mustn't forget to give you this.'

He turns round to his desk and reaches for an unsealed envelope lying next to a black telephone. He laughs nervously as he picks it up. 'To cover your expenses.'

'At least four years' worth I should hope,' Mr OFSTED says

jovially, as he reaches for it. As his fingers graze a corner the telephone rings. The shrill sound makes both men jump and the envelope jerks up and into the air. As it falls, dozens of fifty pounds notes spill from the opening and flutter to the floor.

Chapter Thirteen

'Mum!' I speed after her and Mrs H., dragging my suitcase behind me, as they disappear through a door to the left of the entrance hall. 'Mum, there's something –'

'Sssh.' She gives me a sharp look as I draw up alongside her. 'I'm talking, Drew. Don't be so rude.'

Mrs H. raises a pencilled eyebrow. 'There will be plenty of time for goodbyes in a moment, Drew. I was just telling your mother about –'

'But Mum!' I pull on the sleeve of her grey woollen coat. 'This is important. I just sa–'

'Drew!' Mum grabs me by the shoulders and spins me away from Mrs H. 'Stop. Being. So. Rude.'

'I need to talk to you. Alone.'

She shakes her head, her cheeks reddening under Mrs H.'s judgemental stare. 'Just do what you're told. Please! This is a difficult enough day as it is without you making it harder.'

'Mum, the OFSTED inspector is in Dr Rothwell's office and he just paid him off. I saw the money. Thousands and thousands of pounds.'

My heart thuds in my chest as I wait for Mum to react. This is it. The proof that something dodgy is going on. If Mum rings the police they'll have to shut the school down.

'Mum?' I say as she stares silently at me, her eyes searching my face. 'Did you hear what I just said?'

She swallows, presses her lips tightly together and then, to my utter horror, her eyes fill with tears. 'You don't have to do this, Drew. It's OK to be scared. You're hundreds of miles away from home in a place you don't know, but nothing bad is going to happen to you. I promise. Tony wouldn't have suggested sending you here if he thought you'd be in any kind of danger. I know you don't believe it but he loves you and Mason.'

I laugh. 'Seriously? Mum, we both know that's not true, but this isn't about –'

'So sorry to interrupt.' Mrs H. takes a step towards us. 'But you did say you needed to get off, Mrs Coleman, and it's nearly 5 p.m.'

Mum glances at her watch. 'Oh God, I've got to go! I'm sorry, Drew. I wanted to see your dorm and make sure you were settled in but I can't miss this train.'

'No!' I grab hold of her arm. 'Don't go.'

'I'm sorry, sweetheart.' Mum's eyes fill with tears again as she twists her arm away.

'I love you, Drew,' she shouts as she sprints towards the front door, which Dr Rothwell is holding it open. Beside him is the OFSTED inspector, with the brown envelope tucked under his arm.

'Mum!' I start to go after her but Mrs H. shoots out a hand, lightning fast, and grabs me by the arm and sinks her nails into the thin skin of my wrist. I cry out in pain and Mum glances back but, before I can say anything, the OFSTED inspector sidesteps her, blocking her view.

'How nice to see you again,' he says in a loud pompous voice. 'Dr Rothwell and I are going for lunch in Newcastle. Perhaps we could share your cab?'

'Mum!' I shout. 'Mum, don't go! Mum!'

Chapter Fourteen

As the front door slams shut, Mrs H. releases her grip on my wrist. Four crescent-shaped nail marks are etched into my skin like dirty pink tattoos.

'Oh dear,' she says, peering down at them. 'I'm so sorry about that. I really should get my nails cut. Do you need a hug?'

Do I need a hug? What kind of sick psychopath is she? I move away from her, my hands raised in case she tries to hug or scratch me again. I've got three options:

Run for the door and hope Mum's taxi hasn't left yet

Smack Mrs H. round her stupid 'do you need a hug?' face and tell her that she's not fooling anyone with her 'we're all family' line

Act dumb, play along and go back to plan A – help Mason escape

'Drew?' she says again. 'Do you need a hug?'

I nod my head. (Three, it is then.)

I try very hard not to cringe as Mrs H. puts her arms around me and gives me a squeeze. Her perfume, a vile floral scent, catches in the back of my throat.

'It's tough, I know,' she murmurs into my hair before she swiftly lets go.

'Grab your suitcase, please, Drew.'

She holds the white card at the end of her lanyard against a small black box to the right of the door. It swings open and she ushers me inside.

'Your homesickness will pass quickly, Drew,' Mrs H. says as she follows me into the room. The walls are lined with bookshelves and hundreds of faded hardback books. It smells vaguely musty, like a second-hand bookshop. A man and two women are standing at a large picture window on the other side of the room. They're wearing identical royal blue sweatshirts with a Norton House logo, dark jeans and white trainers. And they all have lanyards dangling from their necks.

'Drew,' Mrs H. says as they walk towards us. 'Let me introduce you to Abi, Stuart and Destiny.'

'Hi,' they chime, flashing ridiculously white smiles.

'Great to meet you, Drew!' Abi steps forward and hugs me. She's early twenties with blonde hair in a ponytail and ridiculously clear skin. She looks, and sounds, like she should work on the Disney Channel.

Stuart steps closer as Abi lets me go and I brace myself. What's with all the bloody hugging? But he doesn't embrace me like I'm some long lost relative. Instead, he nudges my shoulder with a closed fist and says, 'Drew eh? Cool name,' in a thick Scottish accent.

'Nice to meet you, Drew,' says Destiny. She's got a neck tattoo, a septum piercing and long black dreads that are curled into a bun on the top of her head. She shoves her hands into her pockets as she speaks. *Finally*, someone who doesn't invade my personal space.

'Abi, Stuart and Destiny work here,' says Mrs H. 'Officially they're known as support assistants but everyone here refers to them as "the friends". They're responsible for your mental, physical and emotional health and well-being whilst you're in the acclimatization phase of your stay at Norton House.'

'Anything you want –' Abi beams at me '– just ask us.'

'Can I have an iPad and the Wi-Fi password, please?'

She laughs as though it's the funniest joke in the whole world but Mrs H. isn't amused. 'You won't have any contact with the outside world for the duration of your stay, Drew. There are a number of other rules you'll need to abide by but we won't worry about that now. You'll find a welcome pack on your bed when I show you to your dorm.'

Dorm? I have to share with other people?

'You'll get on great with your roomies,' Stuart says. 'Some of the kids make lasting friendships.'

Yeah, right. Not if you're Charlie. Zed told me he wouldn't talk about who he met or what happened at Norton House. Instead, he'd trot out the same stock answer: 'I will forever be grateful to the staff at Norton House for pointing me in the right direction when I didn't even know I was lost.'

I zone out as Stuart continues to waffle on about friendship and sharing and trust. Beyond the two large picture windows on the other side of the room is a large stretch of lawn. Beyond that, about five hundred metres away, a row of conifers bend and sway in the wind. My stomach clenches as I spot the twenty-foot iron fence that runs around the perimeter of the school. The plans I printed out are over thirty-five years old. If the basement of Norton House has been renovated along with the rest of the building, I'm going to have to find a way to get over that fence instead.

'Right then,' Mrs H. says, tapping her foot impatiently. 'We'll just do a quick suitcase search and then I'll show you the rec room.'

*

As I follow Mrs H. across the library, I'm flanked by Abi and Destiny. Stuart walks behind us, dragging my suitcase. Abi went through it and confiscated my e-book reader, two packets of gum, three bars of chocolate and some nail scissors. I wanted to grab everything she'd taken back off her but I didn't move a muscle. I was too busy praying she wouldn't ask me to take off my boots so she could search them too.

Mrs H. slows to a stop as she approaches the wall of books on the far side of the room and reaches for the card on the end of her lanyard. There's another small black box to the right of the door, tucked in between two books on one of the shelves. Three red lights flash at the base.

'You're going to like this,' Abi says as Mrs H. holds her card up to the black box.

There's a click, a clunking sound and a door-shaped section of the bookshelf swings open.

'Holy f–' I press a hand to my mouth, not because the bookshelf contained a hidden door but because I'm hit by a wall of noise as it swings open. Beyond the door is an enormous room, cathedral-big, and it's teaming with kids. There's a sea of blue on the floor – a carpet the same shade as Abi's sweatshirt – broken up by huge circular rugs in red, yellow and green.

Across the other side of the room, there's a huddle of kids

my age, sitting on red beanbags on a red rug. They're wearing headphones, gripping games controllers and staring at half a dozen flat-screen TVs mounted on the wall. To my left, there's a yellow rug where a bunch of kids are lounging around on sofas shoving popcorn into their mouths, headphones clamped over their ears, as they watch TV. Beyond them, the rug is green and there's a pool table, air hockey table, table football game and a huge electronic basketball game. Everywhere I look kids are laughing, chatting, squealing, playing and screaming. It's like an enormous teenaged crèche.

'Wonderful isn't it?' Mrs H. says, completely misreading the expression on my face. 'We're very proud of our recreation room. We deliberately don't have photos of it on our website because, if we did, every kid in the UK would want to come here.'

'Yeah,' I say, but I'm not really listening. I'm staring at the boys playing PlayStation in the red zone. A spotty blond-haired guy is sitting in the same beanbag Mason slouched against in the video they sent Mum. Logically I know he's not here. Mrs H. has already told me he's in the pre-treatment unit, but that doesn't stop me scanning the faces of all the boys in the room.

'What do you think?' Stuart asks from behind me. 'See anything that appeals to you?'

'It looks like my worst nightmare,' I say truthfully. 'Where do you go if you want to be alone?'

Destiny laughs softly.

'We don't encourage our students to isolate themselves,' Abi says. 'But if this is all a bit too noisy for you there are other options.' She points at a line of doors on the wall directly opposite. 'Through there you'll find a café, a bowling alley, a cinema, a gym and a swimming pool.'

'A swimming pool?' I stare at her in astonishment. 'You're kidding me?'

She smiles. 'We're not joking when we say we want your stay to be as enjoyable as possible, Drew.'

'But . . . where are the classrooms?'

'There are classrooms at the rear of the building. You'll only have three hours of lessons a day and one hour of individual therapy every couple of days. The rest of the time is your own.'

'What about the kids in pre-treatment?' I ask. 'Have they got something like this?'

Stuart shakes his head. 'No, the pre-treatment wing is quieter. Students are encouraged to use their time there for quiet reflection.'

'Can I go there now?' I ask and everyone laughs.

'Your time will come, Drew,' Mrs H. says. She indicates to Stuart to pull the door to the library closed, shutting us in the rec room, and then points to her left. 'I'll show you to your dorm now.'

Chapter Fifteen

We leave Abi, Stuart and Destiny in the rec room and head towards the large glass double doors on the left of the room. The wheels of my suitcase squeak as I drag it along behind me and several of the boys playing pool stop and stare as we pass.

'Who's that?' asks a short, dumpy boy in a tracksuit, stretched over the pool table with a cue propped up on his fingers.

'Why?' asks the tall, ginger boy next to him. 'Do you fancy her?'

All the other boys start laughing as I flick them the Vs behind my back.

'That'll be caught on camera!' one of them shouts as Mrs H. waves her card at the black box near the glass doors. 'You'll have to explain your aggressive behaviour to your therapist later!'

'There are cameras?' I say as the doors swing open and Mrs H. steps back so I can walk through first.

'CCTV.' She pats her blonde bob, even though there isn't a hair out of place. 'They're installed in all the communal areas and are monitored twenty-four hours a day to ensure you're all safe.'

Spying on us more like.

'When you say communal areas . . .'

'The rec room, cinema, swimming pool, gym, café, bowling alley and dorms.'

'There are cameras in our bedrooms!'

'Yes.' She smiles tightly.

'So someone will be watching us when we get changed for bed?'

'No one will be *watching* you get changed, Drew. They'll be monitoring for any undesirable behaviour, but if you feel self-conscious you can get changed in the en-suite bathroom. There are no cameras there.'

It's like I've just moved into the *Big Brother* house. With locks on the doors that can only be opened by staff passes and CCTV everywhere escaping is going to be trickier than I thought. And I still have to find Mason.

'Are the dorms up here?' I ask, pointing at the stairs that lead upwards.

'That's right.' Mrs H. gestures for me to go up them.

'And down there?'

Her eyes flit from the top of my head to the black leather boots on my feet. Despite the smile, permanently fixed to her face, she's suspicious of me. I can sense it.

'Those stairs lead to the basement.'

'What's in the basement?' I keep my tone deliberately light. 'More cool stuff?'

'Storage,' she says sharply. 'The kitchen and cleaning staff use it mostly.'

I flash her my sweetest, most innocent smile. 'So nothing I'd be interested in then?'

'The basement is off limits to students.' She gestures, again, for me to take the stairs that lead upwards. This time I do as instructed. I take the first set of stairs, bumping my suitcase behind me, round a corner, take another set of stairs, another corner and yet more stairs. I'm huffing and puffing by the time I reach the top but Mrs H., on my heel, isn't even breathing heavily.

'You can stop here,' she says as I reach a double, frosted glass door. To my right are another set of stairs that lead upwards.

'Staff quarters are on the second floor,' Mrs H. says, catching me looking. 'Nothing *cool* for you up there, either.'

Her stupid sing-song voice is starting to really grate on me. She may as well pat me on the head and tell me to be a good little girl and stop asking any more questions. I wish she'd just leave me to explore Norton House on my own, but it's like being in a prison. I can't go anywhere unless I'm accompanied and I can't get through any of the doors without a staff pass.

'Here we are then,' Mrs H. says, touching her pass to the black box. 'The dorms!'

I raise my eyebrows as the door opens. This place is like a TARDIS. From the outside I was expecting low ceilings, corridors and ward-like rooms, but it's been completely gutted and remodelled inside. They must have knocked two floors together to make a room this big.

'It looks . . .' I stare in shock at the squared horseshoe of doors in front of me. In the centre there are metal stairs, leading up to a second level. 'It looks like a prison block!'

Mrs H. laughs dryly. 'You wouldn't be the first student to say that. But appearances can be deceptive, Drew. The dorms are really quite comfortable. The boys have the dorms on the lower floor, girls on the first floor.'

I say nothing as she heads for the metal stairs. I can't get my head around what I'm seeing. What the hell is this place? Everywhere I look there are small black half-domes affixed to the walls. More CCTV. Mrs H. wasn't joking when she said that the only place to get any privacy is in the toilet. Are we being bugged too? So they can hear and watch everything we say and do?

'Here we are.' She turns left at the top of the stairs and leads me to a door with the number five stuck to the front. In prisons I've seen on the TV there's normally a low fence that runs around the first floor. Prisoners lean over to see what's going on below. Not here though. There's a barrier but it's a six-foot-high clear Perspex wall. Is that to stop us throwing ourselves off or throwing other people off? I reach out a hand and give it a push. It doesn't so much as wobble.

'OK?' Mrs H. glances at me then raps three times on door number five. She turns the handle without waiting for a response. 'Your roomies are waiting to say hello to you.'

My stomach twists as she pushes the door open and the enormity of the situation sinks in. For the next couple of weeks, I'm going to be living with complete strangers. Complete strangers who've been excluded from school for God knows what.

'Girls,' Mrs H. says. 'This is your new room-mate.'

Chapter Sixteen

I step into the centre of the room, dragging my suitcase behind me. I'm desperate to let go of the handle and wipe my sweaty palms on my jeans but I don't want anyone to see how scared I am. I glance back at Mrs H., standing in the doorway. She smiles sweetly. It's almost as though she's enjoying my discomfort.

'The girls will show you the ropes, won't you, girls,' she says, looking from the large, pasty-faced girl on the bottom bunk to my left to the small, skinny girl with a wide mouth on the top bunk to my right.

'Of course, darling Mrs H.' The skinny girl blows a kiss which makes Mrs H. laugh.

'I'll leave you to it then, Jude.' She disappears through the door, closing it behind her with a click.

I fight the urge to throw myself at the closed door and yank it open again. Instead, I take a deep breath. The dorm, like the rec room downstairs, is brightly coloured. The carpet is royal blue, the walls are yellow and the duvet covers are red. There's a pinboard on the wall beside each bunk. Jude's covered hers with photos, postcards and pictures of celebrities, snipped from magazines. The other girl's pinboard is completely bare. In front of me is a door which I assume leads to the en-suite bathroom.

On the right of the door is a bookcase full of paperbacks. On the left there's a shelving unit. Four shelves are filled with folded clothes. At the end of each bunk there's a table. There's an MP3 player docking station on one and three portable DVD players with headphones on the other. There are no windows anywhere. In the corner of the room, fixed between the wall and the ceiling above Jude's bunk is a black CCTV unit. The red light at the base blink-blink-blinks in time with my heartbeat.

I feel like some kind of circus freak, standing in the middle of the room, being watched, and the urge to sit down and hide away is unbearable. But where should I go? Jude has taken the top bunk on one side of the room and I don't want to take the bottom bunk beneath her. Just the thought of lying in it makes me feel claustrophobic. I've got a thing about small spaces. When I was eight I played hide and seek with Mason at our grandmother's house. We were really competitive about finding the best places to hide and, when I discovered a big, old empty chest freezer in Gran's garage, I clambered inside, certain there was no way he would find me there. I was right, he didn't. But what I hadn't anticipated was the fact I wasn't strong enough to push the lid up and off from the inside. I was stuck. I had to stay inside my big, white coffin for nearly an hour until Dad finally heard me hammering on the sides and let me out. He looked absolutely terrified as he opened the lid then, when he realized I was OK, he screamed at me and called me a stupid little girl. It's the only time in my life my dad ever shouted at me.

'You OK?' Jude says. Her voice has the same effect on me as nails being dragged down a blackboard. 'You look like you're about to pass out.'

'I'm . . . I'm fine.' I wipe the back of my hand over my forehead. It's clammy with sweat.

'Can I have this bed?' I touch the duvet on the bunk above the quiet, pasty-looking girl, surreptitiously wiping my sweaty palms on the cool material.

The girl shrugs. She's lying on her side in her bunk, her duvet pulled up to her chin. Her thick brown hair is splayed over her white pillow like tendrils of seaweed on a rock. She has a wide face, doughy cheeks and deep-set eyes.

'Is that a yes?' I ask.

Her amber-coloured coloured eyes flash in my direction then return to the book she's holding in her hands. I guess that's a yes.

'She never speaks,' Jude says, as I haul my suitcase onto the bunk above then scale the ladder. 'So I wouldn't waste your breath if I were you. Her real name's Megan but we all call her Mouse.'

That's original.

'I'm Jude,' she continues. 'I'm sixteen, from London. Mouse is from Cardiff. She won't tell me how old she is. Where are you from? What's your name? How old are you? Why did you get excluded?' She pauses for breath. 'How many schools have you been to? Have you got any brothers or sisters? What do your mum and dad do?'

As she continues to bombard me with questions, I crawl along the bed until I'm up by the pillow. If Mouse is Megan's nickname what's Jude's? Annoying Big Mouth? She's sitting cross-legged on her bunk, watching my every move. She's got small beady eyes, a long, narrow nose and a small puckered mouth that reminds me of a cat's bum. She's one of those twitchy girls, all nervous energy, jerky movements and verbal diarrhoea. The bunk below me creaks as Mouse sighs and changes position.

'Oh God,' Jude says, 'please tell me you're not another quiet one. I swear I'll go out of my mind if you are.'

I look at her lazily. 'My name's Zara,' I say. 'I'm sixteen. My dad was the Duke of Ayreshire. When I was nine years old, me and my mum were involved in a plane crash and we had to take refuge in an ancient Balinese temple. My mum vanished and I still don't know where she is.'

'Woah!' Jude stares at me, her black, beady eyes growing large and round. 'You're kidding me?'

'Yeah,' I say steadily. 'I love making jokes about my dead parents.'

Her gawping mouth snaps shut and her face tightens. She doesn't know whether or not to believe me. I don't know why I just told her such a ridiculous lie. If she knew anything about gaming she'd totally realize where I lifted that from. I didn't plan on lying to her. It just came out of my mouth. Maybe because I didn't like the way she looked me up and down when I came in. Or perhaps it's because I don't like the vibes I'm getting off her. There's something about her that reminds me of Lacey. Something that can't be trusted.

Mouse, in the bunk below, turns a page of her book.

'You said your mum disappeared,' Jude says, 'but what about your dad? How did he die? How did you get back from Bali after your mum disappeared? And you still haven't told me why you were excluded from school.'

She continues to bombard me with questions for a good fifteen minutes. I answer each one without hesitation. Sometimes my answers are directly lifted from the game, sometimes they're totally made up. Finally, Jude gets bored and reaches for a DVD player. As the tinny sound of the film she's watching drifts across the small room I reach for the laminated printout at the bottom of my bunk.

NORTON HOUSE DAILY ITINERARY

7.30 a.m. – wake-up call
8.15 a.m. – breakfast in the canteen
9 a.m. – assembly in the large hall
9.30 a.m. – English or maths
11 a.m. – individual therapy sessions or rec room (check the board in the rec room to find out when your therapy sessions are)
12 p.m. – lunch in the canteen
1 p.m. – English or maths
2.30 p.m. – Sports or outdoor activities
3.30 p.m. – rec room
5 p.m. – dinner in the canteen
6 p.m. – rec room
9 p.m. – dorms for quiet time
10 p.m. – lights out

On the other side of the piece of paper is a list, simply titled,

RULES

Respect other people and your environment (no tampering with the fixtures and fittings)

Intimate relationships between the students are forbidden

Do not verbally or physically abuse other students or staff

You must attend all classes and therapy sessions. Only genuine medical emergencies will be accepted as a reason for not attending

If you feel unwell ask a member of staff to take you to Nurse Jones in the Sanitorium

No smoking, drinking or drug taking (this includes 'legal highs')

No stealing – from other students, staff or any of the rooms

Food is prohibited in the dorms. Cups are available in the en-suite bathrooms if you need water

No dangerous play or games. Any behaviour deemed unsafe will immediately be stopped by staff

No contact with the outside. You are prohibited from

writing letters, making phone calls and using electronic devices that have Internet connectivity (this includes mobile phones, tablets, ipads, laptops etc).

NB: Staff at Norton House reserve the right to place any student who breaks any of these rules in solitary confinement

Solitary confinement? I run my nail under the two words, leaving a dent in the laminate. That sounds scary. I wonder where that is? What else didn't Mrs H. show me?

As a soft snuffling noise suddenly accompanies the tinny sound of Jude's film, I glance across the room. Jude is lying on her back with her eyes closed and her mouth open. The DVD player is on her chest and her hands are hanging loosely at her sides. Watching her sleep makes my eyes feel heavy and I stifle a yawn. According to the schedule there's half an hour until dinner. Maybe Mason will be there too. I'd be very surprised if there are two canteens, even if they do keep the kids segregated into two wings. I shuffle onto my side, being careful not to make the bunk squeak too much, and reach down to my boot. The printout of the pipes and tunnels beneath Norton House should be neatly folded and wedged between my sock and skin. I'm pretty sure I've memorized it but, if Mason's at dinner, this might be my last chance to look at it before I give it to him.

I pull at the leg of my jeans and slip my fingers between my knee-high sock and my calf. For one heart-stopping moment I think it's gone but then my fingertips graze paper and I sigh with relief. Out of the corner of my eye, I see the CCTV unit flash-flash-flash its red light. I'd forgotten about that. I pretend to scratch my leg then take my hand out of my boot and glance across at Jude. She's still asleep. What about Mouse? I can't remember the last time I heard her turn the page.

I shift to the edge of the bunk and peer over it. Mouse's book is on the floor, face down, pages splayed. I can see three fingers of her left hand, fingernails painted a vivid red, hanging over the side of her bunk, half clutching an asthma inhaler. It looks like she's drifted off too but I need to see her face, just to be sure.

I inch closer to the edge of the bed. The mattress squeaks beneath me and I freeze. Across the room Jude continues to breathe heavily. Mouse's hand hasn't moved but that doesn't mean she's asleep. I need to check. Gripping the edge of the metal frame I shift my upper body and, very carefully, very slowly, roll onto my side so my head is hanging over the edge of the bunk.

Mouse stares back at me, her amber eyes narrowed and unblinking.

'There's no way out,' she says. 'You know that, don't you?'

Chapter Seventeen

Mason wasn't at dinner. There were forty-eight kids around the dining table but not one of them was my brown haired, blue-eyed little brother. Jude talked so much on the way to the canteen it made my head hurt. Once we got to the canteen, rather than sit with her and Mouse, I peeled off and sat between two girls who seemed to be studiously ignoring each other. Mouse kept looking over at me as I tried to eat my lasagne and salad but I didn't meet her eyes. I was too freaked out by what she'd said to me in the dorm. Had she seen me fishing about in my boot for my map or was she just stating the obvious? Either way, it had seriously creeped me out.

Dinner's over and a huge crowd of kids are gathered at the door, waiting to be let back into the rec room. Mouse and Jude are at the back, standing slightly to one side. They're both watching me as I dawdle by the huge floor-to-ceiling window. Jude looks away quickly as our eyes meet but Mouse continues to stare.

'Missing home?' Abi asks softly, sidling up next to me.

'Not yet.'

'It's a lot to take in, isn't it? All this?'

'What's out there?' I touch my hand to the glass. 'It looks like a playing field.'

'It is.' She points to a large stretch of grass surrounded by a high, meshed wire fence. 'You can play football or rounders there. Over on the right is the running track. There's also a basketball court and a tennis court. You get an hour a day to go outside and do sports or just walk round the running track and get some air.'

'Like jail?'

She laughs. It's a light, tinkling sound. Very Disney princess. 'No, Drew. Like school.'

'What's over there?' I point to the right of the running track where I can just about make out another stretch of grass.

'That's the West Wing's running track.'

'Right.' I keep my expression neutral but inside I feel a jolt of excitement. The West Wing is where they keep the pre-treatment students. If Mason is allowed out to exercise at the same time as me the only thing separating us is a thin, meshed fence.

I'm desperate to ask Abi when the pre-treatment kids get to go outside but I don't want to raise her suspicions. I'm pretty sure all the friends will have been told that my brother is here too, but I've got no idea whether they know about the note he passed Dr Cobey. For all I know Mason has already been moved to the treatment unit and I've got here too late.

Chapter Eighteen

I barely slept last night, for worrying about Mason, and, when my mind finally went fuzzy and my body relaxed, Jude started snoring and woke me up again. I press a hand to my mouth, stifling a yawn.

'Oi oi!' A black guy with hazel eyes and a ring through his left nostril makes me jump as he plonks himself next to me and points to my plate. 'Are you murdering them or what?'

I look down at my breakfast plate. Beneath the metal prongs of my fork are half a dozen flattened baked beans. I've been mashing them into the plate without even noticing. 'I'm not really hungry.'

'Cool. I'm starving. Can I have the sausage?'

'Sure.'

Jude, sitting opposite me (there was no escaping her on the way to the canteen this morning), stares at him as he whips the sausage off my plate and shoves it into his mouth.

'Are you new?' she asks, narrowing her eyes as she looks him up and down.

He nods, pointing at his mouth as he continues to chew. Finally, he swallows. 'I got here an hour ago, along with those two.' He jerks his thumb further along the table where two other new guys are sitting with their arms crossed and their eyes closed.

I give him a puzzled look. 'What are they doing?'

'They're on hunger strike. See that plate of food at the empty place opposite them? That's mine. I told them I'd go on hunger strike too only I'm bloody starving. Which is why I'm nicking your food!'

He flashes me a smile. He's a nice-looking guy. Cocky, but I like his vibe.

'What are you here for?' Jude asks, tucking her long fringe behind her ear. 'Where are you from? What's your name?'

'All right, darling. Go easy! I thought the interrogation wasn't until 11 a.m.' He looks at me. 'Can I have your bacon too?'

'Sure'

'Israel.' His eyes stay on me as he reaches for the bacon. 'That's my name. I'm from Essex. You?'

'I'm from London,' Jude says. 'So we're not far away. Have you been to the Sugar Hut? I've always wanted to go there. Ever since I saw it on –'

'Yeah, yeah.' Israel waves a hand, as though swatting away an annoying fly. 'Go on,' he says to me. 'You were about to tell me your–'

He's interrupted by the sound of a buzzer.

'Assembly.' Jude reaches for her tray and stands up. 'I can show you where to go if you want, Israel.'

But Israel's already on the move. He's been summoned to the other end of the table by the hunger strike boys. They've opened their eyes and realized that he's missing.

'I suppose you think you're clever,' Jude hisses from across the table as the kids around us reach for their trays and head across the canteen to the stacking units.

I point at my chest. 'Are you talking to me?'

'Well I'm not talking to myself.'

'What are you on about?'

'You know.' Her gaze flicks across the room and rests on Israel. He's heading for the door with the two other boys, his arms casually slung around their shoulders.

'Just don't start with me, Zara. OK?' Jude yanks her tray off the table and hurries across the room. She shoves the tray into the rack then runs her hands through her hair.

'Israel!' she calls as she skips towards him. 'I still want to hear about the Sugar Hut!'

I shake my head as she catches him up. Israel might be a cool guy but if Jude thinks I'm on the hunt for a boyfriend or a hook-up she's completely misguided. All I'm bothered about is –

'Oomph!'

The back of my chair collides with something as I attempt to stand up. Mouse is standing directly behind me, her arms crossed over her chest.

'Sorry,' I say. 'I didn't see you there.'

She doesn't reply. She doesn't move. She just stares at me, her amber eyes pale and unblinking.

'Come on, girls!' Stuart scoots across the room towards us, his white trainers squeaking on the lino. 'Assembly's about to begin and you're going to be late.'

*

Mouse sticks to my side as we file into the huge, wooden-floored assembly room. Unlike school, where we sit in rows during assembly, the kids here gather in a higgledy-piggledy bunch in front of the stage.

'What happens now?' I look at Mouse. 'They'd better not make us sing. My voice would make Simon Cowell cry. And not in a good way.'

The tiniest of smiles appears on her face before she looks away, embarrassed.

'Any chance of a chair?' Israel shouts. He's standing a couple of metres in front of us, still flanked by the boys he arrived with. 'My feet are killing me!'

Several kids laugh, including Jude who's standing next to one of Israel's friends. She senses me watching her and glances back. Her eyebrows flash upwards as she spots Mouse, standing beside me. I'm not sure which of them freaks me out the most – Jude with her mega gob and death stares or Mouse and her freaky, stealth mode. Either way, I'm not going to be here long. As soon as I've made contact with Mason we'll be out of here.

'Ladies! Gents!' The friends circle us, waving their arms to get our attention. 'A bit of hush, please! Assembly is about to begin.'

Abi catches my eye and shoots me a smile as she walks past, then doubles back.

'Everything OK, Drew?'

Mouse, still standing beside me, widens her eyes. Oh no. Abi just used my real name and she heard it. That means that, by the end of the day, Jude will know it too. Great, I can't wait for another game of twenty questions when we go back to the dorm.

I sigh heavily. 'All good, Abi, thanks.'

'Don't forget, if you've got any questions or you need help with anything just come and find me, yeah?'

'Sure.'

Abi nods, satisfied that she's done her friendly duty, and heads off to hug/stroke/simper at a girl with short blue spiky hair who's standing on her own at the edge of the crowd. As she approaches her, the soaring sound of stringed instruments suddenly fills the assembly room. Most of the kids stop talking and turn to look at the stage. The newer students, me included, glance around, unsure what's going on. Israel mimes playing a violin, his raucous laugh cutting through the music. A couple of seconds later, a blue-sweatered friend squeezes his way through the crowd to tap him on the arm and tell him to stop.

Out of the corner of my eye, I spot three boys and two girls – dressed in the sort of outfits my parents wear to work – walking single file down the side of the room. They're flanked by Dr Rothwell and Mrs H. The kids climb the steps onto the stage and stand in a line at the back. The two adults stand side by side at the front of the stage. They're both wearing wireless microphones that curve around their mouths, the sort pop stars wear on tour.

'I hope you're not going to do a dance routine!' Israel shouts. 'Because your backing dancers look rubbish!'

I stifle a giggle and Israel's friends laugh loudly. No one else makes a sound apart from Mouse who's puffing on her inhaler. Jude doesn't so much as glance at Israel. She's staring at the stage, her arms hanging loosely at her sides.

'Students of Norton Hall,' Dr Rothwell says, his booming

voice filling the hall. 'Good to see you again. I'd like to begin by extending a warm welcome to all our new students. You may be feeling scared, apprehensive or even angry about your stay here and that's perfectly natural. In time you'll come to appreciate what an amazing opportunity you've been given and, dare I say it, one day you'll look back fondly on your stay here. In a couple of minutes, you'll have the opportunity to listen to the testimonies of some of the students who have recently completed their treatment but first, Mrs H. has a few words she'd like to say about housekeeping matters. Mrs H.' He gestures at the housemistress. The five students standing at the back of the stage clap politely.

'Thank you, Dr Rothwell.' Mrs H. taps the microphone by her mouth, making a loud crackling noise. 'Can everyone hear me OK?'

Several kids at the front nod.

'Housekeeping issues. Firstly, I'd like to remind you that, if you mislay your welcome pack, duplicates can be obtained from my office. Just ask one of the friends to take you there. Secondly, your individual therapy sessions are listed on the wall of the rec room. Do please ensure you arrive on time otherwise one of the friends will have to chase you down. I mean, come and find you.' She laughs tightly. 'Thirdly, existing students, I really shouldn't have to remind you that food must not be taken into your dorms. Our cleaners are not equipped to deal with insect or vermin infestations in your rooms. Pest control is not part of their job description! I would also request that you take good care of the stereos and DVD players. Accidents can, and do, happen, but if you regularly or wilfully destroy school property you will have such items removed from your dorm. Continued rule breaking will result in isolation. Is everyone clear on that?'

Dozens of kids nod their heads. One or two shift their weight from one foot to the other and hang their heads. It doesn't take a genius to work out that they're the students she's referring to.

'Great!' Mrs H. says brightly. She glances down at the piece of paper in her hands. 'Finally, I have the names of the students who will be moving into the West Wing this morning to begin the pre-treatment phase of their stay.' Mouse, wringing her hands beside me, jolts and looks up. 'Could the following students please congregate at the foot of the stage – Cerys Argent, Ottie Maclean, Kieron Sykes, Ethan Herbert, Tom Macauley, Joe Bradley, Charlotte Tilsley and Logan Hannay.'

There are gasps, squeaks and squeals from the crowd as the names are read out then five boys and three girls push through to the front of the stage. One of the girls, a short redhead in a black jumper and skinny jeans, is sobbing loudly. Everyone else looks excited.

'Were you hoping Mrs H. would call your name?' I whisper to Mouse.

'Sssh.' A fair-haired friend with freckles across her nose puts a hand on my shoulder. 'No talking until you're dismissed.'

'Could everyone please give the pre-treatment students a round of applause,' Dr Rothwell says as Mrs H. descends the steps and gives each of the kids a hug. 'We wish you all the very best of luck.'

They're led from the room by Mrs H. and three of the friends. Poor sods. They've got no idea they're being marched one step closer to becoming brainwashed zombies. That said, I can't help but feel jealous as the door clicks shut behind them. My escape plan would be so much easier if I was in the same wing as Mason.

'Excuse me,' I say to the fair-haired friend still hovering behind me. 'How long do you have stay in assessment before you're moved to –'

She presses a finger to her lips, her dark green eyes stony. 'Sssh!'

She makes a whirling gesture with her other hand, signalling that I should turn round and face the stage like everyone else. It's weird, how well behaved all the other kids are being, considering everyone in this room was kicked out of school for bad behaviour. I'd have expected a few kids to be kicking off or dicking around.

'Next up,' Dr Rothwell says, 'a few words of wisdom from some of the students who have successfully completed their treatment. They will be returning home later this week. Olivia, could you step forward, please?'

A slim girl in a knee-length skirt, thick, grey woolly tights and T-bar shoes I'm sure my mum owns, steps forwards. Dr Rothwell hands her the microphone.

'I . . .' she says then jumps as her soft voice fills the room.

'Go ahead, Olivia,' Dr Rothwell says, touching her on the shoulder. 'Everyone wants to hear what you have to say.'

'I was like you lot once,' Olivia says, staring straight ahead, at some point just over my head. 'I was angry . . .' She pauses to glance at Dr Rothwell, who nods at her to continue. 'I felt lost and alone in the world. I thought no one understood me. I did some stupid things and made some stupid decisions. Being at Norton House has taught me how foolish I was. I have learnt how to be a better person and contribute to society.' She says *be a better person* in a strange, almost robotic way, like she's reading from an autocue. 'I have realized the value of a good education and how important it is to contribute to society. I can't thank you enough for the opportunity to *become a better person*, Dr Rothwell.'

'How much did he pay you to say that?' Israel shouts from the middle of the crowd. The friend standing beside him glares at him and yanks on his arm.

Dr Rothwell ignores him and gestures for Olivia to retake her place in the line-up. He crooks his finger for the next student in line to step forward.

'My name is Alex,' says a tall Chinese boy in a suit. His voice is a monotone and his eyes have the same glazed expression as Zed's boyfriend Charlie. 'When I arrived here I was a degenerate, a waste of space. I was reprehensible scum like all of you.'

There's a collective gasp from the kids on the floor.

'Alex.' Dr Rothwell touches him on the arm. 'Remember what I said about keeping the message positive?'

'Scum?' Israel shouts, yanking his arm away from the friend. 'Who are you calling scum? You don't know the first thing about us.' He shoves his way through the crowd, heading for the stage.

'Come down here and call me scum,' he shouts as he climbs the first step. Alex, still standing on the stage beside Dr Rothwell, stares at him with a look of contempt on his face. Israel climbs the second step, then the third. He glances back and our eyes meet briefly as he scans the crowd.

'No one?' he shouts. 'Is no one else pissed off by what he just said?' The two hunger strike boys shrug their shoulders. 'Come on you lot! They can't force us to stay here!'

He lunges at Dr Rothwell, his outstretched hand reaching for the lanyard hanging around his neck. As he does a wave of blue jumpers storm the stage. Two hands latch onto Israel's ankles. He tries to kick them off but, before he can get free, Stuart flies up the steps and launches himself at him. They're fairly evenly matched, height wise, but Stuart is stronger and he manages to wrap his arms around Israel and lift him clean off his feet.

'Hey!' Israel shouts. 'Get your hands off me. Get your fuc–'

His shout is muffled as he's surrounded by three more male friends then the deafening bleep-bleep-bleep of an alarm echoes around the room.

Dr Rothwell steps away from the kerfuffle on stage and speaks into his mic. 'Could one of the support staff please escort all students back to the rec room immediately!'

The friends circle us, arms outstretched, and herd us like sheep towards the door. Up on the stage, Israel has been lifted into the air and is being carried off the stage by Stuart and the three other men. He's lying limp in their arms, his head lolling on his neck, his eyes closed.

'Hey!' I duck under Abi's arms and double back towards the stage. 'What have you done to him? Hey –'

I jolt backwards as someone grabs the back of my hoody and pulls.

'Leave the room calmly and silently,' Destiny hisses in my ear.

'No. I . . . ow!'

'Calmly and silently, please, Drew,' she says as she marches me towards the door, one arm twisted up behind my back.

Chapter Nineteen

The tension and fear in the rec room is palpable. Everywhere I look there are kids gathered in huddles, wide-eyed and fearful, whispering furtively as the friends attempt to reassure them that there's nothing to be afraid of. Some of the students are muttering that Israel is dead. Others think Dr Rothwell stepped forward and injected him with something.

I slip silently into the cinema. I need to be somewhere quiet where I can process what I've just seen, but I'm not alone. Jude and another girl have claimed two of the seats in the back row. They're chatting animatedly and don't hear me come in.

'They'll put him in isolation,' Jude says as I crouch down in the darkness, my back pressed against the wall. 'He'll be out in a couple of days.'

Her friend shakes her head. 'Nah, they'll claim he tried to attack Dr Rothwell and fast-track him to treatment.'

'They won't do that. They'll want to punish him first.'

'Have you ever seen anyone after they've been in isolation? When they get out they're totally –'

I snap round, sensing someone at the door. If it's Destiny I'll swing for her if she so much as touches me. But it's not Destiny who cuffs a hand against the top of my head as she blinks into the darkness. It's Mouse. I scrabble to my feet and gently shove her back into the rec room.

'Megan,' I hiss, as the door to the cinema clicks shut behind me. 'Could you stop doing that? Seriously, I'm going to have a heart attack if you keep creeping up on me.'

She shrugs. She still hasn't said a single word to me since her creepy whisper on my first night. And I'm starting to wonder if I imagined that. I don't know if she's lonely, bored or just a bit weird, but she needs to stop following me around everywhere. There are shedloads of other girls here that she could be friends with.

'Why do you keep following me?' I say. 'Do you want me to swap bunks or something?'

She shakes her head.

'Well that's good.' I glance up at the huge clock on the wall above the door to the library. It's nearly 9.30, time for lessons. An hour and a half to go until we're allowed to go outside. Mouse catches me looking down at the trainers I put on this morning.

'I'm going to English,' I say. 'Are you coming?'

She shakes her head. Maths then.

'OK then, I'll see you later.' I take a few steps towards the door then turn back. 'Could you like cough or something, the next time you creep up on me? Just so I don't poo my pants?'

She smiles, then stares at her shoes as her cheeks flush red.

*

I suck in deep lungfuls of air as I march around the running track, keeping one eye on the door, to see who else is coming outside, and one eye on the running track on the other side of the fence. It's five past eleven and not a single person has come out of the West Wing door. Tons of kids have spilled out of the East Wing, along with a *lot* of blue sweatshirts. The friends are all dotted around – two or three standing on the touchline watching the football, two throwing balls over the net in the tennis court and another two joining in a basketball game. Then there's Abi, Stuart and Destiny standing by the door that leads back to the rec room. They're all watching me.

I start to jog, the cold air catching in my lungs as my flat feet thump on the track and I half-heartedly pump my arms. It's been a long time since I did any exercise and I feel heavy and awkward. A couple of guys sprint past me. So does a girl with a long, blonde ponytail. But none of them look or laugh. The track's starting to fill up with more kids, walking and running around, or else gathered in the middle to chat. That's good. The more people there are the more chance I have of talking to my brother through the fence without drawing attention to myself. That's if the pre-treatment kids ever come outside. There's still no one on the other side of the fence.

As I continue to run I feel a weird, prickling sensation on the back of my neck as if I'm being watched. But, as I round the bend and catch sight of Stuart, Abi and Destiny again, none of them are looking at me. They're chatting amongst themselves and don't so much as glance at me as I huff and puff towards them. And then I see it, movement at one of the windows on the second floor, and the silhouette of a man, standing in a dark room, looking out. He vanishes almost as quickly as he appeared. I shiver as I continue to jog. This place is seriously creepy.

My heart sinks as time ticks on and I slow to a walk. Most of the other kids who were standing in the middle have wandered off to watch the football or basketball. It's just me, the girl with the ponytail and the two boys who are continuing to plod around the track.

'Five minutes!' Stuart shouts from the doorway to the rec room. 'Five minutes left!'

I stop walking and double over, my hands on my thighs as I suck in the cold February air. I pinned everything on the fact that Mason would exercise at the same time as me. I don't know if that was wishful thinking or stupidity. Of *course* they'd want to keep us separate. But what do I do now? I *have* to give Mason the map of the basement before he's moved to the treatment centre or Mum will be taking two brainwashed kids home with her.

'OK, that's it! Everyone in, please!' Stuart shouts.

I straighten up. As I do, the door to the West Wing opens and a beautiful black girl with a waist-length weave steps out. She's followed by a surly-looking Asian guy, a white guy with closely cropped hair, a massive black guy and – oh my God – it's Mason.

Over on my side of the fence there's a sudden surge of kids coming back into the track field from the football pitch. They crowd around Stuart, Abi and Destiny as they attempt to get to the door.

'Mason!' My bracelets jangle against the metal links of the fence as I run back down the field towards the house. 'Mason Finch!'

For a heart-stopping second, when he sets off anti-clockwise around the track, I don't think he's heard me, but then his head jerks round and our eyes meet. His jaw drops and his eyes widen in surprise. I duck down beside the fence, praying none of the friends clocked his startled expression, and fiddle with my shoelaces. *Walk over here.* I mentally send him a message. *Mason, walk over here.*

A couple of seconds later the fence shakes. My brother is sitting on the ground less than a metre away from me with his back against the wire mesh, his hands on his shoelaces.

'Drew,' he hisses. 'What the hell are you –'

'No time to talk,' I hiss back. Destiny has forced her way through the crowd of students gathered at the doorway and she's heading straight towards me. 'I got your message from Dr Cobey and I've got a plan. You need to get down to the basement. I've got a map of some tunnels that –' As I reach into my bra my brother coughs loudly.

'Drew,' Destiny says, pressing a firm hand to my shoulder. 'It's time to come in.'

Chapter Twenty

'Has anyone seen Israel since this morning?' asks Jake, a fourteen-year-old with a ridiculously cherubic face that makes him look years younger.

Everyone around the table shakes their head. It's 5 p.m., dinner time, and the main topic of conversation is still what happened in assembly.

'He's in isolation,' says Polly.

'No, he's not,' says a boy with a fringe so long it hangs in his eyes. 'They've taken him to the treatment centre. Some girl saw them walking him across the field earlier.'

'Who did?' Jake asks.

Fringe boy shakes his head. 'I don't know but I heard it from Iorwen who heard it from Connor. Apparently some girl was in one of the therapy rooms and she saw Israel through the window. She said he was crying.'

'That's not true,' Polly says. 'You can't see anything through the therapy room windows. She'd have to have been on the first or second floor to see that far across the field. I still think he's in isolation.'

'How do you get referred to pre-treatment?' I ask.

Everyone looks at me in astonishment. It's the first time

I've spoken since we all sat down. Further down the table a boy laughs and jerks his thumb in my direction. I ignore him.

'I'm not sure,' Polly says. 'I think the kids who left this morning had been here for a while. I'm pretty sure they all arrived before I did although –'

She's interrupted by more laughter. The boy who just jerked his thumb at me looks me straight in the eye and cups his hands over his chest, miming big boobs. I check that none of the friends are watching then give him the middle finger. Several kids either side of him laugh. The girl sitting opposite whispers into her neighbour's ear. His eyebrows flash upwards in surprise then he cranes his neck to stare at me.

'Ignore them,' Polly says. 'They're just being dicks.'

But it's not just a handful of kids who are talking about me. The whole length of the table is whispering, pointing and laughing.

'Where's your pistols?' one boy shouts.

'Forget to do your plaits today did you, *Zara*?' shouts another.

Jude, sitting at the far end of the table, laughs so hard she slips halfway down her chair. Mouse, sitting beside her, stares at me with wide, startled eyes then glances away, her cheeks colouring.

Ah, so that's what's happened is it? Mouse has told Jude that my real name is Drew and now Jude has told everyone I think I'm Zara Fox.

'Cuckoo!' One girl makes a circling motion next to her temple with her index finger. 'Cuckoo! Cuckoo!'

I sit very still and stare at a soggy cornflake in the centre of the table as people continue to shout things at me. It's just like school, with Lacey and her cronies spreading rumours about me. I shouldn't have replied when Jude fired all those questions at me on the first night. If you stay silent you don't give someone ammunition to use against you. Which is something Mouse probably knows. I was such a gullible idiot, thinking she was following me around because she was lonely, when all along she was spying on me for Jude. I was an idiot, feeling sorry for her. You can't trust anyone here.

'Show us your special moves, Drew!'

'Where's your combat vest?'

'Did someone deflate your boobs?'

The comments and the laughter just keep on coming. My cheeks are burning and my pulse is thumping in my ears. If I say a word they'll just come back at me with more. If I leave the room they'll think they've won. If I lash out I'll be whipped away to isolation. If I want to save Mason the only thing I can do is sit here and take it.

Chapter Twenty-One

I couldn't get out to the running track yesterday because I had a scheduled therapy session. I sat in a bare, whitewashed room with a woman called Clare who made a strange whistling noise through her nose whenever she exhaled. She asked me about my childhood, my fears and my dreams. After what had happened with the Zara Fox lie I wasn't going to risk making stuff up again so I was monosyllabic instead.

How was my childhood?

Nice.

What were my dreams like?

Scary.

What did I fear?

Freezer.

Clare got very excited when I told her I was scared of freezers. Was it the cold I didn't like? The shape? The low hum? I nearly laughed then but managed to keep a straight face. There was no way I was going to admit to her that I'm afraid of small spaces. That would go straight back to Dr Rothwell and Mrs H. Only an idiot would hand their enemy a weapon to attack them with.

'I would encourage you to be a little more forthright during our next session,' Clare said as the hour drew to a close.

'Why's that then?'

'For your own good, Drew.'

There was something distinctly threatening about the way she said those five words although she kept a smile fixed on her face as she said them.

'Do you work in the treatment unit as well as here?' I asked.

'I do, yes.'

That little creepy smile again. I couldn't help but compare her to Dr Cobey and her honest, open face. Had she told Mason about what went on in the treatment unit? Warned him that she was going to do a runner? It would explain why he gave her the note. She must have really liked him to track me down to give it to me. Or maybe that was her only opportunity to warn someone about Norton House? But why not go to the police or the press instead? If she'd convinced someone to shut the place down instead of giving the note to me she'd still be alive.

I didn't have a therapy session scheduled today but there was no sign of Mason in the West Wing yard. I hung around the fence for as long as I could, until the stroke of 12 p.m., but, while other pre-treatment kids filed out of the door at one minute to twelve, there was no sign of my brother. I tried asking a girl with blonde hair and a pink and white striped jumper if she'd seen him, but Stuart saw us speaking through the fence and came rushing over to tell me it was time to go back in.

I sat alone during lunch. I haven't spoken to anyone since dinner two nights ago. Jude made a couple of comments when we got back to the dorm at bedtime but I blocked her out by putting on headphones and a film. Everyone seems to have forgotten about Israel today and they're all acting like they're in a holiday camp again. The friends have really upped the ante with the entertainment. They wheeled in a candyfloss machine earlier so everyone could stuff their faces with fluffy pink sugar. When I popped my head into the cinema to see what film was playing, several couples were sucking each other's faces off on the back row. According to the rules, students aren't allowed to have relationships with each other but the friends have been blatantly ignoring what's going on. Mouse started following me everywhere again, all rounded shoulders and a face like Droopy. Is she totally stupid? She *has* to realize I know it was her who told Jude my real name. After the third time I spotted her I snapped at her and told her to leave me alone. She scurried away without saying a word.

For the last hour I've been sitting in a corner of the rec room with a book in my hands. But I'm not reading. I'm watching the door that leads to the stairs. I've seen a couple of the friends going up to the dorms but not a single person has gone down to the basement. Even if I do manage to pass the map of the steam tunnels to Mason I'm guessing that the basement door will be locked. We'll both need a staff pass to get in. The friends never take them off unless they're going swimming and, even then, they shut them in a locker with their clothes and keep the key on a rubber band around their wrists.

*

It's 6.55 the next morning and I'm still trying to figure out how the hell I'm going to get into the basement unnoticed. And I've thought of another issue. I know how to get down to the basement but I've got no idea whether Mason will be able to access it from the West Wing.

Jude and Mouse are still asleep in their bunks. I shift to the edge of the mattress as quietly as I can and rest my feet on the first rung of the ladder. I freeze as it creaks under my weight. Beneath me, Mouse stirs in her sleep. She reaches an arm around her pillow and pulls it close but her eyelids don't so much as flicker. I count to thirty then step down the next rung, keeping my eyes fixed on Mouse's face. Jude, on the opposite side of the room, snores so loudly I nearly lose my grip on the ladder.

It takes four stop-start attempts but I finally make it into the en-suite bathroom. There's no lock on the door so I pull it closed quietly then I reach into my bra (I've started wearing it under my pyjama top at night) and carefully pull out the map. I unfold it carefully and lay it on the closed toilet lid. I was hoping it would make more sense now I've got a rough idea of the layout of the ground floor of Norton House, but it still looks like a huge maze. And I've got no way of knowing which parts of the tunnels are accessible from the east and west wings. That's if they're not all blocked up. The pipes at either end of the house seem like they could be accessible from the stairs to the basement, if we can get to them, but the pipework in the centre of the house looks like one big tangle and it's hard to tell which one leads outside. If we can find it we should be able to make our way under the running track, along the field and out towards the shoreline. If we could make it as far as the beach we could double back into the forest and then make our way through the fields until we get to a road. Then we'll have to try to hitch a lift. I press a finger to the map. If that part of the pipe starts at the bottom of the stairs then I'll need to crawl or run for about a hundred metres, turn left, continue on for twenty metres, take a right and –

'Let me come with you,' says a soft, breathy voice in my ear.

I jump so violently I swipe the map clean off the toilet lid and onto the floor.

'It's not . . . it's not . . .' With shaking hands, I snatch it up and shove it down the neckline of my pyjama top. But it's too late. I can tell by the intrigued expression on Mouse's face that she's already seen it.

'It's not what you think it is, Megan.'

'Isn't it?' She plucks at the sides of her pale blue nightdress. On the front, picked out in glitter, are the words *Always be yourself unless you can be a unicorn. Then always be a unicorn.*

I could kick myself for not being more careful. As soon as Mouse tells Jude about the map it'll be all over Norton House by breakfast. The friends will overhear something and I'll be carted off to isolation. Mason could be moved to the treatment centre and I wouldn't even know.

'Mouse . . . Megan,' I stutter. 'I can explain. But, please you mustn't –'

'Take me with you.' She twiddles with her long, dark ponytail.

'Take you where?' Jude's pointed nose pokes around the door and my heart lurches in my chest. 'If you two are going somewhere cool I want to go too.'

Please, I beg Megan silently as her eyes flick towards Jude. *Please don't tell her.*

'Where are you going?' Jude asks again, slipping into the bathroom. 'We don't have secrets in this dorm, do we, Mouse? You wouldn't keep a secret from your best friend.'

Megan's hands twist in front of her and her chin drops. She's going to tell her. Jude's such a big personality there's no way she'd keep something this big from her.

'What's going on?' Jude crosses her arms over her chest. Her eyes narrow as they flit from Mouse to me. 'What are you two up to? Why are you looking so shifty, Mouse?'

I need to say something. I need to come up with a lie that would explain why there's such a tense atmosphere in the room and why Mouse won't meet anyone's eyes. But my mouth is so dry my tongue has stuck to the roof of my mouth and my brain is on go-slow.

'Swimming,' Mouse says suddenly, giving me a sideways look. 'Drew is going swimming today and I want to go with her.'

'Swimming?' Jude's jaw drops. 'Swimming? You?'

She looks Mouse up and down and laughs. It's the ugliest, cruelest cackle I've ever heard.

'Yes, swimming.' The map, shoved down the front of my pyjama top, crackles as I stand up so I wrap my hands around my neck and press my forearms against my chest to silence it. 'So what if Megan wants to go swimming with me? Have you got some kind of problem with that, Jude?'

The laughter stops as suddenly as it started. Her lips thin and her nostrils flare.

'You need to watch yourself,' she hisses. 'There's something weird about you, and I don't mean the fact that you pretended to be a computer game character. There's something snake-like that I don't trust. I'm watching you, Drew.' She points her index finger at me and smiles. 'You're up to something and I'm going to find out exactly what it is.'

Chapter Twenty-Two

'Thank you,' I say to Mouse as we walk side by side through the rec room. It's the first opportunity we've had to talk alone since the incident in the bathroom. Jude has been trailing us all morning. She sat across the table from me at breakfast, glowering silently before she told Polly, in a ridiculously loud voice, that you have to keep your enemies close in a place like this.

'For making up the lie about going swimming,' I add as we pass the games zone.

'Well, we are going swimming, aren't we?' Mouse says, giving me a sideways look. A hint of a smile plays on the edges of her lips. Was that a conspiratorial look I just saw?

'When are you getting your boob job, Zara?' one of the boys playing PlayStation calls as I pull on the door to the gym.

'Right after you get your penis enlargement,' I shout back.

A chorus of laughter follows me and Mouse into the gym.

'I don't know how you can do that,' Mouse says softly.

'Do what?'

'Laugh it off when people make fun of you.'

I look at her in surprise. Is that how I come across? As someone who can laugh off that kind of thing? Did she not see how much I was shaking at the dinner table the other day when the whole Zara Fox thing kicked off?

'It wasn't me by the way,' Mouse adds as we pass a couple of kids pounding the treadmills.

I grab the handle of the door that leads through to the swimming pool. 'What wasn't?'

'Who started the Zara Fox thing. I know you think I told everyone your real name because I overheard Abi call you Drew, but I didn't. I swear. Jez asked Jude what your name and, when she said it was Zara Fox, he laughed and asked her if she'd ever looked up "gullible" in the dictionary and found her own name.'

'I bet that went down well.'

'Jude went bright red. I think she fancies Jez.'

'Let me guess, now she's blaming me for humiliating her in front of him?' As we step into the swimming pool changing room, we're hit by a cloud of hot, humid chlorine-scented air.

'Pretty much. She can be vicious when she thinks someone's done her wrong. That's why she started spreading stuff around about you. She said you were kicked out of school for wearing shorts and a tank top to lessons, that you stuff your bra with socks to look more like Zara Fox, that you're a liar and that you flirted with Israel when you knew she liked him –'

'I thought she liked Jez?'

Mouse dumps her bag on a wooden bench. 'Who knows. I've been here for three weeks and I've lost track of the number of guys she fancies.'

I dump my bag beside Megan's and sit down heavily. Opposite us is a row of ten cubicles. All the doors are ajar.

We're the only ones here. Us and the CCTV unit blinking above the door.

'There are no locks on the cubicle doors,' Mouse says. 'Just in case you were wondering. Oh, and I can't actually swim. I like paddling in the sea but that's about it. Anyway, cold air and water bring on my asthma.'

'I can't remember the last time I went swimming,' I say. 'I haven't been for years. Dad used to take us but then Mason dived into the shallow end of a pool on holiday when he was ten and knocked himself out. He's been afraid of water ever since.

'Megan.' I shift back on the bench so my back is against the wall and pull my knees into my chest. 'Don't take this the wrong way but how come you're so chatty all of a sudden?'

She laughs. It's the first time I've heard it and it's an infectious gurgly giggle. Her laughter stops as suddenly as it starts and she claps a hand across her mouth, her eyes fixed on the CCTV camera in the corner of the room. It's as though she's only just noticed it's there.

'What?' I say. 'What is it?'

She shifts on the bench so her back is facing the CCTV camera then she cups her hands around her mouth.

'You asked, the other day, how long it takes to get moved to pre-treatment,' she says quietly.

I nod.

'Normally it's about ten days. But I've been here over three weeks, longer than anyone else. Everyone I arrived with was sent to pre-treatment ages ago.' She raises her eyebrow and gives me a knowing look.

Oh! I get it now. Mouse chose to keep quiet so she couldn't

be assessed by her therapist and moved onto pre-treatment. Genius. Absolute genius. But she's worried they'll move her on anyway. That's why she was so scared in assembly when the names were read out. She thought she might be on the list.

'You know the post-treatment kids that were in assembly the other day?' Mouse says, her voice so low I have to lean in to hear what she's saying. 'They all arrived here after me. I know what they were like when they got here. And the kids before them. They're not the same people they were when they came in, Drew. It's like they've been brainwashed.'

I lean away so I can see her eyes. Her pupils are huge and filled with fear.

'I know,' I whisper. 'I met someone, at home, who'd had the treatment. He's like some kind of programmed zombie now.'

'I don't want that to happen to me, Drew. I don't want to change.' She reaches into her pocket and takes two short, sharp puffs on her inhaler.

'I like who I am,' she says, as she tucks it back into her pocket, 'no matter what other people may think.'

She looks at me so intently I have to look away. She sounds so truthful. She *looks* so truthful. But I only have her word that she didn't tell Jude my real name. All this could be a ruse. She might already have told Jude about the map of the basement and all this is so she can get more information out of me. But I can't do this alone. I can't see any way that I can get hold of a staff pass, cause a disruption that will distract the CCTV cameras and the friends, *and* slip away unnoticed. I need help.

'Megan,' I ask, 'why did you get excluded from school?'

'Schools,' she corrects me.

'OK. Why were you excluded?'

She plucks at a loose thread on the hem of her jumper. 'You'll judge me if I tell you.'

'I won't. I promise.

'No, I can't.'

'Megan, I want to get out of here and so do you. If you're serious about that you need to be honest with me.'

She's still for a couple of seconds then she shrugs her shoulders. 'Stealing,' she says. 'There you go. Judge me all you like but that's the truth. I was excluded for stealing.'

When I don't immediately reply she looks worried, then perplexed. 'Why are you smiling, Drew? What's so funny?'

Chapter Twenty-Three

'So do you think you can do it?'

Megan grins. 'Of course I can do it. Compared to nicking a watch a lanyard should be a walk in the park.'

It's the day after our conversation in the swimming pool changing rooms and we're sitting up against a wall of the bowling alley pretending to watch the match. The boys are totally showing off, jumping about and high-fiving each other whenever one of them gets a strike. They think we're whispering to each other because we fancy them. Idiots. Hopefully whoever is monitoring the CCTV will think the same.

'How did you learn how to nick a watch, Meg?'

'My dad.'

'Wow. Is he a . . .'

She laughs. 'No, Drew, he's not a thief if that's what you're thinking. He's a magician.'

'Like Dynamo or David Blaine?'

'He'd like to think so, but the nearest he's got to appearing on TV is sitting next to one.' She laughs dryly. 'He does a lot of working men's clubs. He travels all over Wales doing his show but he mostly works in the Rhondda.'

'I bet your birthday parties were fun when you were a kid.'

'Nah, it was embarrassing, having a dad who pulled scarves

out of your mouth for a living. I wanted him to have proper job like the other kids' dads. What does your dad do?'

'He's a psychologist.'

'Like Dr Rothwell.'

I nod. The more Megan opens up to me the more I like her, but I'm not ready to tell her everything about Dad just yet.

'You OK?' she asks.

'Yeah. I was . . . I was just thinking about my brother. I didn't go out to the running track yesterday because we went to the pool instead and –'

'We sat in the changing rooms until Jude came in, you mean!'

'You haven't been swimming you liars, your fingertips aren't wrinkled!' I say and Mouse laughs.

We lapse into a companionable silence that I break by sighing loudly.

'What if Mason was outside yesterday and now he thinks I've been fast-tracked to the treatment centre?'

'He'll be outside today.' She gives me a reassuring smile. 'I'm sure you'll see –'

She's interrupted by the sound of the bell ringing.

'Lunch,' we both say in unison.

*

We don't say a word to each other as we fork overcooked spaghetti bolognaise into our mouths. Megan's been really chatty over the last twenty-four hours and it hasn't gone unnoticed. We've both noticed several kids nudging each other as we've been chatting and I've seen a few of the friends exchange raised eyebrows. We need to be more careful. The last thing either of us need is for her to be moved to pre-treatment before we hatch our plan.

I push the muddy-tasting mince around my plate with my fork. Jude is sitting next to Jez but it's not him she's watching intently. It's me. Ever since she discovered me and Mouse in the en suite she's followed us everywhere, including the swimming pool. The only reason we got to chat uninterrupted in the bowling alley was because she had a therapy session. I glance away. As I do, Mouse nudges me sharply. I pull in my elbows to give her more room. A second later, she nudges me again. This time I give her a look. She's definitely the type to hog the armrest on a train.

'I can't move any further to my left,' I hiss, 'not unless I want to end up on Jake's lap!'

She shakes her head. 'I don't want you to move up. I want to know what your brother looks like.'

'Huh? He's about five eight with brown hair, a floppy fringe and –'

I follow Megan's line of sight and gasp softly. Over on the other side of the canteen a guy with brown hair and a green catering uniform is removing trays from the stand and stacking them up on a low table.

'Is that –'

'Sssh.'

Turn round, I tell him in my head. *Turn round. I need to see your face.*

For several agonising seconds he continues to unload and stack trays, keeping his back to us. My stomach is a tight knot. *Turn around*, I will. *Mason, if that's you, turn around!*

Out of the corner of my eye I see Mouse reach for her tray.

CRASH!

In one quick move, she yanks it off the table and onto the floor. The plate, knife and fork clatter onto the tiles and the plate upends, splattering the ground with mince and spaghetti. The boy by the trays has turned round to see what the noise was.

And he's staring straight at me.

Mason!

'What the hell's happened, here?' Destiny rushes over to us. 'Megan? Did you do this?' She gestures at the mess on the floor.

Megan nods dumbly, a pained, apologetic expression on her face.

'It slipped out of her fingers,' I say. 'When she was trying to get up.'

Destiny shakes her head. She doesn't buy it.

'Over here, please!' She raises a hand and clicks her fingers. 'Mop and bucket as quickly as you can!'

Mason, still staring at me from across the room, visibly starts. His eyes flick towards Destiny and he raises a hand and points to his chest.

'Yes you!' she barks. 'As quickly as you can, please.'

*

I can barely breathe as Mason crosses the canteen with a mop in one hand and a bucket in the other. I'm so terrified that Destiny or one of the other friends will realize we're related that I avoid making eye contact with him and instead continue to push my spaghetti around my plate with my fork.

'Sorry,' Megan says, as he draws closer. 'I've made more work for you.'

'No worries. I was getting bored of stacking trays anyway.'

Tears well in my eyes at the sound of my little brother's voice and I have to bite down on my lip to stop them from spilling onto my cheeks. He sounds normal. They haven't sent him to treatment yet. He's OK.

'Megan, would you please not talk to this student,' Destiny says, sounding flustered. 'He's working here for punishment, not to be fraternized with and – oh for God's sake! Josh! Get down from that chair. If you don't sit down immediately . . .' She rushes off to the other side of the table where Josh and Connor are standing on their chairs and having a sword fight with breadsticks. Several of the other friends rush over to them too.

I can feel Mason standing behind my chair. I can hear him sniffing as though he's got a cold, and the splosh of the mop hitting the bucket. He's so close I could touch him if I reached out a hand.

'It's OK,' Megan hisses, nudging my elbow. 'The friends are all distracted, but be quick.'

I slowly twist in my chair; I don't want to draw attention to myself. Mason's floppy hair looks dirty, there are raised, angry spots on his jaw and dark circles under his eyes. I've never seen him look so pale and unhealthy. As I watch, he slaps the mop onto the tile floor, smearing bolognaise sauce left and right and then dunks the mop into the bucket. He knows I'm sitting here. He saw me from across the room. So why isn't he looking at me?

'Mase,' I whisper. 'Are you OK?'

He doesn't reply. Instead, he twists the water out of the mop head then slaps it back onto the floor.

'Mason. Talk to me, *please*.'

This time he looks up. His blue eyes meet mine and he blinks, once, twice, as his eyes fill with tears.

'What are you doing here, Drew?'

'I've come to help you escape.'

'You?' He laughs softly, dryly.

'What?'

'You were supposed to get help – tell the police, a teacher or social services or someone. Or at least Mum! What good can you do?' He crouches down, picks up the broken pieces of plate and stacks them up on top of each other.

'You were never supposed to come here, Drew,' he whispers, as he reaches between me and Megan and places the broken crockery on the table. 'You're in danger too now and it's all my fault.'

'No, it's not!' I touch the back of his hand. He snatches it away as though electrocuted. 'Anyway, I've got a plan to get us both out of here.'

'Quick!' Megan hisses. 'Destiny's coming back.'

'Here.' I shove the folded map into Mason's hand. 'It's a map of the tunnels in the basement. They lead outside.' Out of the corner of my eye, I see a bright blue sweatshirt heading towards us.

'Steal a staff pass,' I say. 'And we'll meet you down there after dinner, in the central tunnel, under the entrance hall.'

'Thanks for tidying up!' Megan shoves me away and throws her arms around a startled Mason and hugs him close. A second later, Destiny draws up alongside us.

'Megan Jones!' she barks. 'Let go of that boy!'

But Megan continues to hang tightly onto my brother's shoulders. When he tries to wriggle away she tightens her grip.

'Megan!' Destiny yanks at her arm. 'Let go!'

'Would you like a cuddle too?' Mouse says, suddenly letting go of Mason. She hooks one arm around Destiny's neck and the other around her shoulders. Destiny's a strong woman but Mouse has surprise on her side and it takes the friend several minutes to extricate herself from Mouse's death grip. Several of her dreadlocks come loose from her bun during the struggle and when she finally pulls away and stands up her cheeks are flushed.

She glares at Meg, her eyes flashing with anger. 'Give me one reason why I shouldn't throw you straight into isolation.'

'I . . . I . . .' Megan stutters. 'I only wanted to hug you. I thought . . . I thought you needed one.'

Jake, beside me, snorts in amusement then gasps as I elbow him in the ribs.

'Mrs H. did say that the friends are here to support and help us . . .' I tail off as Destiny gives me the evils.

The entire table is silent. Everyone's watching us, waiting to see what Destiny will do next.

'Dest . . .' Abi appears beside Destiny and puts a hand on her shoulder. 'Is everything OK here?'

Destiny blows out her cheeks and reaches for one of her stray dreadlocks. She winds it round her bun and tucks it in, looking seriously pissed off.

'Fine thanks, Abi,' she says tightly then looks back at Mouse. 'Megan, consider this a verbal warning. If I have to talk to you again, I'll send you to isolation. Do we understand each other?'

Megan nods, her expression pure (faked) contrition.

'For a girl who doesn't talk much you've been awfully expressive this lunchtime, Megan Jones. I might have to have a little word with your therapist later. It seems you're making more progress than we thought.'

Megan's hands clench in her lap. Neither of us say a word as Abi walks back to the far end of the table and Destiny leads Mason, with his mop and bucket in his hands, back to the tray stand. As he puts the bucket on the floor he slips a hand into his pocket.

'Thank you,' I breathe. 'If you hadn't launched yourself at my brother like that Destiny would have seen him take the map.'

Mouse turns her clenched fists over and opens her fingers. There's a flash of white then she closes her fingers again. 'You can thank me when you get me out of here, Drew.'

Chapter Twenty-Four

I could barely eat during dinner I was so excited. We'd done it. We'd managed to get the map to Mason *and* Mouse had stolen Destiny's lanyard and staff pass. We decided to sit apart because we didn't want to attract any more attention. My stomach still clenched with fear whenever one of the friends walked past Mouse. Destiny wasn't on duty during dinner but she had to have realized that her lanyard had gone the moment she'd tried to get out of the rec room. There was no sign of her when we were ushered out of the rec room and into the canteen. Maybe she was looking for it.

I kept one eye on the canteen door all the way through dinner, half hopeful I'd see Mason again, half terrified Mrs H. would storm in, demanding we all turn out our pockets. Neither happened and, by the time we filed out of the canteen after stacking our trays, I felt sick with stress. How the hell were we going to get out of the rec room and down the stairs without being seen?

I spotted Mrs H. the second I walked into the rec room. She was standing next to the therapy session board, watching as everyone filed in.

'She knows,' I hissed to Mouse out of the side of my mouth as we passed her. 'Did you see the look she just gave you?'

'She doesn't know anything. Even if Destiny has reported a lost pass they don't know that one of us has taken it.'

'What if they change the door codes?'

'For one missing card?' She shook her head. 'Won't happen. They'd have to reprogram every door in the building and reissue cards to all the staff.'

I wanted to believe her but I couldn't shake the uneasy feeling in the pit of my stomach. Getting hold of Destiny's card had been easy. Almost too easy.

As it was there was no way we could slip out through the doors to the stairs during rec without being seen. The friends seemed to be everywhere and Mrs H. began doing laps of the room. We'd have to go to plan B – try to slip out during quiet time in the dorms.

*

'Have you got it?' I ask Mouse now.

'Yep.' She taps her right boob. 'In my bra.' Her cheeks are flushed and her amber eyes are shining. She couldn't look more different from the pasty-faced girl who stared listlessly at the wall when I arrived a few days ago.

It's 9.09 p.m. We were sent to the dorm for quiet time nine minutes ago but the first floor of Norton House is still ridiculously noisy. There are boys on the girls' floor, girls on the boys' floor; kids popping in and out of each other's rooms constantly, laughing, chatting and listening to music. Destiny reappeared two minutes ago, with a lanyard hanging around her neck. I had to force myself to smile at her when she clocked me walking up the stairs behind Mouse. Jude, who'd kept her beady eye on us in the rec room, followed us into the dorm. She tried to chat to us as we lay on our bunks but soon got bored and wandered off when she failed to engage us in conversation.

'How long do you reckon we've got?' I ask Mouse, as we stand at the glass partition and stare down onto the boys' floor where students and friends are still meandering about. 'Before they realize we're missing?'

She glances at my watch. 'If we go now, hopefully about fifty-one minutes.'

The friends come round to check the dorms to make sure everyone is in the correct bed at 10 p.m. Once the check is complete a buzzer sounds, the doors lock and all the lights go out.

'Do you think we should put pillows under our duvets,' Mouse adds, 'to make it look as though we're in bed? To buy us some extra time?'

'Too risky. If Jude comes back early and pulls back the duvets, she'll tell someone. If we go soon, we've got more than enough time to get down the stairs into the basement, meet Mason and get through the tunnels.'

I sound more optimistic than I feel. There are so many things that could go wrong. The door codes could be changed, Mason might not be able to get down to the basement, and we might get lost in the steam tunnels. That's if they haven't been blocked up. But we have to try. Destiny said Mason was working in the canteen as a punishment. If he's been causing trouble, there's every chance they could fast-track him to the treatment unit.

'Ready?' I glance at Mouse.

'Ready,' she says.

I try to look nonchalant as I stroll along the balcony and head for the stairs. I don't look back to check whether Megan is following me. The plan is to walk separately down to the boys' floor and mill about until we have the opportunity to meet at the door to the stairwell, check no one's watching, use the card, and get out. It's not much of a plan admittedly and there's every chance that the CCTV operator will see us and sound the alarm, but it's all we've got. We considered setting off the fire alarm but neither of us know what happens if that goes off. For all we know any non-emergency exit doors could automatically lock.

The handrail feels slippery under my damp palm as I take the stairs one by one. Abi is sitting on a bunk in the dorm next to us, chatting to Polly. Stuart is standing in the doorway to one of the boys' rooms. There are only two friends on duty tonight and they're both distracted. For now anyway.

'Oi oi!' shouts a familiar voice.

Israel is standing outside one of the boys' dorms, his back resting against the wall and his arms crossed over his chest. I hurry down the rest of the stairs.

'Oh my God, you're back. Are you OK? Where've you been?'

'Isolation.' He smiles, then looks sharply to his left and frowns. 'Did you see that?'

I follow his gaze. He's watching the three boys who are playing cards on the floor. 'See what?'

'The snake.'

'A snake? Where?!'

'On the ground.' He points at the three boys, his index finger quivering in the air. 'Over there.'

I can't see anything. And the three boys don't seem the slightest bit worried.

'Rummy!' one of them shouts, slapping the ground with a card.

'Are you OK?' I look back at Israel. He's stopped staring at the boys and is now gawping at the ground between our feet.

'Man, they're cool,' he breathes.

'What are?' Out of the corner of my eye I spot Mouse pacing back and forth by the door. She looks like a tiger in a zoo, patrolling its cage.

'The little cars,' Israel says. 'Who brought the little cars in?'

'What cars?' I ask, distracted by Mouse making circling motions with her right hand. She wants me to hurry up.

'How do they keep going for so long?' Israel asks, crouching down. 'Are they remote-controlled?'

He swipes at the ground near my feet, forcing me to jump out of the way. What's he talking about? There aren't any cars on the floor. Just like there was no snake near the card-playing boys. Is he trying to be funny? If so, it's not working.

'I'll . . . um . . .' I back away. 'I'll talk to you soon, OK?'

Israel continues to paw the ground, chattering to himself as I walk past the card-playing boys.

'Mouse,' I hiss as I draw closer to her. 'What's going on?'

She makes a sharp nodding motion with her head, up towards the balcony. 'Look. Not straight away. Subtly. Don't talk to me. We're being watched.'

I double back and hover beside the card players. 'Can I have a go?'

All the boys stop playing and stare up at me.

'Do you know how to play rummy?' one of them asks.

'Yeah, my dad taught me.'

He looks at the other boys. They shrug their shoulders then shuffle up to make a space for me on the floor. As I sit down, I glance up, towards the balcony. Jude is sitting on the top step and she's staring straight at me. She probably saw my conversation with Israel and has convinced herself that I'm making another play for him now he's back. Arrrgh! Why can't she just sod off and mind her own business?

I glance at my watch – 9.16 p.m. With Stuart and Abi still occupied now's the perfect time to sneak out of the door – I doubt the card-playing boys would even notice – but not if Jude's watching. One of us could go up the stairs and distract her but then only one could escape and I promised Mouse I'd get her out. There's no point sending her on her own because she hasn't seen the map. She'd never be able to navigate the tunnels to find Mason.

'Here you go,' one of the boys hands me some cards. 'So what you do is . . .'

As he mansplains a game I've played hundreds of times I look over at Mouse and shake my head. We're going to have to abandon the plan. With any luck, Mason will realize pretty quickly that we're not coming and find his own way out of the tunnels.

'Snake!' Israel screams in my ear. A split second later, I'm yanked back by my hood and dragged across the floor.

'Israel!' I lash out at him, but he's already let go of me and is running back to the card circle. He grabs the boy I was sitting next to by the collar and hauls him away from the group.

'You need to run!' he shouts. 'There are snakes everywhere. Get out, man! Get out!'

'Hey!' The second boy he tries to rescue from the imaginary snakes resists and a scuffle breaks out. Fists fly and suddenly everyone is on their feet. Kids fly out of their dorms, startled by the noise. Jude, at the top of the stairs, disappears in a crush of girls hurrying past her. I'm surrounded on all sides by kids baying for a fight.

'Drew!' Mouse grabs my arm and pulls me to my feet. 'What's going on?'

'It's Israel. He's hallucinating. I need to break up the fight and explain why he's being so weird.'

'No!' She yanks on my arm, pulling me back as I try to break through the crowd to get to Israel. 'We can get help when we've escaped. Nothing you do here is going to make any difference.'

'But they're going to beat him. And he hasn't done anything wrong.'

'Stuart's going to stop it. Look!'

There's a flash of blue jumper as Stuart piles into the mix.

'Please, Drew,' Mouse shouts in my ear. 'Please, we need to go.'

Chapter Twenty-Five

'Quick! Quick!' Mouse holds the card to the black box beside the glass door and I say a quick prayer as the red lights flash, once, twice, three times. I give the door the smallest of shoves, fully expecting it to be shut firm but it gives beneath my fingers and opens.

'Go, go!' I bundle Mouse through the door first. I'm too terrified to look back to see if anyone has spotted us so I shove myself up against her, half expecting to feel a hand on the back of my neck as we slip through the gap.

'Shut it!' We slam our body weight against the door, share a split second look – jubilation mixed with fear – and then head for the stairs. My legs feel like jelly as I leap down them, taking them two at a time. I slip as I round the corner of the staircase and only stop myself from falling by hanging onto the handrail. Mouse is close behind me as I take the second set of steps. She's puffing and panting like a steam train but she's keeping up.

'Card!' I say, barely able to speak as we reach the door that leads to the basement. Mouse uncurls her fingers but her hand is empty. Where's the card? I wait, tapping my foot impatiently, as she roots around in her bra. She looks at me with huge, scared eyes and shakes her head. It's gone. Please

God don't let her have dropped it inside the dorm as I shoved her through the door.

I gesture for her to stay where she is then head back up the stairs, scanning the ground for the small, white staff pass. As I reach the second corner I see it, lying on the pale grey tiles. I snatch it up and glance at my watch: 9.21 p.m. We've only got thirty-nine minutes until bed check. Loud, excited voices drift down the stairs from the dorms above. The friends obviously haven't got the situation with Israel under control yet but we're running out of time. If they decide to bring bed check forward we're screwed.

I sprint back down the stairs to Mouse and press the card to the black box next to the basement door. The red lights flash, there's the tiniest of clicks and the door swings open revealing narrow wooden stairs, lit by the dull glow of a circular emergency lamp fixed to the wall. A cold, musty smell hits me as I step through the door and the wall feels damp under my fingertips. I can hear Mouse's raggedy breathing and heavy footsteps behind me as she follows me down, down, down into the bowels of Norton House.

The light fades as we reach the bottom but I can make out four or five cardboard boxes, stuffed with battered cricket bats, broken tennis rackets and volleyball nets, stacked up against one wall. Beside them are three bikes with flat tyres and loose chains, a pile of rusty cooking pots and a tray of assorted cutlery. The walls are brick, the floor is cobbled and, at the far end of the room, an archway opens onto darkness. It has to be one of the abandoned steam tunnels that run through to the centre of the house.

'Megan?' I turn to look at my room-mate. 'Are you OK?'

Meg's hand is pressed against her chest and she's breathing in short, sharp gasps, punctuated by a high wheezing sound.

'Asthma attack,' she pants.

'Have you got your inhaler?'

She pats the pockets of her black cardigan and shakes her head, her eyes wide and panicky. I don't know what to do. I don't want to leave her behind but she can't run if she can't breathe.

'Do you want to go back?' I ask.

She shakes her head, but the panic in her eyes has morphed into fear. I could try to get back into the dorm to get her inhaler but, even if I could get back out again, there's not enough time.

'Let me . . . um . . .' I am frozen by indecision. Mason might be standing in the central tunnel at this very moment waiting for us. I can't just leave him there, not knowing what's going on, but I don't want to leave Mouse either.

'I'll go back upstairs,' Mouse says, struggling for breath between words. 'Go and meet your brother. Send help when you get out.'

'Are you sure?'

She nods her head.

I hand her the card. 'Can you get back upstairs OK?'

'I'll go slowly,' she says breathlessly.

'If you're sure.' I hug her tightly then turn sharply. I can't bear the disappointment in her eyes.

'I'll get you out of here as soon as I can, Mouse,' I call as I start to run. 'I promise.'

*

Within seconds of entering the tunnel, it is pitch black. I can't see my hands as I reach one in front of me and trail the other along the cold, damp wall. The cobbles under my feet are uneven and I have to slow my run to a jog so I don't slip. Water drips from the roof and plops onto my head, my arm, my cheek then my outstretched hand smacks against a brick wall and I stop abruptly. Which way now? Mason's got the map so I have to rely on my memory. Left. I need to go left, then first right. I turn left then take a right as the wall vanishes and my hand waves in the air. I take one step forward, then another and another and then CLANG! My hand hits something hard and metallic. I touch it with both hands, tentatively exploring it with my fingertips. It's some kind of metal grate or door and it's blocking the route out of the tunnel. I weave my fingers into the holes and push. It doesn't move. I yank it towards me. Nothing. My chest tightens and a wave of panic crashes over me. Think, Drew, think. Which way do the other tunnels lead? If I go back the way I came then go straight ahead is there another tunnel that goes right? I try to conjure up the map in my mind and draw a blank. I take a deep breath and blow out slowly and steadily. I need to calm down. I haven't forgotten the map. It's still there, it's still in my head. I just need a second to pull myself together and then –

I've got it! I turn sharply and head back down the tunnel then take a right, a left and another right. It's so dark now I feel like I'm blind. Dark thoughts flash through my mind. What if I've gone the wrong way or there's a hole in the floor and I fall through it? Or something crashes on top of me? Mouse won't tell anyone I'm down here. If I don't come back, she'll assume I've escaped. If something happens to me no one will come and rescue me. I could die down here and no one would ever know.

'Please let this be the right way,' I whisper as I inch my way forwards, hands outstretched. 'Please let it –'

The toe of my boot catches on something and a piercing squeak fills the tunnel, echoing off the low ceiling. Rats! Oh my God!

Every bone in my body urges me to turn and run but, instead, I force myself to take another step forwards. I tense, anticipating another small body hitting my boot, or leaping off the wall onto my arm or my face. Nothing happens so I take another step. Then another.

'Keep going, Drew. Keep going, keep going, keep going.'

After what feels like an age the tunnel ends and my right hand grasps at nothing. If I turn right here, I should end up in the central tunnel, directly beneath the entrance hall.

*

'Mason!' I call softly as I run through the tunnel towards the arched exit. Tiny streams of light, escaping through the gaps in the entrance hall floorboards, illuminate the small square room. 'Mason, are you here?'

I glance at my watch: 9.41 p.m. Where is he? Did he get tired of waiting and escape without me? No, he wouldn't do that. He would have waited.

'Mase?' I run towards the archway that leads towards the West Wing and pause in the entrance of the tunnel. 'Mason?'

My voice echoes off the walls and bounces off the bricks. I stand very still, waiting for a reply or the sound of my brother's trainers thudding towards me. But there's nothing. Not a sound apart from my heart thudding in my ears. Sweat trickles down my back, sucking my T-shirt against my skin. Where is he?

I return to the centre of the room and wait, my eyes fixed on the glass face of my watch.

9.42 p.m.

9.43 p.m.

9.44 p.m.

The sound of footsteps makes me start and I look hopefully in the direction of the West Wing. But Mason doesn't appear in the entrance of the tunnel. Instead, a low voice drifts down through the floorboards.

'The pre-treatment head count is complete,' Mrs H. says, as clear as day. 'All thirty students in the West Wing are accounted for. Stuart just radioed to say that he's calmed down the situation in East Wing but I don't trust that idiot to do the head count. I'm going over there now.'

Chapter Twenty-Six

I stand completely still, one hand clasped over my mouth to silence my rasping breathing.

What do I do?

Escape or go back?

If I escape, I could try to raise the alarm but who would I tell? I can't tell Tony or Mum. And the police didn't believe me when I told them Dr Cobey was deliberately run over. If I went to the press, I'd be laughed at. I need Mason and Megan with me. A newspaper editor might class a single teenager as a time waster or attention seeker but if the three of us made a stink they'd have to listen to us. We could take Zed along too, and Charlie. They couldn't ignore how different he is to Zed's video.

I glance at the tunnel that leads to the outside and make a decision.

Go!

*

All thirty students in the west wing are accounted for. Mrs H.'s voice reverberates in my head as I speed back down the tunnel that leads to the East Wing, both arms outstretched.

That means Mason is still his dorm. Either he didn't make it down to the basement or he went back up when he couldn't find me. And now Mrs H. is on her way to do a head count in the East Wing. I need to get back before she does, but I haven't got the staff pass any more. If Mouse has already let herself into the dorm I'll be stuck in the stairwell.

'Mouse!' I call as I burst out of the final tunnel and sprint across the room. The toe of my boot catches on something on the floor and I lurch to my left, my hands desperately reaching through the gloom as I try to grab something, anything to stop myself from falling. My fingertips graze something solid and, for a split second, I think I'm OK but then – CRASH! – the box of cutlery clangs to the floor. I fall too. My hands and wrists take the impact as I hit the hard cobblestones. I lie still, too shocked to move for a couple of seconds then I tentatively rotate one hand, then the other. I flex and contract my fingers. Nothing seems to be broken. Wincing, I force myself onto my knees and then onto my feet. My left knee twinges as I take a step but I force myself to keep walking. I need to get back to the dorm before Mouse and Mrs H.

I half run, half scrabble up the first set of stairs. 'Mouse?'

But there's no sign of my room-mate outside the door. Or at the bend in the staircase.

'Mouse!' I call, louder this time. 'Mouse, wait! I'm coming.'

The heels of my hands are throbbing and a shooting pain rips through my knee with each step I take but I don't stop running. I grab hold of the handrail and yank myself up, up, up the stairs. 'Mouse! Wait!'

As I round the last bend, I look towards the top of the stairs, desperately hoping to catch sight of the heel of Mouse's trainers or the hem of her black trousers but there's nothing. I've missed her. She's already gone through the door, back to the dorms. I keep low as I climb the remaining flight of stairs then drop to my hands and knees and crawl. When I reach the last step I lower my head and press the side of my face against the cool tile and take a couple of deep breaths. My heart is racing and my back and forehead are slick with sweat. What do I do now?

I raise my head, look through the glass door, spot a pair of white trainers, and lower my head again. That's not a good sign. It means all the other kids have been ushered into their dorms and Stuart and Abi are doing bed checks. If I knock on the door to be let in how do I explain the fact I'm in the stairwell? I could lie and say the door was left open and I tried to get down to the rec room to get help for Israel, but the doors are *never* left open. They close automatically, a couple of seconds after someone walks through them. I'll have to go back down to the basement and try to escape on my own. I never should have let Mouse come back up here on her own. I should have come back up here with her and –

I nearly jump out of my skin as a dark head appears around the corner of the staircase.

'Mouse! What the –'

'I heard . . .' she takes a laboured breath '. . . the . . . crash . . . from the basement. I thought . . .' another breath, sucking in air like a landed fish '. . . that it might be you.'

Her face is pale and sweaty and she's breathing rapidly. She looks bloody awful.

The white trainers pass in front of the glass door again and I duck back down. When I look back up the trainers, and Mouse, have gone.

'Mouse,' I hiss. 'Are you still there?'

'Yes,' says a disembodied voice.

'OK, don't talk any more than you need to. Have you still got the pass?'

She doesn't reply but, a couple of seconds later, her hand appears, sliding the white staff pass along the tiles towards me.

'OK.' I snatch it up. 'We're probably going to have to move quite quickly if we're going to get back in without being seen. Do you think you can do that?'

A strange rasping sound comes from around the corner. I think it's Mouse laughing.

'Great. OK. In a second, I'm going to get up and we're both going to stand either side of the door. I'll check to see if the coast is clear then we both go back in, as quickly as we can.'

Mouse, who must be sitting on the floor with her back to the slim section of wall between my staircase and the staircase to the staff quarters, gives me the thumbs-up.

'Can you stand up OK?' I ask.

Her hand reappears, the thumb-up again.

'OK. On three. One . . . two . . . three . . .'

I skirt over to my left, out of sight of the door, scrabble to my feet and throw myself up the last couple of stairs and against the wall. I press my back to it and look to my left. Mouse is doing the same on the other side of door. Her lips are a weird blue colour and all the tendons in her neck are raised. What the hell was I thinking, letting her come back up here on her own? What if she'd collapsed on the stairs? She could have died. I push the thought out of my mind. I need to concentrate. This isn't over yet. We could still beat Mrs H. back to the dorms *and* avoid any of the friends spotting us. I'll just have to pray that whoever monitors the CCTV is checking their phone or has gone for a wee.

I take a tiny sidestep to my left so the fingers of my left hand are touching the doorframe.

Please, I pray as I grip the staff pass so tightly the edges of the plastic cut into my fingers. *Please don't let anyone see us.*

I twist at the waist and look through the glass door. The boys' floor is empty and all but one door – Israel's – is shut.

'Go!' I whisper to Mouse. At the same time, I press the pass to the black box. The red lights flash once, twice . . . *please don't let anyone come out of the dorms, please don't let anyone come out of . . .* three times. I push at the door, reach for Mouse's hand and yank her through it.

'Up the stairs,' I say, as I shove the pass between the waist-band of my cargo trousers and my stomach.

Mouse stumbles forwards, her hand still in mine. She looks like she's about to pass out. From down here the stairs look like Everest and our dorm, the peak. There's no way we're going to get in there before –

'Girls!'

A thousand icy fingers stroke my spine and I freeze. I know that voice.

I let go of Mouse's hand and turn slowly. Standing next to the glass door with her hands on her hips and her lips pressed tightly together, is Mrs H.

'Come here!' She beckons us with a crooked index finger.

Mouse gives me a stricken look. *Don't panic*, I signal with my eyes but I'm totally faking being calm. I am so ter-rified I feel sick. As we step slowly towards Mrs H., my gaze automatically drops to the floor and I have to force myself to look back up again, into her frosty blue eyes.

'What. Do. You. Think. You're. Doing?' The words come out sharp and clipped, each one a bullet that hits me in the chest. She saw us come in. She was standing at the bottom of the stairs. It's etched into every hard line of her face.

'We . . . we . . .' As I scrabble for an explanation, I feel the staff pass slip from the waistband of my cargo pants and slide down my stomach. I press my thighs tightly together. Please God don't let it drop down my trouser leg and onto the floor.

Mouse doesn't breathe a word. Her chest is rising and falling rapidly. She looks as though she's hyperventilating.

'Mouse . . . Megan . . . she's having an asthma attack,' I stutter. 'She's not well.'

Mrs H. locks eyes with me and a single line of sweat dribbles down my lower back. Why isn't she saying anything? If she's going to send us to isolation or the treatment centre she should just say it, not make us suffer like this. Or maybe she likes the fact we're suffering. Maybe she's enjoying the fact that I'm a sweaty mess and Mouse is about to pass out. Or maybe she didn't see us come in. Maybe we were already at the foot of the stairs when she came through the door. Everyone else is in their dorms, apart from us and she's suspicious. That's why she's having this stand-off. We look guilty and she wants to know why.

I sneak a glance over my left shoulder, towards Israel's open door, and an idea pops into my mind. I'm going to have to lie like I've never lied before but what have I got to lose? If Mrs H. saw us come in she'll punish us, regardless of what I tell her.

I clear my throat. I need to keep it together. I need to

convince myself that what I'm about to say is the truth or Mrs H. will see the lie written all over my face.

'It came on during the fight,' I say. 'Megan couldn't get up the stairs to get her Ventolin inhaler because there were so many kids down here. I took her into Israel's dorm so she could sit down for a bit and catch her breath.'

Mrs H. gives me a long look and then arches an eyebrow. 'Is that right?'

'Look at her!' I touch Mouse on the shoulder, making her flinch. 'She's really unwell, Mrs H. She needs to see the nurse.'

Mouse raises a hand to her mouth and mimes puffing on an inhaler.

'Can I go up to the dorm and get it?' I ask, taking a step towards the stairs. As I do, I press a hand to the top of my right thigh to stop the staff pass from slipping further down my leg.

'Just, one second, Drew.'

I freeze. My forehead prickles with sweat as Mrs H. scans the empty room then looks up at the balcony.

'Stuart! Could you come here for a second?'

Mouse stiffens. She looks absolutely terrified.

'Ah, there you are,' Mrs H. says as the two friends appear on the balcony of the first floor. They both look startled to see Mrs H. and exchange worried glances.

'Stuart, Abi, is the bed check complete?'

'Yes, Mrs H.' Stuart makes a move towards the stairs but Mrs H. raises a hand, telling him to stay where he is.

'Anyone missing?'

'Just . . . er . . . those two. Israel has been taken to the sanatorium along with his room-mate, Jez, who was also caught up in the disturbance.'

'I see.' Mrs H. nods curtly. 'And how long have these two been missing for?'

'We just realized. I just checked their dorm and only Jude is in her bed.'

'So neither of you spotted Drew and Megan in one of the boys' bedrooms?'

'I –' I begin but Mrs H. shushes me. 'I'm not talking to you, Drew. I'm talking to Stuart.'

'Um.' Stuart glances at Abi. She shrugs her shoulders. 'No. Well, I didn't.'

'I didn't see them down there either,' Abi says.

'I see.' Mrs H. raises her eyebrows. The tiniest of smiles prick at the corner of her lips as she turns her attention to me. 'So, if you weren't in Israel's room, Drew, where exactly have you been?'

Mouse makes a noise – half gulp, half snort. Oh my God, she's crying.

'It wasn't . . . Drew's fault,' she says in a breathy voice. 'It was –'

'We were in the en suite.' I grip her by the elbow and give it a short, sharp squeeze. 'That's why Stuart and Abi didn't see us. We had the door shut. Mouse was sitting on the toilet. She didn't want anyone to see her while she was feeling so unwell.'

The smile on Mrs H.'s face slips, just the tiniest bit. 'Is that right?' she says to the friends. 'Was the door to the en suite closed in Israel's room?'

They both shrug.

'I really couldn't tell you, Mrs H.,' Stuart says. 'I can't remember. I passed the room as I was doing the check but, as both Israel and Jez are in the sanatorium, I didn't give it more than a quick glance to check it was empty. If there was someone in the en suite with the door open, I would have spotted them so . . . so maybe it *was* closed.'

'I see.' Mrs H. looks from me to Mouse and back again. *Please*, I beg silently, *please believe us.*

'Abi,' Mrs H. says. 'Would you mind going into Megan's dorm and asking Jude where the inhaler is. Once you've found it bring it down here, please. Megan, would you like to sit down? You can perch on the stairs.'

Megan wipes the tears from her cheeks and nods dumbly. She catches my eye as she passes me on the way to the stairs but her eyes are still clouded with worry. I, on the other hand, feel utterly jubilant and it's taking every ounce of my self-control to stand perfectly still with an expressionless face when all I really want to do is punch the air and scream with relief.

'You can stay where you are, Drew,' Mrs H. says as I turn to follow Mouse. 'I'm going to speak to the CCTV operator now. I think it's a conversation you need to hear. Don't you?'

My heart drops to my stomach as she reaches for the radio, clipped to her belt.

Oh no. Oh no, oh no, oh no.

'Mrs H. to Destiny. Destiny, are you receiving?'

The radio crackles to life. 'Yes, Mrs H. I can hear you.'

'Could you take a look at the CCTV footage for the East Wing, please?' She glances at her watch. 'I'd like you to track the movements of Drew Finch and Megan Jones between twenty-one hours and twenty-two hours, please. Let me know if you see anything unusual.'

The radio crackles again. 'Megan Jones and Drew Finch. East Wing. Twenty-one hours and twenty-two hours?'

'That's right.'

'Shall I radio you back in a bit?'

'No, fast-forward through the footage. I'll wait while you look.'

Her hand, clutching the radio, falls to her side as she gives me a wide smile. She's showing her teeth. Like a shark.

'Are you OK, Drew?' she says, smirking. 'You look a little pale.'

My throat is so dry I have to swallow twice to find my voice. 'I'm just worried about Mouse . . . Megan . . . that's all.'

'What a good friend you are. Didn't I tell you you'd find friends for life at Norton House?'

'Yes, you did.' I clench the fist of my right hand against the fabric of my cargo pants. The hard edges of the staff pass press into my fingertips. Mrs H. is standing between me and the door. If I charge at her, right now, I'd have the element of surprise on my side. I'd be able to knock her to the floor and get out of the door before she had time to recover. But do I get the staff pass out of my trousers now, or after I've pushed her over? If I take it out now she'll be on her guard. I tighten my grip on the card. I'll have to shoulder barge her and then grab the card. Stuart won't be able to get down the stairs quickly enough to –

The radio crackles to life. 'Destiny to Mrs H. Are you receiving?'

My housemistress takes a step backwards, then another. Now she's only inches from the door. She's trying to block my escape route. She can see the fear in my eyes.

She raises the radio to just beneath her chin. 'Yes, Destiny, I can hear you.'

'I'm . . . um . . . I can't, um . . . I can't seem to access the footage between those times.'

'I'm sorry?'

'There's footage of the West Wing between twenty-one hours and twenty-two hours but the footage of the East Wing cuts off at twenty-one nineteen.'

Mrs H. angles herself away from me. 'Could you repeat that, please?'

'There's no footage of the East Wing between twenty-one nineteen and twenty-two zero nine. It just cuts out.'

'There's nothing?'

'No. Nothing. Just grey fuzz.'

'Are you quite sure?'

'Yes. I checked twice.'

'Were you at your desk between those times?'

'No. Stuart radioed me to help out in the East Wing. Israel was acting peculiarly and –'

'I know what happened with Israel,' Mrs H. snaps. 'Destiny you are *never* to leave your post when you're on CCTV duty. Never. First you wipe your staff pass by leaving it too close to your credit card and now this. Report to my office immediately.'

'Mrs H., I'm sorry. I know I was on my final warning but I really love this job and –'

'*Now*, Destiny.' Mrs H. whips round as I clear my throat. 'What are you staring at? Get to your dorm. Now!'

*

Wow. Destiny lied to Mrs H. She must have told her she'd

accidentally wiped her staff pass because she was on her final warning and she knew she'd be fired if she reported it as lost or stolen. She must have shat her pants when she realized it had gone. And now she might be fired. That has to be the best news I've heard all day.

I glance at Mouse, walking alongside me up the stairs. Now she's had a couple of puffs on her inhaler the colour has come back into her cheeks and she's stopped making that horrible rasping noise. I shoot her a smile, even though Abi is walking directly behind us. I cannot *wait* until I tell her about the conversation I overhead between Mrs H. and Destiny. I wonder why Destiny was on her final warning. Maybe she was caught twisting another student's arm behind their back?

'In you go, girls.' Abi shepherds us towards our dorm. 'Please settle down quietly. I think we've all had quite enough drama for one night.'

Mouse steps through the doorway to our dorm and immediately throws herself face down onto her bunk. The door clicks shut behind me as I walk through too, then clunks, locked.

'Well, well, well . . .' says a whiny, annoying voice as I climb the ladder to my bunk. 'If it isn't Thelma and Louise.'

'Sod off, Jude.'

'Can't, we're locked in for the night. So go on then? Where've you been?'

I sigh. 'Nowhere.'

'That's not true, is it?'

I roll onto my side and stare at her. She's sitting on her bunk cross-legged, still dressed in her day clothes. 'What are you on about, Jude?'

'I heard you tell Mrs H. that you and Mouse were in Israel's en suite.'

'You eavesdropped at the door. Congratulations.'

'You were lucky that's all I did.'

'What's that supposed to mean?'

She smirks. 'Well, Stuart and Abi might not know whether you and Mouse were in the bathroom but I know for a fact that you weren't.'

'No you don't.'

'Don't I?' She raises an eyebrow. 'That's funny, because I was sitting on Jez's bunk after he was punched on the nose by Josh. I had to go into the en suite to get some toilet paper to help stop the blood. And I didn't see either of you in there.'

'You're lying.'

'No, Drew.' She shifts forward. '*You're* lying. And you're going to tell me exactly where you were or I'm going to have a little word with Mrs H.'

Chapter Twenty-Seven

For the last ten minutes Mouse and I have been sitting on beanbags in a corner of the rec room pretending to read the books on our laps, trying to work out what the hell we're going to do about Jude and her threat to expose us.

'I think we should ignore her,' Mouse says. 'She hasn't got the first clue where we were last night.'

'No, but she knows where we weren't and if she tells Mrs H. or one of the friends –'

'Then what? No one can prove anything. The CCTV was down.'

I give her a sideways look. 'That was a lucky coincidence, wasn't it?'

'Huh?'

'The timing. The CCTV was down for the exact length of time that we were in the basement.'

'Oh, right.' She raises her eyebrows. 'Do you think it was Mason?'

'Must have been. But why would he go to the CCTV room, wherever that is, instead of the basement?'

'Maybe he wanted to give us a better chance of escaping.'

I laugh. 'Have you met my brother? He's not exactly the selfless type.'

She shrugs. 'Maybe Destiny turned it off on purpose.'

'To help us escape? Are you kidding? She nearly twisted my arm off the other day.' I slump back against the beanbag and stare at the smooth white ceiling. 'Whatever happened, it doesn't help us with the Jude problem.'

'You know what we need to do?' Mouse raises her book so the cover shields her face from the CCTV camera on the other side of the room. 'We need to kill her.'

'What?!' I stare at her in horror.

'No? You don't like that idea? How about we cut her tongue out? Or cover her mouth in duct tape and hide her body somewhere?' She laughs. 'I'm *kidding*, Drew.'

I smile. 'You look remarkably normal for a psychopath.'

'Appearances can be deceptive, Ms Finch.'

We lapse back into silence again and I glance at my watch. It's 11.58 a.m. and Jude is having a therapy session. In another two minutes she'll be free to start stalking us again. We need to think of *something*.

'Could we get her fast-tracked to treatment?' I say.

'How?

'I dunno. We stage something. Make it look like she's broken one of the rules.'

'It would have to be pretty bad to get her fast-tracked.'

'Isolation then. Israel was sent to isolation for speaking up in assembly but we can't make her do something like that. We can't force her to *do* anything.'

'Oh!' Mouse says, her face lighting up. 'She really fancies Jez. We could convince him to kiss her in front of Mrs H. or Doctor Rothwell.'

I shake my head. 'He'd get into trouble too. And anyway,

you only got a warning for hugging Mason. What else is on the rules list?'

'Breaking stuff?'

I shake my head. 'Nah.'

'Food in dorms?'

'Not bad enough.'

'Contacting someone on the outside?'

'How could we do that?'

'I don't know.'

We fall silent again, both of us racking our brains for a solution.

'Stealing!' we both say in unison.

'Yes.' I grip Mouse's arm, making her squeak. 'We could nick stuff from the other students and plant it in Jude's bunk.'

Mouse raises her eyebrows and nods slowly as though considering the proposition. 'I could certainly help with that . . .'

'And then we "discover" it and report it to Stuart or whoever.'

'I like it. But how do we keep her off our backs until then? We won't be able to get into the dorms until later tonight.'

'I'll think of something,' I say.

*

'You were trying to escape?' Jude says, her eyes lighting up. 'How?'

Mouse, sitting at the lunch table on the other side of her, flashes her eyebrows at me, horrified.

'Jude.' I press a finger to my lips. 'Keep your bloody voice down.'

'OK, OK.' She scans the faces of the kids sitting opposite us to check they're not listening then hisses in my ear, 'How were you trying to escape?'

'We were going through the dorms,' I whisper, keeping one eye on Abi who's standing at the end of our table trying to encourage a sobbing new arrival to eat something. 'We were looking for weapons.'

'WEAPONS!'

I slap a hand over Jude's mouth. 'For God's sake. Can you please keep quiet? This is the exact reason we didn't tell you about the plan. You're a such a bloody big gob.'

'What weapons?' says Polly, across the table, laying down her fork.

'The ones you need to complete level four of "Bloodborne",' I say, removing my hand from Jude's mouth. 'I don't want the boys to know.'

'Oh.' She looks away again, disinterested.

Mouse leans forward and gives me a puzzled look. As far as she knows the plan is still to nick stuff and plant it in Jude's bunk. The bell rang for lunch before I could tell her about my new and improved plan: Jude steals things herself and gets caught in the act.

'What do you need weapons for?' Jude asks, keeping her voice low.

'Why do you think?' I say. 'We need to get one of the friends to hand over their staff pass so we can get out.'

'It would never work.' She shakes her head but her eyes are wide and intrigued.

'Why not?'

'They'd be on you like flies. You wouldn't get through more than one door before they shut the whole place down.'

'Not if we lured Abi or whoever into an en suite and took it from her there.' This part of the plan is a lie. We won't be collecting weapons or tying up any of the friends, but I'm astonished at how quickly I'm making this up. If they let us do things like this for English GCSE I'd get top marks.

'You'd need rope or masking tape,' Jude says. 'If you wanted to stop her from raising the alarm.'

Jesus, what is it with my room-mates and their love of tying people up?

'That's right. And that's where you come in. We'll source the weapons and you'll source the other stuff – hairbands, dressing gown ties, whatever you can find.'

'Cool, cool . . .' Jude twists round to look at Mouse. 'I'm in on the plan.'

Mouse frowns. 'What plan?'

The excited look in Jude's eyes fades and her expression grows hard and suspicious as she looks back at me. 'Is this some kind of a wind-up? Like your Zara Fox story?'

'No. I swear. Look, Jude, if you don't want to be part of this you don't have to be.'

'If it is true what's to stop me telling someone?'

'Nothing, nothing at all.'

'I don't get it. Something about this doesn't add up.' Her eyes narrow as she studies my face. My stomach clenches in response. Telling her a half-truth was a big risk. There was always the possibility she'd tell on us but I've been studying Jude since I got here. She hates feeling excluded. She has to be part of everything or she feels like she's missing out. Despite her bravado it really bugs her that me and Mouse have grown so close. But is her desire to screw things up for me greater than her need to belong?

'Tell someone if you want, Jude,' I say. 'But if Mouse and I are sent to isolation or treatment we'll still find a way out and you'll end up like those brainless zombies at assembly.'

'No, I won't.' She pulls a scornful face. 'No one's going to change me. They can make me go to therapy or give me pills to swallow but, whatever the treatment is, I'll still be me. I'm stronger than you think, Drew.'

'I'm not doubting your strength, Jude. But you didn't see what those post-treatment kids were like when they got here. Mouse did. Didn't you, Mouse?'

I lean back in my chair as Mouse tells Jude what the post-treatment kids used to be like. It's freezing cold in the canteen today and I'm shivering despite my T-shirt and hoody. As Mouse continues to talk to Jude, I scan the canteen. There's been no sign of Destiny all day and –

My breath catches in my throat as the door to the rec room opens and Mason, flanked by Stuart, walks in. He's wearing a canteen staff uniform again – green trousers and a pale green polo shirt. His eyes rest on me as he walks directly past our table but his face doesn't register any emotion. He thinks the plan to escape was a wind-up. He probably hates my guts for telling him to go down to the basement and then abandoning him there.

'Drew?' I feel a sharp pain in my side. 'Why are you staring at that boy? Do you fancy him or something?'

Jude is staring at me, irritated. 'Did you hear a word I just said?'

'Sorry. Sorry. I was . . . I was just lost in thought. Thinking about the plan, you know.'

Her frown remains but her voice loses its irritable tone. 'I was just saying that I can't believe more kids don't know about the treatment. I can't believe we're all being kept in the dark about it. Someone needs to tell them about it.'

'You can't tell them,' I snap. 'There would be a riot.'

'Well maybe there should be.'

I stop listening as she continues to argue her point. On the other side of the room, Mason is stacking trays with Stuart glued to his side. Only Stuart isn't paying him any attention. He's scanning the faces at the table, looking for someone.

'Drew!' Jude tugs on my sleeve. 'If you think ignoring me is going to make me shut up about this then you've got another thing coming. Jez is being let out of the san later today, I'm definitely going to tell –'

'Megan!' Stuart slaps a hand on her shoulder, making us all jump. 'I am the bearer of good news.'

'What . . . what news?' She stares up at him with startled eyes.

'Don't look so scared! It's good news, I said. Guess who's off to pre-treatment after tomorrow's assembly?'

All the colour blanches from her cheeks. 'Me?' She points at her chest with a quivering hand.

'Yes, you. It's normally a surprise but you've been here so long I thought I'd let you know. Save you feeling anxious tomorrow. You're one step closer to going home, Megan Jones. Congratulations.'

'But . . . but . . .' Megan's eyes meet mine. I have never seen her look so scared. This changes everything. We need to leave *tonight*.

'Excuse me, Stuart.'

I jolt at the sound of my brother's voice. He's standing directly behind my chair.

'Should I clear the tables of trays? I've stacked up the ones that have already been returned.'

'No, no.' Stuart waves him away. 'People are still eating. Go and wait by the stand, please.'

Mason, I mentally plead as my brother walks away, *Mason, turn around.*

But he doesn't turn round. He spends the whole of lunch with his back to me. He doesn't look at me once, not even when the bell rings for lessons and we file out of the room.

Chapter Twenty-Eight

I don't know how Mouse was feeling during maths but I wrote the same word three times in English before I realized what I'd done. Concentration isn't one of my strongpoints in lessons anyway, but it completely vanished today. I was told off twice for staring into space and only paid attention when the teacher told me she'd give me a verbal warning if I didn't start listening. I did as I was told but my subconscious was still whirring away, trying to work how to keep Jude quiet, get in touch with Mason, and hatch an escape plan before Mouse is transferred to pre-treatment tomorrow. We were lucky things kicked off in the dorms last night, but there's no way we'll be that lucky again. We'll have to try to sneak out during rec. But how?

*

Mouse sidles up to me as I walk through the rec room, towards the door that leads to the café.

'We haven't got long to chat,' she says, her voice tight and small. 'I managed to get out of maths before Jude but she'll catch up with me soon. What are we going to do?'

My heart twists at the sight of her desperate, hopeful face.

She's relying on me to come up with a plan and I haven't got one.

'I don't know,' I say, then lower my voice as Josh and Callum push past us in their hurry to get to the pool table first. 'But we need to leave tonight.'

'How?'

'I don't know.'

The light fades from Mouse's eyes. Jude is pushing her way through the crowd at the door. She raises a hand and waves.

'Meg, could you keep Jude distracted, just for half an hour or so so I've got some time to think.'

'Sure.' She nods. 'I'll ask her if she wants to go to the cinema.'

'Cool.'

'Have you got any ideas at all?' she asks desperately.

I shake my head. 'Mouse, I'm sorry I –'

'Hello, hello!' Jude skips up to us and grabs us both by the elbows. 'So? Any news on the . . .' she looks around furtively – she couldn't look dodgier if she tried '. . .the you – know – what?'

'Not yet,' I say.

'Oh.' Her face falls.

'Look, Jude, what you said during breakfast about telling Jez. Were you serious?'

'I haven't decided yet.'

I try very hard not to roll my eyes. Asking Mouse to tell her about the treatment was *such* a bad idea. We stood on either side of her during assembly to make sure she didn't talk to anyone but Mouse took a risk leaving her behind in maths. She could easily have blurted something out to another student, or worse, a teacher. But by keeping her close we're never going to get the chance to escape. It's catch-22. The only solution is to take her with us and I really, really don't want to do that.

'I'm going to the cinema,' Mouse says brightly. 'Apparently they're showing a short film about a woman on a series of disastrous blind dates. Want to see it with me, Jude?'

Jude looks at me. 'Are you going?'

'Yeah. Yeah, I am,' I lie.

'Then why are you both heading for the café?'

'Snacks,' I say. 'And drinks.' I glance at my watch. 'Didn't you say it started at 11.15, Megan? You'd better get going. Want me to get you anything, Jude?'

'I'll come to the café with you.'

Mouse, standing behind Jude, flashes me a look of despair.

'You can come if you want, Jude,' I say casually. 'Actually, I think Jez and Polly would appreciate a bit of alone time.'

'What?' She narrows her eyes.

'Yeah . . . um . . . I heard Polly saying they were going on a first date when Jez gets out of the san. It was the cinema, wasn't it, Mouse? Not a stroll round the running track later?'

Mouse doesn't get chance to reply. Jude takes off like a bullet from gun.

*

It's 2.30 p.m. and I still haven't come up with an escape plan. During lunch I had to listen to Jude's increasingly paranoid ramblings about Jez and Polly and how, whilst she hadn't caught them in the cinema together, she could tell that Polly fancied him because she kept looking at his empty seat during lunch. Actually she was doing no such thing – I'd made up the thing about the first date – but at least it had stopped Jude from talking about the escape plan and who deserved to know about the treatment. I didn't come up with any ideas during maths either, and now it's time for outdoor activities.

I stare desperately at the door to the West Wing as I walk round and round the running track with Jude gabbling away in my ear. I still can't shake how weird Mason was at lunchtime. He had loads of opportunities to make eye contact with me but it was like he was deliberately avoiding looking at me.

'Do you think Jez will get out of the san this afternoon?' Jude asks. 'Because I want to talk to him before Polly does.'

I shrug. 'No idea.'

'Mouse?' She looks at Megan, walking on the other side of her. 'What do you think?'

'I thought you said Stuart told you he was getting out this afternoon.'

'Yeah, he did.'

'What about Israel?' Mouse asks. 'Is he getting out too?'

'I didn't ask about him.'

I start at the mention of Israel's name and a wave of guilt washes over me. I should have realized something was up when he started mentioning snakes and little cars but I was so wound up about the escape plan it was easier to believe that he was winding me up. Being in isolation had messed with his head. I'd read about extreme isolation and how it warps the mind in one of my psychology books before I left home. There was an experiment run by McGill University Medical Center in Montreal where students were isolated in soundproof cells and their perceptual stimulation was reduced to a minimum through gloves, visors and a humming air-conditioning unit. After just a few hours the students became restless and started talking to themselves or singing to stimulate themselves. Some of them started to hallucinate – sounds and visions – and they all became really anxious or overly emotional. The experiment had to be cut short. Most of them didn't last more than a few days and none of them lasted a week. Poor Israel, going through something like that. I shiver and pull up my hood.

'Drew!' Jude nudges me. 'What's that?'

She points at a tiny piece of paper on the ground beside my foot. It's not much bigger than a stamp. 'It fell out of your hood when you just put it up.'

I stoop to pick up what I assume is a bit of napkin or tissue but, as my fingers close around it, the hard edges prick at my fingertips. It's a folded piece of paper. My instinct is to open it but a tiny voice in the back of my mind tells me not to, so I shove it into my pocket and continue to walk.

'What was it?' Jude asks.

'Nothing. Just a bit of rubbish. One of the lads must have slipped it in for a joke.'

'Probably Callum. He's always dicking around.'

'Yeah.'

Mouse gives me a sideways glance but says nothing.

*

Once we're back in the rec room I slip away to the toilet and take the folded piece of paper out of my pocket. I've been clutching it so tightly it's become soft and damp. I unfold it quickly, telling myself not to get too excited. It's probably nothing. But it's not nothing. It's a note from Mason. He must have slipped it into my hood when he came over to talk to Stuart. That's why he didn't make eye contact with me. He didn't want anyone to think he was acting suspiciously. I scan the words, scrawled on the tiny bit of paper in blue biro:

Couldn't get to the basement last night but will meet you there at 9.10 tonight. We will need to RUN. M.

Chapter Twenty-Nine

9.10pm. We go up to the dorms for quiet time at 9 p.m., which means we have next to no time to get down the stairs, through the tunnels and into the central chamber to meet Mason. I don't know why he's specified such an exact time but we can't be late.

The second I step out of the toilet I run into Jude. She must have been standing outside the door, waiting for me.

'Jez isn't coming out of the san today,' she says mournfully. 'I just spoke to Abi. She said he'll be back tomorrow.'

'Right.'

'You know Mouse is going to pre-treatment tomorrow?'

'I do.'

'So when are we going to . . . you know . . .' She mouths the word 'escape'. 'You two still need to find weap–'

She squeals as I shove her into the toilet cubicle and shut the door behind us.

'Jude!' I give her a wide-eyed glare. 'Stuart was standing about three feet behind you. You *can't* keep mouthing off about this.'

It's *so* frustrating. If Stuart had only told Mouse about her pre-treatment a couple of minutes earlier I wouldn't have had to make up a story about weapons and tying up friends to keep Jude off our backs. I feel like my head's going to explode, trying to juggle everything that's going on.

'I just want to know what the plan is,' Jude whines, twisting out of my grasp. 'You tell Mouse everything but you can't keep me in the dark for ever, Drew. You need to tell me what's going on or . . .' She tails off but the threat is there.

We could just kill her. Mouse's words float around in my head but I mentally shake them away. No one's going to get killed but Jude's a bloody liability. I was hoping that Jez *would* get back from the san this afternoon so he could distract her, but now she has no reason to stop bugging me.

'Tonight,' I hiss. 'When we get back to the dorms you find the . . . you know. And Mouse and I will get the rest.'

'No.' She shakes her head. 'I'm searching with you. Mouse can find the other stuff.'

God. This lie is getting more and more out of hand and *I still don't know what to do!* I still don't have a plan and there are less than six hours until we need to meet Mason.

'Fine. You search with me.'

'Really?' She looks at me suspiciously, like I've agreed too easily.

'Yes. Or search with Mouse. I don't care either way.'

'Oh, right. Like that is it? So what happens after we've got what we need?'

I whisper some stuff about how we're going to tell Abi that Mouse is having another asthma attack then bundle her into our room and tie her up. When I finish speaking, Jude's cheeks are flushed pink. She's thrilled at the thought of attacking a member of staff and tying her up. *Such* a sick puppy.

'Then,' I say, 'we run down the stairs, use the pass on the

door, go down through the rec, out through the library, into the entrance hall and out the front door.'

'You think Mouse can deal with all that running?'

'Yes,' I snap. 'I do.'

'OK then. But I'm not getting caught just because she's fat and unfit. I want to be the one to hold the card.'

I swallow down my irritation. 'OK.'

I bundle her back out of the toilet before she can ask another question then pull on her arm and hiss in her ear, 'Don't screw this up, Jude.'

She pulls away and grins at me. 'I won't. Believe you me, I won't.'

*

I could cry. For the last hour and fifteen minutes I've been sitting on a beanbag in the corner of the rec room, with Mouse and Jude either side of me, watching the clock.

8.54 p.m.

8.55 p.m.

8.56 p.m.

8.57 p.m.

There is no way Mouse and I could have escaped from the rec room without one of the friends seeing us. Some new friend, a big ginger bloke with a beard – Destiny's replacement, I assume – has been standing by the door to the stairs since we arrived and Stuart has been playing PlayStation in the red zone. If we so much as stepped towards the door to the library he'd see us.

Three times I tried to get away from Jude so I could have

a word with Mouse alone but she saw through every ruse I came up with. She insisted on coming to the café with me to get hot chocolate, then she decided that she needed the loo at the same time as Mouse and I. And then she hovered by the table when I challenged Mouse to a game of pool. I could tell by the tight set of Mouse's jaw that she was frustrated too. She's pinning everything on my escape plan to avoid going to pre-treatment tomorrow and I still don't have one. I'm beginning to think we're going to have to go with the stupid, made-up plan about kidnapping Abi that I told Jude. But even if we did that we'd still have Stuart to contend with and, whilst the CCTV conveniently went down the last time we went to the basement, we can't rely on that happening again.

8.58 p.m.

8.59 p.m.

Dozens of ideas flash through my mind and I dismiss them almost as quickly.

Start another fight?

No.

Set fire to something?

How?

Set off the fire alarm?

We can't. The ginger friend is standing right next to it.

Pretend to be ill?

We'd be escorted to the san.

Just go?

We could try to peel away from the crowd and sneak downstairs as they shepherd us upstairs for quiet time. It's all I've got but it'll have to do.

I glance across at Mouse. She is twisting the hem of her

cardigan as she stares at the door. I can't tell her what the new plan is. I'll have to just shove her towards the basement stairs and hope she gets the message. Jude will have to come too. Let's hope she's as good a runner as she says she is.

9.00 p.m. The bell sounds and loads of kids groan. Not Jude, she grins and jumps to her feet.

'Ready?' she says, winking ridiculously.

Mouse shakes her head but says nothing.

'Have you . . . um . . . have you got your inhaler?' I ask.

'Yeah, why?'

'You might need it.'

She raises her eyebrows. 'Oh.'

I hold out a hand. 'Can I have it?'

'Why?' she and Jude ask simultaneously.

'Backup plan.'

*

'What are you doing?' Jude hisses, as I grab hold of her sleeve and tug her out of the front of the queue to get up to the dorms.

'Change of plan.'

She looks confused, and ever so slightly pissed off, but she follows me and Mouse to the back of the queue without saying a word. I gather my room-mates closer to me and drop my voice.

'So what's happening now is –'

I glance over my shoulder. Abi is standing directly behind us. She gives us a wide, fake smile then looks at her watch and gazes over our heads towards the front of the queue. She

168

looks as though she can't wait to get us all into the dorms so she can sign off. We might have to push her out of the way to get down the stairs. I know she's as fake as an Essex tan but the thought of giving her a shove doesn't sit well with me. She probably doesn't even know what happens once we're shipped off to the treatment unit.

I turn back and raise my eyebrows at Mouse and Jude, signalling that they should pay attention. Then, keeping my hands low and out of sight of Abi and the CCTV cameras, point at them, my eyes and my chest. *Don't take your eyes off me.* I touch my lips, point at them again and mime running by scissoring the fingers of my right hand. *When I tell you, run!*

For a split second they both look confused but then they nod. They've got it.

I glance over my left shoulder again, to check that Abi wasn't watching but we're good. She's looking at her watch again.

'Alreet, Abi?' The big ginger friend strolls down the queue and stops beside Abi. Up close he's enormous; at least six foot four with shoulders like boulders and the thickest forearms I've ever seen in my life. He'd better not be escorting us upstairs too.

'All the better for seeing you,' Abi simpers.

'That's what all the lasses say.'

'Well this *lass* –' she does such a crap Geordie accent it makes me cringe '– is off to get a glass of wine. You sure you're OK doing the cool down routine? It doesn't always go exactly to plan.' She laughs.

Ginger runs a hand over his hair, preening himself. He must fancy her. 'I'll let you know I've worked with hardened crims. How bad can this lot be?'

'You'd be surprised.'

'Well, I'm sure I'll be fine. You get yourself off. Enjoy your wine. Maybe I'll see you later.'

I hear the soft pad of Abi's trainers on the lino as she crosses the rec room, heading for the library door. The sound gets quieter and quieter and then stops.

'Alreet, lasses.' A heavy hand on my shoulder makes me almost jump out of my skin. 'It's my first night on the job. Be gentle with us, won't you?'

'Yeah, 'course.' Jude flutters her eyelashes at him from under her fringe. She has no idea how much Ginger's appearance has just screwed up my plan.

*

I follow Mouse through the open door and feel Jude press up against me as we shuffle into the stairwell. As normal, the other students are taking their time getting to the dorms and we're backed up with about ten others, waiting to go up the stairs.

'Come on, kids!' Ginger Beard shouts, pulling the door closed behind him. 'Get a move on! The slower you go the less time you've got to chill out before lights out.'

I nudge Mouse with my elbow, urging her to take a step to her left, closer to the basement staircase but, as she does, Polly shoots her a smile.

'Apparently you're off to pre-treatment tomorrow. Congratulations!'

'Thanks.' Mouse smiles tightly.

'No time for chit-chat!' Ginger orders. 'Up the stairs. Quick as you can.'

The kids standing at the base of the stairs shuffle up a step. As they do, Ginger slips from behind me and stands on the left of Mouse, effectively blocking our route to the basement. Damn it. We could still chance it. We could rush him and hope at least one of us gets past him, but there's only one staff pass and it's in my bra. If he catches me, Mouse won't be able to get out. It's too risky. Plan B it is then.

I take a step to my right, knocking into Jude, then shout out in pain.

'Drew?' Jude stares at me, her eyes wide. 'What the –'

'You stepped on my foot.' I duck down and touch the toe of my right trainer with my left hand. At the same time, I plunge my right hand into my pocket, pull out Mouse's inhaler and shove it behind me. It spins along the tiles then lies still in the corner of the stairwell.

'Drew?' I feel Mouse's hand on my shoulder and look up. 'Are you OK?'

'Yep, yep, yep.' I get up quickly as Ginger's hairy face peers over the top of Mouse's head.

Please don't let him have seen the inhaler. Please, please.

'What's up?' he says.

'She stood on my foot!' I flick a thumb towards Jude.

'No I didn't! Why would you lie about something like that?' She glares at me, her expression changing from affront to suspicion in a millisecond. She doesn't know what's going on and is worrying that this is all part of a plan to escape without her.

'It's not a problem.' I flash my eyebrows at her. 'It was just an accident. Wasn't it?'

'No,' she hisses from between tight lips, 'it wasn't. Because

I didn't step on your foot. Don't accuse me of things I didn't do, Drew. You might not like the repercussions. Do you get what I'm saying?'

Ginger Beard looks from me to Jude and frowns. 'Everything OK with you girls?'

'Fine.' I take a step towards the stairs. Polly is already at the top and now it's only me, Jude, Mouse and Ginger Beard in the stairwell. Without so many bodies crammed into the small space the blue inhaler looks really conspicuous in the corner of the stairwell.

'Come on, guys.' I reach for Mouse's and Jude's hands and, feeling like a mum dragging her kids to the doctor's office for an injection, pull them up the first few steps.

I let go of their hands as we round the corner and look at my watch: 9.04 p.m. We've got six minutes left to meet Mason. Mouse and Jude continue to walk beside me, glancing at me with every step they take, their eyes fixed on my hands, waiting for the signal to run. It's not going to come, girls. Not with the Jolly Ginger Giant right behind us with his arms spread wide. All I've got left is Plan B and, as plans go, it's pretty crap.

I slow my pace as we reach the bottom of the last set of stairs. There's a massive huddle of kids standing in the stairwell outside the dorms. Why have they all stopped? What's going on? I look back at the Ginger Giant give him a questioning look.

'What's going on?'

'Pat down.'

'WHAT?'

He laughs. 'Mrs H.'s orders. One of the support assistants left today and she didn't hand her pass in.'

'And Mrs H. thinks one of us has got it?' My heart's beating so quickly I feel sick. Of course Destiny didn't hand in her 'wiped' staff pass when she left – it's sitting between my boob and my bra.

'I know you've got it.' Ginger Beard narrows his eyes and holds out a hand. 'Hand it over.'

My forehead prickles with sweat. How does he know? Did CCTV catch me fumbling around under my pyjama top as I changed my bra? No, I'm sure I went into the bathroom. I always go into the bathroom. He has to be bluffing.

'Ha ha!' I point at his pass and fake a laugh. 'You think I'd still be here if I had one of those, Kyle?'

He laughs – a real, bellowing guffaw. 'True. True. Anyway, up you go. Stuart's checking the boys. Stella's doing the girls.'

I continue to keep my smile fixed on my face as I take step after step after step until I'm in the stairwell, then I head to the right, annoying the other kids as I squeeze past them to get to the base of the staff quarter stairs. We're so tightly packed up here that, if one person fell over, there would be a domino effect and we'd all tumble to the ground. When I reach the wall I turn round, to check that Mouse and Jude are following and, sure enough, here's Jude, batting people of the way like she doesn't give a damn and Mouse, apologizing profusely, as she trails in her wake.

'Are we still going ahead with you know what?' Jude says, as she squeezes up beside me.

'Yeah.'

I turn my back to her and shove a hand up my long-sleeve T-shirt. I fumble the staff pass from under my bra, palm it and give Mouse a nod to come closer. As she does, I knock

173

my hand against hers and signal with my eyes that she needs to take the pass. She shakes her head. No, she doesn't want to or no, she doesn't understand?

'Tell Kyle you dropped your inhaler,' I whisper as I press it into her hand. 'You'll find it in the corner of the stairwell downstairs. Once you've got it go and find Mason.'

She gives me a startled look. 'What about you?'

'I'll stay here. It's the only way.'

'No!'

'Hey?' Jude says from behind me. 'What are you two up to?'

I twist round. 'I'll tell you in a minute.'

'To get out of the tunnels,' I whisper into Mouse's ear, 'you go straight ahead, take a left, then another left, then a right, then another right. Left, left, right, right. OK?'

'So it's straight ahead then –'

'Hey!' Jude shoves her way between me and Mouse. 'Tell me what's going on. I'm sick of you leaving me out of things.'

I give Mouse a gentle shove. 'Go, now!'

'Go where?' Jude reaches out to stop her but Mouse is too fast. She sidesteps her and heads towards Kyle, still standing on the steps.

'Jude!' I grab her arm. 'It's OK. She's only gone to find her inhaler. She's dropped it somewhere.'

'I don't believe you. This is part of the real escape plan, isn't it? You're going to leave without me.' She shakes her head slowly back and forth, her eyes narrowed. 'I knew you couldn't be trusted, Drew. I knew it the second I set eyes on you.'

Mouse has reached Kyle now. He's shaking his head and she's remonstrating, miming taking an inhaler whilst pointing down the stairs. He seems to relent, gesturing with his head that he'll go down and look with her. Damn it. That wasn't part of the plan.

'Drew!' Jude shoves me in the chest. 'You're ignoring me again! What did I tell you about ignoring me. Hey!' She twists away and raises her hand high in the air. 'Hey, Kyle! Come over here. You need to hear this. Drew's planning on kidnapping one of the –'

I'm sorry, I say in my head, as I hook a foot around one of Jude's and shove her in the chest, hard. Her eyes meet mine, glassy and terrified, as she tips backwards. Her outstretched arms swipe at one, two, three students as she falls. Kids try to twist out of her way but there's nowhere to move and she smacks into the boy who's standing on tiptoes, trying to see what's going on in the doorway. The weight of Jude's falling body unbalances him and he lurches to his left, knocking over the short girl beside him. Down they fall, bodies tumbling like dominos, almost in slow motion.

'Go!' I mouth at Mouse. 'Go now!'

As she flies down the stairs and a startled Kyle leaps forward to catch three kids who are tumbling towards him, I inch to my left, ready to follow Mouse down the stairs as soon as there's a gap in the bodies. Out of the corner of my eye, I see movement, a flash of grey, at the top of the stairs that lead up to the staff quarters. A pair of trousers. A shiny black shoe. A grey sock. And a flash of curved metal where the other foot should be.

Chapter Thirty

$D_{ad?}$

I take the steps two at a time. That was my dad I saw at the top of the stairs. He always refused to wear a realistic prosthetic leg. 'Why hide something I'm not ashamed of?' he used to say. 'Why conform to society's view of normal?'

But why would he be here?

'Dad! Wait!' I shout, but my voice gets lost in a wall of sound as the students in the stairwell below continue to scream and shout.

I reach the top of the first flight of stairs in seconds and speed across the second-floor stairwell. As I reach bottom of the next set of stairs, I scream my dad's name but there's no one here. Whoever it was has already passed through the door to the staff quarters. It's open but it's starting to close.

'Dad, wait!'

I haul myself up the steps but, before I reach the top step, the door swings shut. The three red lights on the locking unit flash once, twice, three times.

Locked.

'No!' I power up the last few stairs and yank on the handle but it holds fast.

'Dad!' I pound on the door with closed fist. 'Dad, I know it was you. Open up! Please, Dad! Please! Please open the door.'

Angry, desperate tears roll down my face as I slam myself against the door, over and over again. Why won't he open it? He must have seen me standing at the bottom of the stairs, outside the dorm. He must know that it's me.

As the noise from the floor below dims to a low hum, I drop to my knees. It can't have been Dad. He wouldn't abandon me again.

*

I sit with my back to the door for what feels like hours but it must only be minutes before I hear the sound of footsteps.

'Hey!' Kyle climbs the stairs purposefully, his arms pumping until he stops about a foot away from me. 'Do you want to tell me what's going on?'

I drop my head and stare at my arms, hugging my knees to my chest. It's all over. For me, anyway, but I can still help Mouse and Mason escape. If I keep Kyle talking that'll be one less person looking for them.

'Have you been crying?' Kyle drops his voice as he crouches down beside me.

I shake my head but I know my eyes must be red and puffy, my nose swollen and my cheeks streaked with tears. I always look a mess when I cry.

'What are you doing up here . . .' He pauses. 'Sorry, I don't know what your name is.'

His big, brown eyes are full of concern and his brow is furrowed with worry but I've seen all that before. Destiny made out she was all nicey-nicey – until she decided to twist my arm behind my back.

'Drew,' I say softly. 'Drew Finch.'

'Cool name.' He smiles. 'Mind if I sit here?' He gestures at the wall beside me. 'My back's killing me. Side effect of being the beast from the North-East.' He laughs and runs a hand over his beard.

'If you want.'

He lowers himself to the ground, keeping his radio tightly gripped in his hand. I glance at his staff pass, on the end of the lanyard, sitting on his stomach. I could grab it and make a run for it, but there are more footsteps on the stairs now, and adult voices, calling to each other.

Kyle touches his staff pass. 'Don't even think about it, Drew. I could see you looking,' he adds with a half-smile.

'Yeah, well.'

Abi appears at the bottom of the stairs. Her ponytail has come loose and tendrils of hair are hanging over her cheeks. She moves to climb the stairs but Kyle raises a hand.

'I've got this.'

'But . . .' She glances to her right, as though checking with someone else. I can't see who it is because of the angle of the stairs.

'Seriously, Abi,' Kyle says, 'I've got this.'

'Is there anyone else up there?'

'No, just me and Drew.'

'OK.' She tucks her hair behind her eyes. 'But radio if you need backup. We've just done bed check. Another student's missing. Megan Jones. Short girl, long brown hair, light brown eyes, on the heavy side.'

My heart skips a beat. *Run*, I send Mouse a silent message. *Just run.*

'OK. I'll keep an eye out.'

'Why'd you push Jude?' he asks, as Abi disappears again.

'She was annoying me.'

'You could have killed someone. Josh would have fallen down the stairs if I hadn't caught him.'

I hang my head. 'I didn't mean for anyone to get hurt.'

'No. I don't imagine you did. But that's no excuse.'

I lean my body away from Kyle's then shift over a couple of inches. I'm still close enough that he could grab me if he wanted but we're not sitting so close that I feel uncomfortable any more. 'What's going to happen to me?'

He shrugs. 'That's not down to me.'

'Mrs H.?'

'You'll need to speak to her and Doctor Rothwell, yeah.'

'They're going to send me to isolation, aren't they?'

'Like I said, Drew, I don't know. But you broke a pretty major rule. It could have ended badly.'

'I know, and I'm sorry. Is Jude OK?'

'She's fine, they're all fine. I got everyone into the dorm in one piece.'

We lapse into silence.

'Do you know Israel?' I ask, breaking the silence.

'The country?'

'No, the boy. He's in the san.'

'Not . . . er . . . no . . .I haven't met him.' He shakes his head. 'I was shown around the san and there a boy in one of the beds but I was asked not to talk to him.'

'He had a psychotic breakdown. Caused by whatever happened to him in isolation.'

Kyle smiles. 'Is that the new rumour doing the rounds?'

'It's not a rumour. I talked to him before he went in. He was normal. He was funny. And you . . . you lot, you broke him. He was decent and you've screwed him up.' I can't hide the anger in my voice.

'Or maybe it was Israel's problem with weed that caused his illness?' Kyle gives me a long look. 'Did that ever occur to you?'

'What?'

'I probably shouldn't be telling you this. I *definitely* shouldn't be telling you this, but the nurse told me it was on his record. Israel's. He was a heavy smoker . . . toker . . . before he came in. That can lead to psychotic breakdowns, particularly, y'know, the strong stuff. Skunk.'

'Well that's convenient.'

'Sorry?'

I laugh dryly. 'His record saying that. If Dr Rothwell tells you guys Israel likes the odd joint you're not going to question his weird behaviour, are you? You'll accept that's what caused his psychosis. Have you actually seen the isolation room?'

'I don't see how that's relevant, Drew.'

'Have you seen it or not?'

Kyle's face shuts down. I'm being too bolshy. I can't talk him round to being on my side. He's one of them. He might be new but he's no fool.

'I'm not having a go at you,' I say quickly, 'it's just that –'

I'm interrupted by the sound of Kyle's radio crackling. It's Abi, asking him to respond.

'Yes, Abi.' He raises the radio to just below his chin. 'I can hear you.'

'Please take Drew Finch to the library and wait there until you're called into Dr Rothwell's office. We've found Mason Finch and Megan Jones.'

Chapter Thirty-One

'Sit down, please, Drew.'

Dr Rothwell and Mrs H. are sitting side by side behind Dr Rothwell's large oak desk. They both have notepads in front of them and their forearms on the desk. They look like a couple of local newsreaders, waiting for the red light on the camera to come on so they can smile and read the news. But they don't smile as Kyle ushers me into the room. They track me with their eyes, neither of them saying a word until I take a seat in the soft, padded leather chair opposite them. I'm so scared I have to press my hands between my knees to stop them from shaking. An hour. That's how long I had to sit in silence in the library with Kyle. He wouldn't let me get up to look out of the window. He wouldn't let me take a book off the shelf. He wouldn't let me do anything and he ignored every question I threw at him.

'Where are they?' I say. 'Megan and my brother?'

'You don't need to know that,' Mrs H. says evenly, her blue eyes narrowed.

'Yes I do.' I jolt forward in my chair and grip the edge of the desk. 'I need to know they're OK. If you've –'

'Drew.' Kyle grips my shoulder, gently, but firmly enough that I know he's serious. 'Sit back in the chair, please.'

I glare at him but shuffle back into the chair and grip the arm rests. He's such a sheep, just like Abi and Stuart. Destiny was a cow but at least she wasn't as brain dead behind the eyes as the rest of the 'friends'. If Dr Rothwell asked them to march us off a cliff they'd ask which one.

'Megan and Mason are safe,' Dr Rothwell says, pressing his glasses up towards his nose. 'We've spoken to them both and they've told us everything. We know all about the escape plan. Now we have a few questions for you.'

They haven't told you anything, I think. And you must think I'm really stupid if you think I'm going to fall for that. I've watched third rate TV detective shows too, you know.

'We've reviewed the CCTV footage of the stairs and stairwell,' Mrs H. says in her perfect, clipped tones. 'We saw you, Jude and Megan standing at the bottom of the stairs that lead to the staff quarters. We then saw Megan approach Kyle.'

'She said she'd dropped her inhaler outside the rec room,' Kyle pipes up.

'Yes, Kyle.' Mrs H. smiles tightly. 'We'll talk to you in due course. Let's just focus on Drew and what she has to say for now. If that's all right?'

'Yes, yes of course.' He takes a step back, chastened.

'So,' Mrs H. continues, 'when Megan was talking to Kyle you decided to push Jude. Why was that, Drew?'

'Because I don't like her.'

'Interesting, when we spoke to Jude she said she likes you very much.'

I stiffen. They've talked to Jude? I force my raised shoulders down and try to relax. Dr Rothwell hasn't said anything for a couple of minutes but his eyes haven't left my face since

I sat down. He's analysing me, trying to work out if I'm lying or not.

'I don't know why Jude would say that. She definitely doesn't like me.'

'Why don't you like her?' Dr Rothwell asks, leaning forwards slightly.

'Personality clash,' I lie. Well, it's a half-truth. Our personalities clash because she's a nosy, jealous big – mouth and I'm a secretive, laid-back loner. Well, maybe not so laid-back.

'Hmmm.' He leans back again.

'Why did you run up the stairs after Megan ran down the stairs?' Mrs H. asks.

'I didn't know Megan ran down the stairs.'

'But the first question you asked,' Dr Rothwell says, 'when you entered this room was "Where are Megan and my brother?"'

Did I? Yes, I did didn't I? Um . . .

'That's because I overheard Abi on the radio. She told Kyle that you'd found them. I want to know where you found them. I want to know what's going on, the same way you do.'

A bead of sweat dribbles down the centre of my back. I'm having to think very quickly to talk my way out of this. One wrong word and they'll twist it around.

'OK then, Drew.' Mrs H. rubs her hands together. They make a horrible dry sound that reminds me of the leaves in the park when I went to meet Zed. 'Why did you run upstairs?'

'Because everyone was falling over after I pushed Jude. It seemed the safest place to go.'

'How did Drew seem when you found her upstairs, Kyle?' Dr Rothwell asks.

'She was upset. She looked as though she'd been crying.'

'Why was that, Drew?'

'Because . . . because I was scared.'

Dr Rothwell looks at me for a long time then runs a hand over his beard. He tugs lightly at the end then says, 'And why was that?'

'Because I thought I'd hurt everyone.'

The beard tug again. 'Is that so?'

Mrs H. leans towards him and whispers something in his ear that I can't hear. A frown crosses his brow then, barely perceptible, I hear him say the word 'impossible' in reply. As they continue their whispered conversation my palms grow sweaty against the polished wood of the chair arms. My stomach is a tight knot. I need to know where Mason is and that he and Mouse are OK. I don't care if they ask me a million questions or interrogate me for hours but not knowing what's happened to those two is torture.

The enormous grandfather clock in the corner of the room tick, tick, ticks as Dr Rothwell and Mrs H. continue to talk quietly. I was kept in the library before I was brought in here so Megan and Mase can't be there. They could be in the café, or Mrs H.'s office. Maybe they're keeping them in the basement? Oh God. *Please* don't let them be in isolation.

'Where's my brother?' I ask.

'Drew.' Kyle touches my shoulder and shakes his head.

'I need to know. All this whispering and secrecy is driving me cra–'

I break off as Dr Rothwell gives me a slow smile. I've shown him where my weakness lies. I've given my enemy a weapon to attack me with. Damn it. Why couldn't I just sit here and play dumb? Because I'm not a robot, that's why. I love Mason and if they've done anything to hurt him I swear I'll . . . I'll . . .

'Do you know what this is?' Mrs H. slides a small plastic card across the desk towards me.

'It's a staff pass.'

'Do you know how Megan Jones got hold of it?'

I pause before answering. Do I tell her I stole it to stop Mouse getting into trouble? Or do I pretend I've got no idea. Which answer would help Mouse? This is like a terrifying version of one of those choose your own adventure games – open the door on the left and fall into a fiery pit, open the door on the right and run to freedom.

'No,' I say.

If they have put Mouse and Mason into isolation there's no way I can help them if they lock me up too. Although that's almost a certainty. They've got CCTV footage and witnesses who saw me push Jude. 'No harming the staff or students.' It's one of the major rules.

'Do you know what this is?' Mrs H. pushes a crumpled piece of paper across the table. It's my map of the steam tunnels. They must have taken it from Mason.

'No.' I look Mrs H. straight in the eye as I ball my hands into fists and squeeze my fingernails against the palms of my hands. They know everything.

'Have you had any contact with your brother since you entered Norton House?' Dr Rothwell asks.

'No.'

He raises his dark eyebrows.

'I . . . I saw him in the canteen if that's what you mean. But we . . . we didn't talk to each other. It wasn't allowed.'

'Would the CCTV footage corroborate that?' Mrs H. says. 'If we checked it.'

'Yes, it would!' I stand up and grip the edge of the desk. It scrapes across the wooden floor and Mrs H. and Dr Rothwell both put out their hands to stop it from hitting them in the stomachs.

'Drew. Sit down.' Kyle reaches an arm in front of me. What does he think I'm going to do – crawl over the desk and attack them?

'Don't do that.' I swat at his arm but it's like pushing against a wall. 'Please.' I appeal to Dr Rothwell whose expressionless face is preferable to Mrs H.'s narrow-lipped irritation. 'Just tell me what's going on. I'm sorry I went up the stairs instead of into the dorm, OK, but you need to tell where my brother and Mouse are.'

'We don't need to do anything, Drew,' he says, calmly. 'You don't get to come into my school and bark orders at me. You don't get to decide what information we choose to share with you. You don't get to display anger and get away with it.'

'I'm not, I'm just . . .' Tears prick at my eyes as I sink back into my seat. I'm so angry. I've never felt so powerless or frustrated in my life.

'Your brother and Megan Jones have been transferred to the treatment unit,' Dr Rothwell says.

Oh God. I slump back in my seat and close my eyes. My worst fear has come true.

'What about me? Am I going there too?'

'No.'

I open my eyes. Oh God, the isolation room.

'We're not sending you to the isolation room either,' Dr Rothwell says, as though he just read my mind.

'What? Why?' It doesn't make sense. What I did to Jude was way worse than what Israel did in assembly. Why send him to isolation and let me walk free?

Mrs H. smiles her slow, shark smile. 'You need to ask Jude that.'

'Ask Jude what?'

'She's more of a friend than you think, Drew. She begged us not to send you to isolation. She said there had been a misunderstanding and she didn't want you punished for it. Despite the severity of what happened we don't think you deliberately set out to harm your fellow students and, given Jude's desperate plea for clemency, we're going to give you one last chance. But one more false move from you and you'll be fast-tracked to treatment. Do you understand?'

I nod dumbly.

'OK, Drew,' Dr Rothwell says. 'You may go.'

'One more thing,' Mrs H. adds as I push back my chair and stand up. 'The locks have all been reprogrammed and new cards have been issued to all staff. Oh, and all tunnels in the basement will be sealed tonight. Just in case Mason and Megan have inspired you to plan a little escape attempt yourself.'

*

I walk up the stairs to the dorms in a daze, Kyle following close behind me. I don't get it. I saw the rage in Jude's eyes when she thought that we were double-crossing her. Right before I pushed her she tried to tell Kyle about the fake plan to escape.

She would have relished watching me go to isolation. I can't think of a single reason why she'd beg Mrs H. not to send me there. Unless she's still hoping to escape and she thinks I can help her. But that doesn't feel right. She's more motivated by revenge than freedom.

'OK, in you go.' Kyle gestures at the open door to my dorm. All the other doors are closed and the wing is silent, other than the odd cough, sneeze or snore.

'Behave yourself, Drew,' he adds, as I step into the room and the door clicks shut behind me. Out of the corner of my eye I can see a Jude-shaped lump in the top bunk on my right. Her duvet is pulled right up over her chin but I know she's watching me. There's a strange atmosphere in the small room, like a malevolent tension building under the silent, sleepy surface. I glance towards my bunk, then my eyes flick, automatically, towards Mouse's bed. My breath catches in my throat. I thought it would be stripped bare, along with all Megan's belongings, but her duvet is still on the bed and there's someone lying beneath it.

'Meg?' I whisper.

She doesn't reply. She doesn't pull the duvet from over her head. It continues to rise and fall with each breath she takes. I take a step towards her.

'Megan, are you OK? I thought they'd sent you to treatment.' I reach a hand to the duvet and pull it back.

'Hello, Andrew.' Lacey sits up, brushing her black hair away from her shoulders as Jude screams with laughter. 'Fancy seeing you here.'

Chapter Thirty-Two

Lacey and Jude tore shreds off me for hours last night. They made comments about me, laughed at me, goaded me and sniggered at private jokes. In the hour I'd sat in the library Lacey had told Jude *everything* about me. Jude, in turn, had told her everything that's happened here.

At first I ignored them. Then I put headphones on and tried to watch a film under the duvet. When Lacey started pushing her feet against the springs of my bed I had enough.

'Stop it,' I snapped, leaning over the edge of the bunk.

'Or what?' Her snidey voice rang out in the darkness.

'Are you going to hit her again?' Jude said from across the room. 'You like pushing people around, don't you?'

'Go on, Drew,' Lacey chided. 'Do it. But don't forget, there's two of us and only one of you.'

'And I only need to say the word to get you shipped off to isolation. You're going to have to be very nice to us, Drew, if you don't want to turn into a total headcase like Israel.'

'I think it would be nice if she cleaned the toilet with her toothbrush. What do you think, Jude?'

'Nah, I think she should use her tongue.'

They exploded with laughter then the springs of my bed started creaking again as Lacey pounded them with her feet. It took every ounce of willpower not to leap off the bed and slam my fists into her stupid, hysterical face. I didn't care if she and Jude jumped me. I wasn't bothered by how much it would hurt or how humiliated I'd feel. But if I was sent to isolation I wouldn't be able to stop Mouse and Mason being brainwashed. If I lost my temper, I'd lose them too. For ever.

Please, Dad, I silently begged as I jiggled up and down, up and down, up and down, *if you are here, please help me. I don't think I can take any more.*

Finally, when I thought I'd go insane if Lacey kicked my bed one more time, she and Jude fell silent. A couple of minutes later the soft sound of Jude's snoring filled the room. I didn't sleep. I lay on my side and watched the red blink of the CCTV camera lights in the corner of the room. Dad wouldn't help me. That wasn't who I'd seen walking up the stairs. It was wishful thinking. The only person I could rely on was myself.

*

'In a hurry, Andrew?' Jude says trailing behind me as I march around the running track. 'Lacey was just wondering if one of the friends could lend us a camera. Apparently you like having your photo taken. You might want to change into a skirt first though.'

I clench my fists as Lacey squeals with laughter. Jude's braver now she's got an accomplice. Yesterday she was terrified that we'd escape without her if she took her eyes off us. Now she's following me around because she's getting a kick out of tormenting me. I actually hate her more than I hate Lacey. Lacey's a ringleader and a bully but Jude's a vicious coward. She'll only attack if someone else can offer her protection. Or she'll start a whispering campaign and then deny all knowledge. She's always watching, always waiting for an opportunity to turn the knife. I don't know why she is the way she is but Jude's infinitely more dangerous than Lacey. And the quicker I get away from her the better.

Lacey and Jude continue to insult, berate and bully me as I approach the three friends, guarding the door to the rec room. Today it's Stuart, Kyle and Abi. They're all rubbing their arms and stamping their feet, despite their thick, blue anoraks. I give them a wide smile as I pass them. Kyle's the only one who smiles back. The other two look suspicious. Great. Now I can be sure they're watching me.

I glance behind me, to check on Lacey and Jude. They're still close behind. They break off from chatting to each other to glare at me. I smile back at them then break into a run. I hear Lacey's laugh and Jude's whiny voice as my trainers pound against the track and I pump my arms, but then I'm away and all I can hear is the wind whistling in my ears. A sudden, terrifying flash of doubt passes through my mind – this could go wrong, this could go horribly, horribly wrong – but I push it away. This is the only chance I've got.

I pump my arms harder and increase my stride. I was always rubbish at sports day but there was one sport I wasn't completely terrible at.

The long jump.

As the tip of my right trainer hits the edge of the track where it curves to go left I launch myself forwards and upwards – legs outstretched in front of me, fingers reaching. I don't jump more than a couple of metres off the ground but it's enough to propel me up and into the metal fence. It clangs as my hands and feet smack against it and I cling on, weaving my fingers through the gaps, grabbing onto the cold, hard metal. I ram the tips of my trainers in too then feel myself lurch backwards as the fence sways under my weight. I don't let go. Instead, I start to climb. The gaps in the fence are narrow and, more than once, my trainers slip out and my fingers burn as I scrabble to get them back in again. Beyond the fence and across a field that must be at least four hundred metres wide, is the low, squat red-brick building that's holding Mason and Mouse.

As shouts ring out from behind me, I hasten my climb. I glance over my shoulder as the voices get louder and louder. Lacey and Jude have stopped, halfway up the track, gawping at me. Kyle, Stuart and Abi brush past them. Abi is waving her arms, Stuart's face is bright red and Kyle looks as though he's running into battle. I ignore them and continue to climb. I'm over halfway up the fence now and it's shaking. Each time I take a step upwards I'm either catapulted forwards or rocked backwards and it takes all my strength just to cling on.

'Drew!' Abi shouts, sounding breathless. 'Come down!'

I ignore her and continue to climb. The low rumble of Kyle's and Stuart's voices drifts upwards and I brace myself. Kyle wants to come after me but the other two aren't so sure. Stuart says something about health and safety then Abi radios for backup. She wants at least three more friends on the other side of the fence. And a first aid kit.

I grab the top of the fence and pull but, as I do, there's a sudden pain in my left shoulder blade as though something hard just bounced off the bone. I twist sharply, only for something small and grey to whizz past my head. A group of kids have gathered halfway down the track. One of the boys, his arm pulled back, launches another stone at me.

'Oi!' Stuart runs towards them, waving his arms. 'Harry Meadows. I saw that! Do that again and you'll be in isolation.'

'Drew!' Abi shouts from beneath me. 'Drew, don't do this. You'll hurt yourself.'

'I don't care!'

Lacey and Jude, out of Abi's eye line, exchange a look and smirk. They're totally loving this.

'Why are you doing this?' Kyle shouts, gripping the fence. He looks like he's readying himself to climb after me and, with Stuart on crowd control, there's no one to lecture him about health and safety.

'I've had enough,' I shout back. 'I can't take it any more.'

'Who's her therapist?' Abi hisses. 'We need her out here.'

Kyle shakes his head. 'I've got this.'

'Drew!' he shouts. 'Come down and let's talk about it.'

'No.'

I shiver, despite my warm hoody. The wind's more powerful up here and it's whipping my hair around my face. I can barely feel my fingers and my thighs are starting to cramp from holding this position. Gripping the top of the fence with both hands, I attempt to throw my left leg over the top. But I'm not strong enough and I lurch to the side as my left foot clangs against the fence. The gasps from below are drowned out by my blood thrumming in my ears as I try to jam my foot back into a gap. I can't do it. I'm too tired. As I twist and turn and kick at the fence, my right foot comes loose too and I drop like a stone. I scream in pain as the wire cuts into my fingers, my hands taking the full weight of my body. I can't let go. I'll break my ankle if I fall from his height. But it hurts so much.

'Drew!' Kyle shouts. 'Don't move. I'm coming to get you. Don't move!'

The fence sways violently as he launches himself at it. I close my eyes and cling on for dear life as he powers his way up to me, huffing and puffing and swearing under his breath. Finally, just when I don't think I'll be able to hold on a second longer, I feel his hand on my ankle.

'There!' He shoves at my feet, jamming them into the fence then continues to climb, pinning me against the fence with his body. 'Someone get a ladder!' he shouts. 'Then let's get her down.'

*

I am half carried, half dragged out of the gate near the football pitch and into the field, kicking and screaming the whole way. Kyle has his hand under one armpit, Stuart the other.

'It's for your own good, Drew,' Mrs H. hisses, her high-heeled shoes sinking into the soggy grass as she attempts to keep up. 'We gave you a second chance, you can't say we didn't.'

'Take me back!' I shout twisting my upper body to look back at Norton House. 'Please! Please just take me back.'

A light flickers in one of the staff quarter rooms and the silhouette of a man appears in the window. He gets smaller and smaller as I'm marched towards the low red-brick building of the treatment centre.

Chapter Thirty-Three

There was a moment, when Mrs H. came rushing out of the rec room and onto the running track, her blonde hair flying behind her, her face pinched with anger, when I felt sick with fear. I'd pinned everything on her sending me to the treatment centre for trying to escape. What if she didn't? What if she sent me to isolation instead? What if she saw through my 'desperation' to go home and realized that it was all a ruse; that what I actually wanted was to be reunited with Mason and Mouse so we could all escape together. But she didn't. She reacted instinctively, fuelled by rage.

'Get her down and take her to the treatment centre,' she screamed. 'And get everyone else back in the rec room. *Now!*'

She continued to rant – about how ineffective and useless the friends were and how she was considering sacking the lot of them – all the way across the field to the treatment centre. Only now, as Stuart and Kyle set me down on my feet outside the heavy black door, does she pause to draw breath.

She presses a buzzer on a metal grille to the left of the door. 'It's Evelyn Hatch. We've got a new student for you, Drew Finch.'

There's a pause then, 'Sorry, there's no Drew Finch on our list.'

'That's because it's an emergency referral. I radioed over the request ten minutes ago.'

'Has the referral had authorization from Dr Rothwell?'

'Of course it has. Oh for goodness' sake just open the door.'

Another pause then there's a buzzing sound and the black door clicks open. Stuart and Kyle usher me in, not taking their hands off my shoulders. A long white corridor stretches ahead of us with a door at the far end. Directly to our right is a glass window. Sitting behind it is a woman in a white uniform, her hair pulled back tightly into a bun. She looks me at me then at Mrs H.

'The authorization from Dr Rothwell has just come through,' the nurse says sharply. 'In future, please wait until we have confirmed a residency before bringing a student over. We can't always guarantee that we'll have a room ready.'

Mrs H. opens her mouth to reply but, as she does, the door at the end of the corridor opens and two men, also in white uniforms, walk towards us. Kyle tightens his grip on my right shoulder. He's as clueless as I am about what happens next.

'We'll take over from here,' says the man on the right. He's got deep-set eyes, slightly too close together, and a heavy brow that makes him look like a caveman.

'Come with us, please,' says the taller man on the left. He's got close-cropped blond hair and thin, arching eyebrows.

Stuart's hand falls from my shoulder. So does Kyle's.

'It would be in your best interests to cooperate,' says the blond man, staring, unblinkingly, into my eyes. 'We will restrain you if we have to.'

'I'm not . . . I'm not going to run. I'll come with you,' I stutter. This man couldn't be more different to the friends with their fake, happy smiley personalities. The complete lack of emotion in his eyes is unsettling. It makes him impossible to read.

He doesn't reply. Instead, he points towards the door at the other end of the corridor.

I start walking, aware that the men in white are following close behind me. When we reach the door a buzzer sounds and the door swings open. No staff passes here. The woman behind the glass wall must have buzzed us through.

'Where now?' I ask, as I step through the door into another long white corridor. The blond man points for me to walk straight ahead. I continue to walk, memorizing the route as we take a right, a left and another right, passing through doors that magically swing open as we approach them. Finally, when we reach the fourth corridor, the blond man holds up a hand for me to stop. He points to a door on my right with the number six embossed on the outside. The red lights on the CCTV unit on the ceiling flash once, twice, three times, then the door clicks open. The caveman pushes it open and gestures for me to go inside.

I hesitate. 'I want to see my brother first. I need to check he's OK.'

He shakes his head, gesturing again for me to go inside.

'No, I won't. You need to tell me where Mason and Mouse are. You need to –'

I'm shoved hard, between my shoulder blades, forcing me into the room. The door clicks shut behind me then I hear a clunk-click sound. I'm locked in.

*

A white ceiling with inset lights but no light switch. A shiny metal floor, slanted at a strange angle. White walls, covered in some kind of soft, quilted plasticky material. It gives slightly as I press a hand against it. On three walls there are strange black and white pictures, screwed to the wall at odd angles. They're of geometric shapes, wavy lines and repeated patterns. They make my eyes go weird if I look at them too long. There's also a metal bed in the corner of the room with a single rough, grey blanket folded on top. No windows. A metal hatch low down in the wall to my left. I pull on the handle but it doesn't open. A metal toilet in the opposite corner of the room. Thick, waxy toilet paper. A sink with no plug. Only the cold water tap works. I pace the room, touching and testing the few bits of furniture in the room. The bed is fixed to the floor. So are the toilet and sink. There are no air vents but there's a black CCTV unit on the ceiling near the door. Out of curiosity I run from the hatch to the opposite wall and barge into it with my shoulder. I bounce straight off.

'Hello!' I shout. 'Can anyone hear me?'

My voice reverberates off the padded walls but no one answers. The CCTV unit continues to blink.

'Hello! What am I supposed to do now?'

Still no reply.

I walk laps around the room. I sit on the floor and pull at the hatch, jamming my feet against the wall and tugging with all my might. It doesn't budge. I throw myself at a different wall and bounce off. I tug at the door handle.

'I know you're watching me! Just tell me what I need to do, OK?'

No one replies and nothing happens. I sigh heavily as I

plonk myself down on the hard, metal bed and pull the itchy grey blanket around my shoulders. Is this it? Is this *the treatment*? I'm almost disappointed. If they think they're going to brainwash me by leaving me alone in a white room for a few days they've got another thing coming. They might have been able to scramble Israel's brain by isolating him but he didn't know what was going to happen to him. He wasn't prepared. I studied brainwashing before I left. I need to keep my brain busy. I need to hang onto my sense of self. I'm not going to let them beat me.

*

I jerk awake, smacking my hand against the cold, padded wall as I sit up. At some point while I was singing 'Ten Green Bottles' I must have fallen asleep. I glance at my watch: 4 p.m. Wow. I was asleep for two hours. I must have needed it. I roll my shoulders backwards and forwards and then stretch my hands above my head. My whole body feels tight and sore from sleeping on the metal bed. I need to do some stretches and maybe some jumping jacks or press-ups or something.

I scoot off the bed and stand in the middle of the metal floor.

'One, two, three, four,' I count out loud as I pretend to jump rope then burst out laughing at the image of the CCTV operator watching me jump an imaginary skipping rope. In a weird way I'm kind of enjoying this and –

I jolt in surprise as the hatch in the wall suddenly slides open and a voice booms, 'Remove the uniform from the hatch.'

'Ok.' I pull a white long-sleeved T-shirt and a pair of white leggings from the hatch. 'Now what?'

'Change into the uniform and deposit your own clothing, including jewellery, watches, belts, shoes and laces in the hatch.'

I shake my head. 'I'm not doing that.'

Talk about predictable. If you strip a prisoner of their own clothes you're stripping them of their individuality and sense of self.

'Remove your clothing and place it in the hatch.'

The voice seems to be coming from beneath the CCTV unit.

'No,' I say, looking directly at it. 'I've got no privacy. You can't make me do that.'

I wait for them to respond.

Nothing.

'I'm not giving you the white stuff back,' I say. 'It's freezing cold in here and if you're not going to turn the heating up I'm going to wear this stuff under my clothes.'

Still, nothing.

What is this? Some kind of call my bluff game?

'You may as well shut the hatch,' I say, 'because I'm not giving you the – Aaarrgh!'

It's as though the soles of my feet have been stung by a thousand bees. The sensation travels up my legs and my body jerks up and into the air. When I land it happens again. It's an electric shock, conducted through the metal floor.

'Stop it! Stop!' I launch myself across the room and onto the bed but that's made of metal too. So are the toilet and sink. There's literally nowhere to escape. My teeth judder against each other and I wince in pain as I'm shocked and shocked and shocked. 'Please, please,' I beg in between shocks. 'Please stop. I'll put the clothes on. I'll do it.'

The shocks stop as suddenly as they started I slump onto the blanket, sobbing and exhausted.

'Put on the uniform *now*,' the voice orders.

'OK, OK.' I tentatively place a foot on the floor then, turning my back to the CCTV camera and throwing the blanket over my head, I strip off my hoody, trainers, jeans and T-shirt. I unfasten my earrings and bracelet and slide my rings off my fingers then yank at my watch strap. I stare at the shiny, glass face. If I give them the watch, I'll lose all sense of time. But if I try to hide it – in my mouth or under the band of my bra – and they discover it, they'll shock me again, or worse. I need to act like I'm playing along. If they think I'm subservient and obeying orders they'll go easier on me.

I shuffle over to the hatch, the blanket still over my head, and drop my clothes, jewellery and watch into the square, metal basket, then I pull on the leggings and long-sleeved T-shirt.

'There.' I pull the blanket from head and look up at the CCTV unit. 'I've done it.'

'Open your mouth and your hands,' says the voice.

I do as I'm told.

'Now sit on the bed.'

The moment my bottom makes contact with the metal bed the hatch slides shut.

'Now what?' I say.

But the voice doesn't respond.

Chapter Thirty-Four

'You are not an individual. You are not free. You do not have control over your life.'

The cold, emotionless voice in the corner of the room has been repeating those three phrases over and over again for what feels like hours. At first I replied, shouting back, 'Yes, I am,' after every statement. Then, when my throat became scratchy and sore, I put my hands over my ears and began humming every song I could think of – the entire backlist of my favourite band and then, when I'd done that twice, all the nursery rhymes I could think of. At some point, I fell asleep and dreamed about white robots with red eyes marching towards me, repeating the phrases over and over again. In the dream the words were red ribbons that they fired at me. I tried to run away but the ribbons wrapped themselves around my arms and my legs, my face, my eyes, my ears and my mouth. I woke up gasping.

I force myself to get off the bed and march round the room with the blanket draped over my shoulders. It's still freezing cold and the bland, tasteless egg salad that was shoved through the hatch a while ago didn't help. It came in a white, polystyrene box – the sort you get a takeaway in – and there wasn't any cutlery. I took it out of the hatch and put it on the floor. There was no way I was going to eat it, not when it could have been laced with something, but when the voice ordered me to eat or I'd be shocked, I shoved every last bit in my mouth and then threw the container back into the hatch. The food doesn't seem to have affected me. Other than making me feel a bit sick.

When I haven't been singing, shouting or humming I've been thinking about Mason and Mouse. I was an idiot to think they'd let me see them before starting my treatment. Poor Mouse will be absolutely terrified by all this and I can't stand the thought of my brother being in pain or upset. Other than the voice, I haven't heard a single sound since they shut me in here and, if Mason and Mouse are in identical cells to this one, they won't even know that I'm here. I just have to hope that they're strong enough to resist the brainwashing.

'You have let down your family,' the voice says. 'You have disappointed everyone who loves you. You have failed your mother and father. You have failed your brother. You have failed your friend. You acted aggressively. You have no self-control. You have an inflated sense of your intelligence. You are proud. You are a failure. You are alone. No one is proud of you. This is all your fault. You have let down your family. You have disappointed everyone . . .'

What? I look in horror towards the CCTV unit. No. That's not true. I haven't . . .

'You have failed your brother.'

'This is all your fault.'

'Failed your mother and father.'

'Failure.'

I press my hands to my ears to try to block out the voice but it only gets louder and the words seem to burrow themselves into my brain. I haven't failed Mason. I've been trying to help him. OK, so the escape didn't work out as planned but that wasn't because . . .

'You have an inflated sense of your own intelligence.'

Maybe I do.

No. I don't. I'm not the most intelligent person in the world, or even in my school, but I'm not stupid.

'You acted aggressively.'

I hit Lacey. I pushed Jude. But I had to. I was tired of being pushed around. I was tired of feeling afraid. Of being a victim.

'You have no self-control.'

I do. Don't I? Yes, I've been controlled before. No, that's not what I mean. I had self-control . . . I had to be controlled when . . . when . . . the voice is so loud I can't think straight.

'I am kind,' I shout as I wrap the blanket around my head and continue to march around the room. 'I am loving. My dad would be proud of me. Mason knows that I did what I did for him. I tried to help Mouse. I am not a bad person. I haven't done anything wrong.'

But even as the words leave my mouth the voice continues to burrow its way further and further into my brain, spreading unease and doubt, until, finally, it settles in my heart.

*

'Sit in the centre of the floor,' the voice commands.

I drag myself off the bed and onto the metal floor. I pull the blanket tighter round my shoulders but it does nothing to stop the shakes and shudders that pulse through my body and make my teeth chatter. I was asleep. Or I think I was asleep. When I close my eyes I see white. When I open them I see white. I hear words. I see words. They're imprinted in the whiteness. I cry words. No, no. But I do cry. I've been crying a lot. This is all my fault. I could have stopped Mason being sent here. I was pleased because he was annoying and I thought he deserved to be taught a lesson. I should have stood up to Tony. I could have convinced Mum not to send Mason away but I didn't. I was selfish. I was only thinking about me. And Dad. What would he think if he knew what I'd done? He'd be horrified if he knew that I'd hurt people. That wasn't how he brought me up. I've made a lot of mistakes. I've screwed up and I've only got myself to blame.

'Repeat after me,' the voice says, 'I was wrong.'

'I was wrong.'

'Repeat. I have no free will.'

I shake my head.

'Repeat. I have no free will.'

I shake my head again. I have free will. I know I have free will.

'Aaaagh!' I scream in pain as an electric shock pulses through my body.

'Repeat. I have no free will.'

'I have no free will.'

'Repeat. Everything I believe is wrong.'

I pull the blanket tighter around my shoulders and grit my teeth. I'm not going to say that. It's not true. Not everything I believe is wrong.

'Aarrgh!' I flip onto my side, the force of the electric shock is so strong. It's as though a thousand tiny wires are threading their way inside my body.

'Everything I believe is wrong!' I scream.

'Repeat. I do not know what is best for me.'

'I DO NOT KNOW WHAT IS BEST FOR ME!' Tears stream down my cheeks as I shout the words. I thought I was stronger than this. I thought I could withstand anything. Mason would be so ashamed if he could see me now, his big sister crying and screaming and denying everything she believes in. My dad would be so disappointed. He brought me up to believe that I could do anything, that I could be anything, but I'm not indestructible, I'm not undefeatable. I'm shallow and weak and I just want them to stop. I don't want them to hurt me any more.

*

I don't know what day it is. I don't know what time it is. Sometimes, when I open my eyes, I think I am upside down and I reach my feet towards the lights on the floor and I try to stand up. I have stopped humming and singing. My voice sounds strange, as though it belongs to someone else. When I try to say a word, it is shapeless and nonsensical, a raspy, squeaky sound that reverberates from my throat to the roof of my mouth and out of the top of my head. Food. Food is limp, wet, dry. It lies on my saliva-less tongue, like it's waiting for orders. I tell my teeth to mash together and my throat to swallow. When it gets stuck because I forget to do the second part properly I have to put my lips to the tap and wash it down with water. I cry continuously and I don't know why. The padded walls pulse. In, out, in, out. I match my breathing to the motion. It's the only way I can stay calm. I know they've forgotten about me. The other people. The voice hasn't spoken in years. A robot puts the food in the hatch. There are no humans here. I am the last one. They are never going to let me out.

'I can help you.'

I sit up suddenly, too suddenly, and black spots appear before my eyes. I sink back onto the bed and close my eyes. I thought I heard the voice but I must have imagined it.

'What do you miss about home?'

I open my eyes again. The black thing in the corner of the room blinks its red eyes at me. It's speaking to me again.

'What do you miss about home?' it asks again.

I part my lips, inhale, then exhale heavily, forcing a word out. 'Everything.'

'Look in the hatch. I have a gift for you.'

I attempt to swing my legs out of the bed and land in a heap on the floor. I crawl towards the hatch. The voice is tricking me again. It's asked me to look in the hatch before and there's been a spider, an eyeball, an image of a child screaming. I hook my fingers over the metal and peer inside. A single piece of paper. A glossy piece of paper. Colours. Faces. It takes my eyes a couple of seconds to focus in on it. It's a photograph of my family. My real family. Mum and Dad, me and Mason. We're on a beach. Dad's squinting into the sunlight with one hand curved over his eyebrows. Mum is wearing shades. Mason's sticking out his tongue. I'm holding a bucket and spade.

I reach out a hand then snatch it back quickly. The voice is going to sting me again. It's a trick.

'You may take it,' the voice says.

I shake my head. I don't want to be hurt again.

'You can trust me. It's a gift. Take it.'

My hand darts towards it. I snatch it back. I try again. The edge of the paper grazes my fingers. I snatch my hand back. On my third attempt my fingers grip one corner of the photograph and I hug it to my chest, waiting for the shock. But none comes.

'Thank you,' I whisper. 'Thank you so much.'

'You're feeling a lot of pain inside,' the voice says, as I stare at the photo, my eyes blurred with tears. 'Would you like me to help you get rid of it?'

I nod my head. 'Yes. Yes, I would.'

'Repeat after me. I am not a bad person.'

'I am not a bad person.'

'But my belief system was wrong.'

'My belief system was wrong.'

'I did some stupid things and made some stupid decisions. Being at Norton House has taught me how foolish I was. Now I want to learn how to be a better person and contribute to society.'

I nod in agreement as I repeat the sentences, word for word.

Chapter Thirty-Five

I do not jump as the door slowly swings open and a man with a bald head and a neatly trimmed beard steps into the room. Instead, I stand up, smile, reach out a hand and cross the room.

'Doctor Rothwell, how wonderful to see you.'

He shakes my hand. It is the firm, confident handshake of an admirable man.

'Drew.' He smiles warmly. 'How are you?'

'Very well, thank you, Doctor Rothwell. And you?'

'Well, quite well.' He looks over his shoulder and nods at the two orderlies standing behind him. I have the distinct impression that I've pleased him in some way and feel a warm glow of happiness.

'You've been given an opportunity to reflect on the past and your future during your stay with us, Drew,' he says, looking back at me. 'Would you mind sharing any insights you've had with me?'

'Of course. I was very troubled when I came here, Doctor Rothwell. I was full of rage, self-loathing and resentment. I had a very narrow, very blinkered outlook on life and I was unable to see the bigger picture. I didn't appreciate how much those around me were doing for me. I didn't realize that all the decisions they were making were with my best interests at heart.'

'And your brother? Did they also have his best interests at heart?'

'Absolutely. Mason was as immature as I was. Sending him to Norton House was the best decision my mother could have made. We're both extremely lucky to have had this experience.'

'And the future? How do you feel about that?'

'I'm very excited. I'd like to do a degree in psychology and then work here. If you'd have me. Or perhaps a role in Government. I'd love to work with the Home Secretary. I think he's doing such valuable work. If he can get the National Service Bill through Parliament I think it would transform this country. Such an incredible opportunity for non-academic students to contribute to society.'

'Well, well, well. Isn't that wonderful.' Dr Rothwell's face lights up and I couldn't be more delighted. He approves of my career choice. 'I think you'd be a valuable asset wherever you decide to work.'

He nods at the orderlies again. 'She's ready. You can put her in with the rest now.'

*

I make small talk with the orderlies as they lead me down a series of white corridors. They look at each other and grin when I apologize for not immediately complying with their orders when I first arrived.

'At least you didn't try and punch us,' the blond one says. I look at him in shock. 'People do that?'

He smirks, but I'm not sure why. I feel dazed, as though I've just woken from a long sleep. 'Yes, miss. They do.'

'Did I say something amusing?'

'No, miss.' He pushes at a white door. There's a sign above it that says 'Lounge'. He indicates that I should go in. 'If you wait in the lounge someone will show you to your room.'

'My room? I thought I'd be going home immediately after treatment. I'm keen to see my mum and stepdad again. You're not the only people I need to apologize to.'

'You'll need to stay here for a week or so first,' the blond orderly says. 'Just to, you know, acclimatize.'

I glance down at my clothes. I'm still wearing the long-sleeved top and leggings I was asked to change into when I arrived. 'Will I be given something else to wear? I had a . . . a suitcase. Clothes and some personal items although . . .' I tail off. I feel embarrassed now, remembering the clothes that I wore when I arrived. I looked like such a scruff. Sixteen years old and dressing like some kind of down and out when I should be portraying a much more polished, professional demeanour if I want to be taken seriously.

'Don't worry,' the dark-haired orderly says. 'You'll be given clothes. And if you're feeling self-conscious, don't bother. All the kids in here arrived in the same kit as you. They won't give you a second look.' He pushes the door further open.

The lounge is full of teenagers, my age and younger. They're playing chess, reading newspapers, doing puzzles and reading books. The only sound is the gentle swish of a page being turned or a chess piece being pushed across the board. It's an oasis of calm. I scan the room, looking for a spare chair. There are two people – a young man and young woman – sitting either side of a sofa with a space between them. The girl is writing in a notebook. The boy is staring into space with the smallest of smiles on his face. I head towards them, stopping short as I get closer. The boy is Mason, my brother. The girl is my old room-mate, Megan. Something sharp and desperate sparks inside me but the feeling dulls quickly and then disappears. Mason senses me watching him and looks up. He smiles warmly.

'Hello, Drew. I didn't expect to see you here.' He leans across the sofa and touches Megan on the arm. 'Megan, this is my sister Drew.'

She nods. 'Yes, I remember you. Lovely to see you again, Drew.' I feel the spark again, at the sound of her soft Welsh accent. I liked her. We were friends. But we were also incredibly stupid. Mason too. If our escape attempt had succeeded we would have remained naive and unenlightened, with no purpose in our lives. Thank goodness Mrs H. took such decisive action when she discovered what we were planning. I won't mention it to them though. I imagine Mason and Megan feel as embarrassed about what happened as I do.

Megan smiles politely then returns to her writing.

'Would you like to do a puzzle?' Mason asks. 'There's a thousand-piece jigsaw that I'd like to.'

'Yes,' I smile. 'I'd love to.'

*

We've just completed the outer square of the jigsaw when Stuart walks into the room.

'Megan, Mason, it's time for you to do your assembly,' he says.

Megan and my brother share an excited grin and the other students applaud politely. I join in, even though I feel a frisson of envy. I wish I could share the insights I've gained with the pre-assessment students. Megan and Mason say goodbye to me and cross the room, chatting excitedly and then disappear into the corridor. As the door closes, I return my attention to the puzzle and try to push down my feelings of disappointment. It's not a productive emotion. If I want to achieve great things I need to work harder but, for now, the jigsaw is a socially acceptable way to spend my free time.

*

I place the last piece in the puzzle. Mason and Megan have still not returned from assembly and, with all the newspapers being read and no desire to play chess, I approach the orderly sitting on a chair by the door.

'Hello,' I say. 'I'd like to read a book. Is that allowed?'

'There's a bookshelf over there.' He points across the room. 'What do you like reading?'

A memory flashes through my brain – of me giving a book to Mum when we arrived at Norton House. It was an important book. I was studying it on the train and I needed her to return it to the library for me. Why can't I remember what it was? I dismiss the thought. It won't have been important.

Nothing I did, nothing I said, nothing I thought before treatment was important.

'I'm not sure what I like reading,' I say. 'What would Doctor Rothwell approve of?'

Chapter Thirty-Six

My free time didn't last long. After half an hour I was approached by an orderly and handed a pair of green overalls to change into. Now I am walking across the field to Norton House with a bucket and mop in one hand and a cleaning tray in the other.

'You're new, aren't you?' says the mixed-race girl beside me, matching me pace for pace.

I shoot her a puzzled look. 'I've been here for several weeks.'

'No, to cleaning duty. I haven't seen you on rota before.'

'Today is my first day.'

The orderly, walking ahead of us, clears his throat and my stomach clenches with anxiety. Are we not supposed to talk? I've read the welcome booklet several times and I don't remember reading anything about whether talking is acceptable outside of the lounge. I did read that community service was character building and an important way of giving back to society but there was no mention of whether . . .

'We're allowed to talk,' the girl says, reading my fraught expression. 'Don't worry. You won't get into trouble. I'm Mia by the way.'

'Drew.'

We follow the orderly through the gate at the side of the football pitch, across the running track and into the part of the building that houses the swimming pool. There are no students in the water and the only sound as we cross the wide room is the squeak of our trainers on the tiles.

'OK,' the orderly says, as he flashes his pass at the door and ushers us into a white corridor, 'over there is the sanatorium.' He points at a white door directly in front of us.

'And those are isolation units.' He points further down the corridor at a series of doors. 'Mia, I'd like you to mop the floor and scrub down every surface in the first isolation room. Drew, you can do the san. I'll wait out here. Any questions, just ask.' He opens a cupboard door to his right and pulls out a folding chair. He props it against the wall then holds his staff pass to the lock on the right of the san door. 'In you go then.'

*

Unlike the swimming pool, which was flooded with light from the floor-to-ceiling picture window, the sanatorium is dark and gloomy, despite the white walls, tiled floor and cotton bedlinen. Other than one bed, with lumpy bed sheets, none of the beds look slept in and the room seems fairly clean. It shouldn't take me long to mop the floor and wipe everything down. I put down my cleaning tray then cross the room, mop and bucket in hand, and head for the large metal sink. I squirt bright pink floor wash into the bucket then run the tap. When the bucket's half full with hot foamy water I lift it out of the sink and plunge the mop head inside.

'Oi oi!'

The sound of a male voice makes me jump so violently I yank at the mop handle and tip over the bucket, covering my feet, legs and the floor with white, foamy water.

'Sorry!' the voice says from across the room. 'I didn't mean to make you jump.'

A young black man is sitting up in the bed nearest the door, his arms folded over his chest, his bed clothes gathered around his hips. Israel. His name comes to me like a lightning flash. He was a disruptive student who was sent to isolation for punishment. I remember Kyle telling me that he has a drug problem. There is a part of me that feels sorry for him but the larger part feels irritated. Israel was gifted with an amazing opportunity to better himself when he arrived here and he's squandering it. From the inane grin on his face he's obviously unrepentant.

'I'm sorry if I disturbed you.' I sweep my mop over the spilled water and squeeze it into the bucket.

'You didn't. It's good to see you. I haven't talked to anyone apart from the grumpy nurse in days.'

'We shouldn't insult our elders and betters.' I attack the spilled water again, sweeping the mop from left to right to try to absorb as much as possible, but there's too much water. It's going to take me a while to mop it all up.

'Our elders and betters!' Israel laughs. 'Since when did you get so posh?'

I glance at him over my shoulder. 'There's nothing wrong with good manners.'

'Oooh!' He pulls a face. 'Who made you the Queen of the World? Seriously –' he swings his legs out of the bed and crosses the room towards me '– is this some kind of wind-up? Why're you being so weird, Drew?'

My skin prickles with irritation as he plonks himself down on the nearest bed and stares at me. I don't want to talk to him. I just want to get on with my job.

'Drew,' he says again. 'Why are you being weird? Is it because you think I'm mad?'

I straighten up. 'I don't think anything.'

'No? Because I thought we were mates and you're looking at me like something you just picked off the sole of your shoe.'

'I'm not the same person I was, Israel. I've done a lot of growing up in the last few days. I've got different priorities now.'

'What? Like being a dick to your mates?'

'You're not my mate. You're an acquaintance. If that.'

'Ouch!' He mimes pulling a knife out of his chest. 'Jesus, you don't pull any punches, do you, Drew?'

I shrug my shoulders. 'I don't know what you mean. I'm just being honest. And honesty is good.'

'Honesty is good?' He opens and closes the fingers of his right hand as he speaks. 'You sound like some kind of parrot.'

'Obedience, compliance and honesty. They're the bedrocks of society. Doctor Rothwell thinks that the most important –'

'Oh!' His lips part, forming a perfect circle. 'I get it. You've been for treatment, haven't you? You've got that same weird, glazed look in your eyes as those freaks who stood on the stage in assembly. And the same horrible, condescending manner.'

'I'm not condescending, Israel. I'm enlightened.'

He roars with laughter and tips back onto the bed, pulling his knees up to his chest as he rolls from side to side. 'You're unbelievable.

'Seriously –' he props himself up on one elbow and stares at me '– I shouldn't laugh. This is the saddest I've ever seen. I wish the old you could see the Drew you've turned into because –'

'Israel! What are you doing out of bed?' A short, stout woman in a white lab coat with her dark hair curled into a bun, appears in the doorway to the right of the sink.

'I was . . . er . . .' Israel pulls himself into a sitting position, his eyes wide and fearful. 'I was just . . . chatting to the . . . um . . . the cleaner.'

The nurse turns her attention to me. 'Was he distracting you from your duties?'

I nod. 'He was, yes.'

'Right, Israel.' She crooks a finger at him. 'Come with me.'

'I wasn't doing anything wrong. I was just chatting. You don't need to medicate me. I'll go back to my bed. I won't say another word. I promise.'

The nurse's eyes turn steely as she takes a step towards him. The fingers of her right hand tighten on her radio. 'Are you going to come with me or am I going to have to call some of the friends to help me?'

'There's an orderly in the corridor. I could get him for you,' I suggest helpfully.

'Thank you.' She smiles tightly. 'That won't be necessary. Will it, Israel?'

His head drops and his shoulders slump as he inches

himself off the bed and slopes across the damp tiles towards the nurse.

'Thanks, Drew,' he mutters as he passes me. 'Thanks a bloody bunch.'

I say nothing as he and the nurse disappear through the open door. Instead, I slide my mop back and forth over the slippery floor then squeeze the excess water into the bucket. It's nice and quiet in the sanatorium now and I can work unimpeded.

Chapter Thirty-Seven

Lightning rips through the sky, slashing dark clouds and illuminating the fields. Then, as though the clouds have been torn open, heavy rain begins to fall. I look at Mason, standing beside me at the window, and smile.

'Isn't it amazing?'

He nods. 'I love storms.'

'Me too.'

It's the day after his assembly. When I asked him how it went he told me that he'd delivered a heartfelt and powerful speech but the response from the pre-assessment students had been disappointing. They'd stared at him with vacant eyes and gawped.

'They don't understand,' he said. 'But they will.'

I agreed. It's sad to think how close minded and unenlightened they are but we were like that once. We were trapped in our small lives, distracted by our childish concerns. My uncomfortable altercation with Israel yesterday reminded me as much. Unlike Israel, my eyes have been opened by Doctor Rothwell's treatment. No one person is more important than society. Dissenting voices should be quashed, not listened to. In order to be happy we need to work hard, and work as one. The Government knows what's best for us and it's our responsibility to offer them our support. Together we can make this country great.

I sense someone standing to my left and turn my head. 'Hello, orderly.'

The blond man smiles. 'You can call me Steve.'

'OK.'

He looks me up and down. 'You've got some clothes now I see.'

'Yes. There were several outfits to choose from in my wardrobe.' I touch the thick material of my navy blazer. 'I like this a lot.'

'Great, well, it's time for community activities again. What would you like to do? You could help with cooking, cleaning or maintenance.'

I shrug my shoulders. 'I don't mind. I'm happy to do any of those things.'

'OK, cool. Well, you can do cleaning then.' He hands me some green overalls. 'Change into these then come and find me in the staffroom and I'll tell you what to do.'

*

'Right, so, this is the cleaning cupboard. You'll find all the supplies you need in here – cloths, sponges, cleaning fluid, mop, bucket etc.'

I nod. 'I was shown the cupboard yesterday.'

'We've got some new students coming in for treatment this afternoon and I need you to prepare the rooms. The walls and floors need to be washed down. The sinks and toilets need to be scrubbed down, the blankets need to go to laundry and the beds need to be cleaned.'

'That's fine.'

He hands me a washing-up bucket containing a pair of washing-up gloves, a sponge, a cloth, cleaning fluid and polish. 'I suggest you do the sink, toilet and bed first then come back to get the mop and bucket for the walls and floor. The cupboard is locked overnight but I'll leave it open for the next couple of hours so you can get what you need. When you're done come and find me.'

'Will do.'

*

I tie my hair back with a band that I found in my room when I was getting changed into my overalls, then get to work. The sink doesn't take long to clean but the toilet's another matter. It's splattered with vomit and other bodily excretions and I have to concentrate very hard on the reason why I'm completing this task to stop myself from gagging. It's important that the room is a safe and sanitary place for the new student to undertake their treatment and, by cleaning it, I am helping to enhance their experience.

It seems to take for ever until the toilet is sparkling clean, but finally it is done and I turn my attention to the bed. I deposit the blanket in the laundry room as requested then get to work with the polishing spray and cloth. The storm is still raging outside, I glimpsed it through the window in the laundry room, but, inside the treatment room it's silent and there are no distractions so I work quickly and efficiently. I gather up all my cleaning supplies and carry them back down the corridor to the cleaning cupboard. I place them on the floor and open the door. I can see the mop and bucket, propped up in a corner and step inside to retrieve them, keeping one hand on the door to keep it open. I grab the base of the bucket but the handle of the mop is wedged against the shelf above. I pull and pull then let go of the door and yank at it with two hands. The door clicks shut behind me, instantly plunging the cupboard into darkness. I don't panic. Steve the orderly said he was going to leave the door open. I turn the handle and pull but nothing happens. I run my hands down the wall on the left of the door, searching for a light switch. There isn't one. My heart hammers in my chest and a wave of panic flashes through me. I reach for the door handle again, jiggle it up and down and pull with all my strength. The door doesn't move.

'Help!' I pound on the door with my clenched fists. 'Steve! I'm locked in the cupboard.'

I stop pummelling the door and listen. Nothing.

I bang on the door again. 'Help! I'm trapped! Help! Help!'

I'm breathing quickly now, each inhalation short, sharp and desperate and when I pass a hand over my forehead it's slick with sweat. I need to think clearly. I need to calm down and wait. Someone will realize that I'm missing and come and find me, but what if the air runs out? The door is sealed shut. If light can't get in, how can air?

'Help!' I pound on the door again. 'Help! Help! Help!'

I need to slow down my breathing. The faster I breathe the quicker I'll use up the air. But I can't slow my breathing down. I feel hot and faint and the tips of my fingers are tingling. If I don't sit down I'm going to fall down so I sink to my feet and rest with my knees pulled up against my chest. I count to ten then I brace myself with my hands and slam both feet against the door. Thud. The sound fills the small space but still no one comes. I kick at the door again.

Thud.

I kick it again.

Thud.

And again.

Thud.

My feet smack against the lid of the freezer. I'm desperately trying to do a shoulder stand so I can reach the lid but I'm not strong enough to hold the position and each time I kick out I lose my balance and my knees smack against the side of the freezer. I roll onto my knees, crouch, and then pop up like a jack-in-the-box, slamming both palms against the lid. The seals hold fast and it doesn't move.

'Dad!' I scream. 'Dad, I'm in here! Dad! DAD!'

I'm only little but I know I will eventually run out of air. I don't want to die in here, alone, cold and afraid. I want my dad. I need my dad. I don't want to die.

Thud.

I kick at the lid again.

Thud.

And again.

Thud.

'Dad! Dad, help! Help me, Dad! Please!'

Thud.

The walls of the freezer are damp with condensation. It smells musty, like death.

Thud.

Where's Mason? Has he given up on our game of hide and seek and gone back into the house to get something to eat? Or maybe he's watching TV, pleased that he can watch what he wants without his big sister snatching the remote. Or is he still hiding? He gets really cross if he's the one that's found first. Sometimes he cries, even though he's seven years old. He's such a cry baby sometimes. I need to get out to make sure he's OK. Mum will kill me if anything happens to him. I'm his big sister. My job is to look after him. That's what she always says.

Mason.

His face morphs in my mind, from seven years old to fifteen. Long, floppy fringe. Sullen blue eyes, fringed with dark lashes. *Help me, Drew. You need to help me.*

He needs my help. I need to get out of the freezer to . . .

More images flash into my mind:

A note. Mason's handwriting.

A woman, staring into my face, her long, brown hair swept into a sweaty ponytail.

I clutch my head. What's happening to me? I feel as though a film of someone else's life is being screened inside my brain. It's bright and vivid and I can't turn it off. The voice is shouting in my head – *I did some stupid things and I made some stupid decisions.* It's trying to distract me from the film but I can't stop watching it.

A train. My hands. Holding a book. I see the cover as I close it. *Pavlov's Dogs: An experiment in classical conditioning.*

Power lies in submission, the voice shouts. *Obedience is good.*

My mum, walking away from me. A pained expression on her face when her eyes meet mine.

I press a hand to my knotted stomach. I don't want her to go. She mustn't go.

We must all contribute to society, the voice whispers. *We will make this country great.*

Jude, on her bunk, staring at me. Mouse, gripping my hand. A tunnel. Mason.

A fence.

A room. A white room.

'Drew!' The door opens suddenly, flooding the cupboard with light and slamming into my feet.

I shuffle backwards, pulling my knees into my chest, blinking as a head appears around the open door.

'Drew, are you OK?'

A blond-haired man wearing a white uniform stares at me in concern. I press my palms against my temples and screw my eyes up tightly against the throbbing pain that's radiating across my head. It's so intense it makes me retch.

'The storm caused an electrical outage,' the man says. 'All doors locked automatically. It's in case of security breaches. I heard you knocking on the door. Have you been in here long? Are you OK?'

I open my eyes and look into the face of the man who escorted me to my treatment room. Eyebrows. That's what I called him.

'I'm OK,' I say, scrabbling to my feet.

'What about your head?' He looks at my hand, still clutching the side of my head, and his brows furrow with concern.

'I hit it when the door shut,' I lie.

'Do you need to see the nurse?'

'No, I'll be fine. Would you like me to continue with the

cleaning? I was about to mop the floors and ceiling in treatment room ten.'

He laughs. 'You obviously didn't lose your memory when you hit your head.'

'No.'

I turn and yank the mop and bucket from where they're wedged under the shelf, smiling to myself as they come free. I haven't lost my memory. I remember absolutely *everything*.

Chapter Thirty-Eight

It's strange, and more than a little bit scary, being the only non-brainwashed person in the room. I feel like an alien, masquerading as a human – a Cylon in *Battlestar Galactica*. I look like everyone else, I sound like everyone else but, if they discovered who I really am, they'd turn on me. I only have the vaguest memory of how I felt when I was brainwashed. I can remember feeling really calm and in control of my emotions but that's about it. So that's what I'm doing, acting calm and in control. I'm not speaking until I'm spoken to and then I'm keeping conversation to a minimum. Mouse isn't all that chatty so she's not a problem but Mason does like a rousing 'aren't we wonderful, enlightened people' conversation. It's freaky, looking into his brainwashed eyes, and seeing absolutely nothing. It's like all traces of his personality have been wiped out. Scary to think that that happened to me too. So much for my 'I won't be brainwashed, I've read a few psychology books' bravado. A few days, weeks, hours – however long it was – of electric shocks, starvation and sleep deprivation and I was broken. I would have said or done anything for them to stop.

I take a seat on the sofa between Mouse and Mason and resist the urge to scratch at my horrible, itchy skirt and jacket. I look like I'm playing a Fifties housewife in a school play.

In a minute one of the orderlies will come in, asking which community activities we'd like to do today. Thank God for the storm when I was cleaning yesterday. If I hadn't ended up locked in a cupboard, I'd still be spouting crap about *Making Britain Great* like Mason.

It was fear that reversed my brainwashing. I was reading about it on the train up here. Back in the Twenties a Russian physiologist called Pavlov was researching the way that dogs salivated when they were fed. He noticed that the dogs salivated whenever he walked into the room, whether he had food with him or not. He began to ring a bell when he fed the dogs and noticed that, whenever he rang the bell, the dogs would salivate, expecting food. The dogs had been conditioned to salivate whenever they heard the sound of a bell. One day the laboratories where the dogs were kept were flooded and the dogs had to swim to the top of their cages to avoid being drowned. Pavlov's assistants realized what was happening and saved most of the dogs by submerging them into the water and pulling them out. Later, when they repeated the ringing bell experiment on the saved dogs, they didn't salivate. The fear the dogs had felt during the flood had reversed their conditioning.

And that's exactly what happened to me. All I need to do now is watch what I say, stay out of trouble and sit it out until they release us. With any luck Mum will be alone when she comes to pick us up. I've got the entire train journey home to tell her what's happened. There's no way she'll be able to deny what they're doing here when she sees the difference in Mason. I'll ask her to drive me straight to the police station once the train arrives then we'll get Mason to a proper psychologist who'll know how to reverse his conditioning. I'll have to get Mouse's home phone number so Mum can call her parents and let them know what's happened too. And then I'll need to get in touch with Zed to see if –

'Are you looking forward to it?' Mason says, making me jump.

'Looking forward to . . . what?'

Mouse gives him a look and shakes her head. 'They haven't told her yet. And it isn't your place, Mason.'

'What should I be looking forward to?'

Mason is jiggling up and down in his seat he's so excited. 'The evaluation at the end of the week.'

'For what?'

'Students suitable for Home Office training.'

'What?' I say the word so loudly several students look round in surprise. I need to keep it together but I can't believe what I'm hearing. I assumed we'd be going home after we completed our treatment. Charlie did. But then again, Charlie decided he wanted to be an accountant.

'Home Office training?' I repeat.

'Yes, Drew. The Home Office.' Mason smooths his fringe across his forehead. Not that there's a hair out of place. He looks like he's just stepped out of a Forties men's clothing catalogue in his grey suit and waistcoat, white shirt and oiled hair. 'They are responsible for immigration, security and law and order.'

'But you're fifteen. You can't get a job.'

'It won't be a job. Yet. It's training.'

'In what?'

'I'll find out when I get there.'

'*If* you get there. There's no way Mum will agree to that.'

'She already has.'

I stare at him in horror. I can't believe it. I won't. Agreeing to a short stay at Norton House is one thing but the Home Office is in London. He's fifteen years old.

'How long is the training?' I ask.

'A year.'

'You can't go away for a year. You'll miss Mum.'

'No more than I do now.'

'And your friends?'

'I'll make new ones.'

I feel sick. I can't believe what he's just told me. If he passes the evaluation, I won't see him for a year. I won't be able to get him to a psychologist to reverse his brainwashing. And Mum won't be able to see how much he's changed. She's not going to believe me if I tell her what's been happening here. She didn't believe Mason when he sent the note. Oh God. I slump forward and rest my elbows on my knees. If I say a word, Tony will convince her to send me straight back.

'Drew?' Mason touches me on the back. 'Are you OK? Are you feeling unwell? Should I call for an orderly?'

'No . . . no. I sit back against the sofa and stare straight ahead. I want to cry, to scream, to shake Mason by the shoulders until his stupefied brain rattles in his skull. But I can't. I am dying inside and no one can know.

'Will you apply?' Mason asks. 'Megan is. Wouldn't it be wonderful if we all passed the test?'

I don't answer. Instead I stand up, walk to the window and press my hands to the glass. I'm going to have to try to reverse Mason and Mouse's brainwashing myself. But how? I could start a fire. If I volunteer for cooking duty, I might be able to get my hands on a lighter or a box of matches. The orderlies in this unit don't watch us as closely as the friends did in the main building. Why would they? We've been brainwashed to do what we're told and not cause trouble.

A fire though. It's risky. I'd never forgive myself if someone died. I'm going to have to target Mouse and Mason individually but the only time I see them is in this stupid lounge. Unless I want to try to frighten them to death with a chess piece I've got no hope. Although . . . if I'm given the same community activity as them I could do something. If we were given maintenance duty maybe I could push them off something or pretend to hit them with a spade. Oh God, I don't know. I'll think of something. I have to.

'OK, ladies and gents.' Eyebrows appears at the door. He's holding his hands up for hush, which is pretty stupid considering no one is speaking. 'It's time to assign community activities for today.' He consults the clipboard in his right hand. 'OK, so, hands up for cooking. I need four volunteers.'

Mouse and Mason don't move a muscle so I keep my hands at my sides.

'Winston, Nesta, Sanj, Camille, OK, good.' He clicks a pen against his teeth and scribbles on the board. 'Maintenance?'

Several hands shoot into the air, but not on the sofa. They must be holding out for cleaning duty. Weirdos.

'Cobey, Lou, Paddy, Hari. Great. So now we have . . . well, it's a bit of an unusual one. Several of the friends in the main block are doing training today so we need three of you to stand in for them. Do we have any volunteers?'

Mason and Mouse's hands shoot straight up. Mine joins

them a split second later. This could be perfect. If we're taking the place of friends that means we'll be given staff passes. If I can convince Mason and Mouse to leave the building with me I can work out how to reverse their brainwashing later. The main thing is for all three of us to get the hell out of here before Mason is shipped off elsewhere.

'Okayyyy . . .' Eyebrows says, looking around the room. 'We've got five volunteers for three opportunities. Right . . . um . . .'

His eyes flick from Mouse to me to Mason and then over to the window where two girls are sitting at a table holding a half-finished jigsaw puzzle. I stretch my hand higher into the air and give him a dazzling smile then promptly adopt a neutral expression. Mouse and Mase couldn't look more serious.

'Mason.' Eyebrows waves a hand towards my brother. 'Megan and . . .'

I clench my teeth together to stop myself from shouting, 'Me! Me!'

'And . . . Rae.'

What?

'Drew and Takesha, you're on cleaning duty with the others.'

'But . . .' I barely breathe the word but Mouse and Mason immediately give me questioning looks.

'Is there a problem?' Mouse asks.

'Should we inform the orderly?' Mason says.

'No.' I look him straight in the eye, softening my gaze to match the blank expression in his eyes. 'I enjoy any activity that benefits the community.'

He nods approvingly and looks back at the orderly. That was close. One false move and these two will blow my cover. I need to be more careful. But I'm not letting them go to the main house without me. This might be my only opportunity to get my hands on another staff pass.

'Please return to your rooms to change into your overalls,' Eyebrows says, passing out the vile green outfits. 'Cleaners report to Ian. Cooks to Anabel. Maintenance, you're with me. Mason, Megan and Rae, you should go to the front desk and wait to be escorted to the main building.'

*

I hang back until Rae gets up from her chair then follow her out of the lounge. She stalks, rather than strolls, down the corridor – her back ramrod straight, her overalls under one arm, the arm. My room is on the opposite side of the corridor but no one questions me as I walk in the wrong direction. I match Rae for pace, close enough to keep up with her but not so close that she notices me. When she stops outside a door labelled 'Post Treatment #17' I walk straight past. As the door clicks shut, I double back. As I do a tall, gangly black guy walks past me. He doesn't question why I just did a sudden about turn. He's too focused on getting to his room to get changed.

I walk back to door number seventeen and stop. My heart feels like it's going to beat itself right through my chest but I raise a hand and knock. I can do this.

The door opens.

'Yes,' Rae says. She's already removed her white blouse

but she doesn't seem to be the slightest bit bothered that she's answered the door in her bra.

'I was . . . um . . .' I swallow nervously. 'Do you have any toothpaste? I appear to have run out.'

'Toiletries can be obtained from the front desk. That information was made available to you in your welcome pack when you were assigned your room.'

Uh oh.

'Yes, that's true. But they are awaiting a delivery. The orderly requested that I should ask a fellow student.'

'Did he?' There's the faintest flicker of suspicion on her face.

'He did. Yes. As you know the welcome pack also states that we should be properly turned out at all times. If I don't clean my teeth, I will lower the standards of Norton House.'

The flicker of suspicion fades.

'In that case,' Rae says, 'I will lend you my toothpaste but you must return it after dinner.'

'That won't be a problem.'

She turns and crosses the room, heading for the open door of the en-suite bathroom. Her bed, to the right of the door, has been neatly made. On the chair to the left of the door is her blouse, neatly folded. Nothing in the room is out of place. There are no photos from home, no books, no jewellery. It is as devoid of personality as Rae herself.

When she reaches the sink, she looks back, hearing the click of the door as it closes behind me.

'Drew.' She glares at me indignantly. 'It is not permitted for other students to enter –'

I leap forward, slam the door to the en suite shut and reach for the chair. The door handle wiggles up and down as I jam the top of the chair under it.

'Open this door!' Rae calls from inside. 'Open it immediately!'

The door shakes as she shoulders it but the chair holds firm. I strip off my clothes, my shaking hands fumbling at the buttons on my jacket and skirt, and pull on my green overalls. It's only a matter of time until the cleaning duty orderly realizes that I haven't turned up and sends out a search party.

Chapter Thirty-Nine

'Rae was taken sick?' Mouse asks *again* as we walk across the field towards the main house.

'Yes.' I fight to keep my tone even. I'm terrified that, any second now, an orderly will come flying out of the treatment centre, screaming that I imprisoned another student. I desperately want to glance over my shoulder to have a look but if I don't walk with my shoulders back and my chin slightly tipped up – like Mouse and Mason – I'll draw attention to myself.

'Yes, Megan, Rae was sick. As I told the nurse at the front desk, she began vomiting when she returned to her room. That's when I was asked to take her place.'

'She seemed well earlier,' Mason says. 'She was doing a puzzle with Takesha. I was watching.'

Of course you were watching, you freaky robot boy. Once upon a time you'd have been checking her out because you fancied her, now it's because you're itching to report someone for antisocial behaviour.

'Who's taking over your cleaning duty?' Mouse asks and it's all I can do not to sigh. God knows how I'm going to convince these two to leave the house with me. Maybe I'll have to do something really *antisocial* so they run after me.

'Let's uh . . .' Kyle, who's leading us back to the house,

glances back. 'Let's not get too tied up with cleaning rotas and stuff, guys. You're going to be friends today so you need to listen while I tell you the ropes. OK?'

Mason and Mouse nod.

'Of course,' I say.

*

By the time we've walked through the playing fields and reached the doors to the rec room Kyle has given us each a map of the building and told us what he expects us to do. Basically, we're to keep an eye on the pre-assessment students (ensuring that they're content, amused and not breaking any rules), deal with any non-emergency situations and radio one of the proper friends if there's a query or problem we don't know how to deal with. Mason and Mouse are buzzing with the power and responsibility.

'If I could change one student's attitude towards social responsibility,' Mason says as we walk through the door into the rec room, 'then I will have achieved something.'

Kyle glances back. 'No lecturing,' he mutters. 'That's not your job.'

Mason shrugs. He might be brainwashed but he's still got attitude. He reveres Dr Rothwell and he does what the orderlies tell him to do but I can tell that he doesn't respect Kyle. He probably thinks he's superior to him.

I sneak a look over my shoulder before I step into the rec room. The field is still empty but it's only a matter of time until they come looking for me.

'Who are they?'

'What are they doing here?'

'Why are they wearing overalls?'

The questions from the pre-assessment students come thick and fast as Kyle positions me, Mouse and Mason around the rec room. Mason is stationed in the café, Mouse in the cinema and I'm asked to stand by the door to the library. Unlike the friends, who almost blend in their blue identikit sweatshirts and white trainers, we look like great green plants, dotted around the building.

'I'll be over there,' Kyle says, gesturing towards the games zone. 'Shout if you need me.'

He moves away, almost knocking into two girls in his desperation to stop an argument that's broken out between two boys playing *Final Fantasy*. The shorter of the girls flicks her hair away from her face as she gives him a winsome look. I'm so distracted by what's going on between the two boys that it takes me a second to realize that it's Jude.

'Well, well, well,' Lacey says, nudging her, 'look who's back.'

They swagger towards me, all smug grins and twitching eyebrows.

'Still here are you, Andrew?' Jude says.

Lacey laughs. 'We saw your little escape attempt. What happened? Couldn't get your fat arse over the fence?'

'Nice outfit. Where'd you get it, the garden centre?'

My hands twitch at my sides and my stomach twists into an angry knot but I force myself to stay calm. Post-treatment

Drew wouldn't react. She'd feel as detached and superior as Mason does.

'Hello,' I say. 'Lovely to see you both again.'

For a second they're both stunned into silence then Lacey wrinkles her nose.

'She thinks she's being funny. And you're not funny are you, Andrew? Not unless you're the butt of the joke.'

'It's a shame you left when you did,' Jude says. 'We had a lot of fun stuff planned, didn't we, Lacey?'

Lacey nods. 'Yeah. The toilet still needs cleaning though, if you fancy it!'

I look straight through her, as though she's not real. Keep it coming, Lacey. There's nothing you can say that's going to get a rise out of me.

'Did they punish you?' Jude asks, her scrawny little rat face screwing up with excitement. 'When they took you to the treatment centre? What did they do to you, Andrew?'

'I enjoyed my stay at the treatment centre, thank you. I think you'll both find it a worthwhile experience too.'

They both burst out laughing.

'Not if I turn out like you,' Jude gasps, between giggles. 'You're even weirder than you used to be.'

Lacey crosses her arms over her chest and looks me up and down. 'I think this is all a big lie. This polite act. I know you, Drew Finch. You may look like you don't care but inside I know you're itching to punch me.' She leans in close, so her face is inches from mine. I can feel her hot breath on my skin. 'Go on then. Give me a smack. You know you want to.'

I don't move a muscle. Instead I continue to stare straight ahead, into her single blurred eye.

'Why so quiet all of a sudden?' She pulls away. 'Cat got your tongue has it, or did they cut it out in the treatment centre? Let's have a look.'

She reaches out a hand and grabs my lower lip. She yanks it down towards my chin as I clench my teeth. Rage pulses through me and my right hand clenches instinctively. I mustn't react. I mustn't react. I mustn't –

We all jolt as the door to the library swings open and two men step into the rec room.

'Ladies?' Dr Rothwell frowns at Jude and Lacey as they jump away from me. He does a double take when he spots me. 'Drew Finch? I thought you were . . .' He tails off and looks at the man who's walked through the door with him. 'Jeff, this is David Finch's daughter.'

I look sharply at him at the mention of my dad and have to fight not to show surprise on my face. Dr Rothwell knows my dad?

'Is it?' says the other man. 'Well I never.'

'His son's here too.'

'Best place for them, I imagine.'

The two men share a look and then laugh.

I recognize him, the smartly dressed man with greying hair, glasses and a bottom lip that looks too large for his face. It's Jeff Kinsey, the Home Secretary. I only know who he is because Tony always points him out when he's on the news and says, 'I know him. A great man, a truly great man.'

'Drew's been through the treatment,' Dr Rothwell says. 'Haven't you?'

'I have, yes.'

Across the room I can see an orderly talking to Kyle. He's

gesticulating wildly with his hands and pointing at me. Oh no. They must have found out what I did to Rae.

'I was going to take you over to the treatment centre,' Dr Rothwell says to the Home Secretary, 'but seeing as we have one of the students here with us – an interesting case to say the least – why don't we have a little chat with her back in my office. I'll take you across the field later. Are you happy to talk to Mr Kinsey –'

'Dr Rothwell, excuse me, Dr Rothwell.' Kyle hurries over, cheeks blowing, and taps him on the arm. Behind him, puffed up with his own self-importance, is Ian, the orderly I was supposed to report to for maintenance duty. A jolt of fear, as powerful as electricity, courses through my body and I take a step backwards, but I'm already backed up against the wall and the heel of my trainer catches against the skirting board. They've discovered Rae, locked in her bathroom, and put two and two together. I can't escape. With Lacey and Jude to my left, Dr Rothwell and the Home Secretary to my right and Kyle and Ian in front of me, I'm surrounded on all sides. I look desperately around the room, searching for an escape route or someone who can help me but there's nothing, no one. Jude was right about one thing, I should have told all the students what was going on here. I could have planned an uprising. Forty kids against ten members of staff. We could all have escaped. Polly is sitting on a beanbag in the gaming zone, staring at us. When I catch her eye, she gives me a curious look and then glances away. Jez does the same. So does Callum. At some point in my stay all three of them have tried to befriend me but I've kept them at arm's distance because I didn't want to have to rely on anyone else.

Because I didn't trust them. Now I'm going to be carted off to isolation or stuck back in a treatment room and it's all my own fault.

'Yes.' Dr Rothwell turns sharply so Kyle's hand falls away from his arm. 'What is it, Kyle?

'There's been an incident in the treatment unit. This student was supposed to –'

'Kyle, a word, please.'

Dr Rothwell grips Kyle's shoulder and angles him away from Jeff Kinsey. He keeps his voice low enough that I can't hear everything he says but I catch the words 'Home Secretary' and 'don't embarrass me' and I can tell from the expression on Kyle's face that he doesn't like what he's hearing. He grimaces as he glances at the Home Secretary.

I reach for the staff pass, hanging round my neck. If I give it a quick tug when no one's watching me, the catch at the back of my neck will release. If they throw me into an isolation room I might be able to escape but where can I hide it? My sleeve? Inside my overalls?

'Drew?' Dr Rothwell turns to look at me and I freeze, my hand on my pass.

'Yes, Dr Rothwell?'

'I'd like you to come to my office, please.'

Kyle and Ian, standing behind him, are stony faced. Jude and Lacey are clasping each other, expressions of sheer delight on their smug faces.

'Your office?' I say.

'Yes, please, Drew.' Dr Rothwell presses his staff pass against the lock and the door to the library swings open. He opens his arm wide, ushering me inside. 'After you.'

Chapter Forty

'Sorry we were so rudely interrupted, Jeff,' Dr Rothwell says as we walk into his office. 'Normally our support staff are perfectly adept at dealing with issues and problems but Kyle's new, he's still finding his feet.'

'I totally understand.' Jeff Kinsey crosses the room and settles himself into an armchair near the window, without being asked to sit down. He has the air of a man who's used to doing exactly what he wants, when he wants.

'Take a seat, Drew,' Dr Rothwell says, touching the back of the chair nearest his desk. As I sit down, he takes the seat opposite. 'As I was saying,' he says to the Home Secretary. 'This is David Finch's daughter. She's also the most recent of our students to have completed treatment.'

'Ah, I see. Great.' Jeff Kinsey looks me up at down, his rubbery lips pressed together, his nostrils flaring as he evaluates me. Beneath the leather armrests my palms are slick with sweat but I don't wipe them on my overalls. As far as both men know I am a perfectly behaved zombie. And zombies don't feel fear.

'The last time you were in my office,' Dr Rothwell says. 'We were investigating an escape attempt.'

'Escape?' The Home Secretary raises an eyebrow.

'A failed attempt,' Dr Rothwell says quickly. 'This place is like Fort Knox but we have learned from the experience and taken all necessary precautions to avoid it happening again.'

He's being all chummy with Jeff Kinsey but I can tell by the way he keeps touching his tie that he's not comfortable. Self-soothing, that's what Dad taught me about repetitive movements, like stroking your beard, running your hands through your hair, touching your tie. Dr Rothwell knows he's not the most powerful man in this room but he still wants to impress. He probably wants to ensure the Home Secretary keeps Norton House open.

'Tell us about the escape attempt, Drew,' he says. 'And how you feel about it now.'

'It was a mistake,' I say levelly. 'I was uneducated and uninformed. I wanted to return home because I was scared that the treatment would change me and I didn't want to be changed. Now I am thankful for the treatment. It has opened up a world of possibilities I didn't know existed.'

'What kind of possibilities?' Jeff Kinsey sits forward in his armchair and rests his elbows on thighs.

'The opportunity to give something back to society, to contribute in a meaningful way.'

Both of his eyebrows flash upwards and he nods. 'Nice, Phil. Very nice.'

'They're not just treated, Jeff. They're reformed. And totally biddable. They respect authority unquestioningly.'

'No.' Jeff Kinsey looks genuinely impressed.

'Seriously.'

'She'll do anything you tell her to.'

'I don't believe you.'

'Try. She won't question it. She'll just do it. Just, um, obviously –' he clears his throat '– within certain boundaries.'

'Of course. Absolutely.'

'Right, well.' The Home Secretary stands up. He circles my chair, looking me up and down. He leans in close, his breath hot and damp in my ear. 'Do you know who I am, Drew?'

I keep my gaze fixed on the stag's head, mounted on the wall opposite. It's got horrible glassy eyes but it's not nearly as creepy as Jeff Kinsey, who smells of expensive aftershave, cheap whisky and gingivitis.

'Yes, sir. I do. You're Jeff Kinsey, the Home Secretary.'

'What would you do if I asked you to stand up?'

'I'd do as I was told.'

'OK.' I hear him take a step back. 'Stand up.'

I stand, nerves fluttering in my stomach like butterflies in a net.

'Hop on one foot!'

I raise my right foot and hop three times.

'Continue hopping,' he says, as my right foot touches the floor again.

I continue to stare at the dead stag as he rounds the desk and I continue to hop, hop, hop but, out of the corner of my eye, I register the impressed expression on his face. He looks from me to Dr Rothwell and shakes his head. 'She really doesn't mind, does she?'

'No. As I said, the implications are . . . well . . . limitless.'

'If I asked her to put her hand over a candle would she do it?'

'Absolutely.'

'She has no free will?'

'She does, but within certain constraints. She may show a preference for one task over another but, ultimately, everything she chooses must be for the good of her country.'

Jeff Kinsey sits back down on the armchair and rubs his hands together. 'How many of these kids have you got?'

'We've treated a hundred so far. Seventy have returned home but, since the call from your secretary, we've kept a number back as requested.'

'This changes everything.' The Home Secretary is breathless with excitement. 'MI5, the secret service, the police, terrorist investigations, immigration – the implications are huge. Once trained these kids could be . . . they could . . .'

'Drew, stop hopping and sit down, please,' Dr Rothwell says.

As I sit back down he leans towards Jeff Kinsey. Small pink patches have appeared on his cheeks and the base of his neck. He's thrilled by how excited the other man is. 'The hopping, that's physical, a trick you might teach a dog, but what's really special about these kids is their emotional restraint. Watch this.'

I smile stiffly as Dr Rothwell perches on the desk in front of me.

'What was your relationship with your father like, Drew? Before he disappeared.'

I swallow hard. Why's he asking me about my dad? I'm not sure I can do this.

'I was very close to my father,' I say, forcing myself to look Dr Rothwell in the eye. I mustn't cry. I mustn't cry.

'Did you love your father?'

An image of my dad's face flashes up in my mind – his

tanned, lightly lined skin, his dark hair, his warm yet mischievous eyes. And that smile. A smile that made my heart leap whenever he flashed it in my direction. I so wanted to make my dad proud. All I've ever wanted was to make him proud.

'Yes, I did. Very much.'

I swallow as my mouth fills with saliva and my throat constricts. I can feel Jeff Kinsey's eyes on me, his intense stare boring into my brain. If I keep thinking about my dad I'll cry and Dr Rothwell will realize that I haven't been brainwashed at all. I need to think about someone else. Someone I can't stand. I grit my teeth and force the image of Dad's face out of my mind. Lacey's face takes its place and the heavy feeling in my chest dissipates, almost instantly.

'Where is your father, Drew?' Dr Rothwell asks.

'I don't know. Nobody knows. My mother thinks he's dead.'

'And you? What do you think?'

Please forgive me, Dad.

'I think he's dead too.'

'Where does your loyalty lie, Drew – family or society?'

Inside I relax a little. Thank God he's stopped asking me questions about my dad.

'My loyalty is always to society first, family second.'

'Good.' Dr Rothwell nods. 'Very good. One final question, Drew.' He glances over at the Home Secretary who nods. 'What would you say if I told that your father helped develop the treatment programme at Norton House and that, at this very moment, he's residing in his room in the staff quarters?'

First there is shock, a cold blanket that wraps itself around my heart. Then it's as though a knife has been plunged repeatedly into my stomach. That's the only way I can explain the punctured, wounded feeling that rips through my body. Dad's alive. He's here. He's been here the whole time. It was his leg I saw at the top of the stairs. His face I saw at the window. My dad's here. Oh my God. Oh my God. Oh my God.

I don't show any of this on my face, or in the hands that lie loosely on my lap. I don't give Dr Rothwell any indication that I am anything other than totally apathetic whilst inside I am being torn apart.

'No reaction?' Dr Rothwell shifts forward and peers at my face. 'No reaction at all?'

'I am pleased that my father has aided the programme,' I say stiffly.

'Pleased?'

I look him straight in the eye as doubt gnaws at my gut. Was that the wrong thing to say? Have I shown too much emotion? 'Yes. I am pleased.'

'Excellent, excellent, excellent!' He claps his hands together, jumps off the desk and looks at Jeff Kinsey with an expression of unrestrained delight. 'You see, Jeff? You see what we've accomplished? Did you see that reaction? I just told her that her father is still alive after eight years of thinking that he was dead and she couldn't be more nonplussed. That's the power of the treatment, Jeff. Society before family. We're turning antisocial teenagers into model citizens; young people who drained this country of its resources now actively want to contribute.'

'Well.' The Home Secretary eases himself out of his seat and holds out his hand as he approaches Dr Rothwell. 'You've got me convinced. Bloody well done.' He grips his hand and squeezes him on the arm. 'We're proud of you, Phil. You're doing amazing things here. Absolutely amazing.'

'I'm so glad you think so.' Dr Rothwell couldn't look more proud. 'Now, I think we've got just enough time to show you the treatment centre before you need to get back to London. We'll go out the front door so you can take a good look at the grounds.' He doesn't so much as glance at me as he guides Jeff towards the door. 'You can find your way back to the rec room, can't you, Drew?'

Chapter Forty-One

As the front door clicks shut behind them I look from the staircase to the library. Which way do I go? Up the stairs to find Dad, or back into the rec room to get Mason and Mouse? If Kyle and Ian are still in the rec room they'll grab me the second I set foot through the door, but I can't escape with Dad and leave Mason and Mouse behind. We all need to go, together. But I haven't got long. As soon as Dr Rothwell hears about what happened to Rae he'll be straight on the radio to the friends and they'll hunt me down.

The radio! I completely forgot that Kyle gave me one.

I reach into my pocket and turn the dial to five, the number Mason was assigned, and then hold it near my mouth as I press the button. 'Mason, can you hear me?'

There's a crackling sound then, 'I can hear you, please identify yourself. Over.'

'It's Drew, your sister. Where are you?'

'You didn't say "over". Kyle specifically told us to end each conversation with "over" to signify the end of speech.'

Oh for God's sake, of all the times to be pedantic, Mason!

'Drew to Mason. Where are you? OVER.'

'At the swimming pool. Over.'

'Where's Mouse . . . I mean, Megan? Over.'

'Also at the swimming pool. We are supervising during activity time. OVER.'

'But you can't . . .' I almost drop the radio as an idea so brilliant it's ridiculous pops into my head.

'Sorry,' Mason says. 'I didn't catch that. Over.'

I leave him hanging as I shove the radio back into my pocket and pull out the map that Kyle gave us. To the right of the staircase, next to the door to the East Wing is another door. It leads to a long corridor, sandwiched between the assembly room and the isolation rooms then runs along the canteen, past the cinema and straight up to the swimming pool. The sound of a door squeaking on its hinges makes me look up sharply. The door to Mrs H.'s office is opening.

***

I sprint down the corridor, barely glancing to the right as I pass one, two, three, four, five isolation rooms. When I reach the corner I spot a door marked 'Sanatorium' and stop running. Through the glass window in the top of the door I can see ten beds, each made up with crisp white sheets and blankets, five along each wall. All of the beds are empty apart from one. Israel is lying on his back on the bed nearest to me, staring at the ceiling, his arms folded behind his head. He looks so fed up and depressed my heart twists in my chest. I can't leave him behind. I'm pretty certain I said some awful things to him yesterday and I still haven't forgiven myself for abandoning him the last time I tried to escape.

'Israel?'

His head turns sharply as I tap on the glass.

'I'm getting you out of here,' I mouth, praying that he's well enough to understand me.

He sits up and glances to his right, towards the door I assume leads to the nurse's office, then back at me.

'Eh?' he mouths, shrugging his shoulders.

'I . . .' I point to myself. 'Will . . . get . . . you . . .' I point to him. 'Out.' I gesture towards the windows at the back of the building.

'No.' He shakes his head. 'You're a weirdo.'

'I'm not. I'm back to normal. Look.' I point at my eyes as I blink repeatedly, scrunch them up then roll them from left to right. Israel continues to look wary so I stick my tongue out as far as I can, put my thumbs in my ears and waggle them back and forth, like a four-year-old pulling a silly face.

And there it is – the mischievous grin he gave me when he asked if he could steal my breakfast.

I hold up a hand to the window, my fingers splayed. 'Five minutes.'

He nods and gives me the thumbs-up.

Please let this work, I silently pray as I head off again. I duck down as I reach the window to the canteen and continue to run. I speed past the red-brick wall of the cinema and then I'm there, outside the door to the swimming pool. I press my staff pass to the lock and push on the door. It swings open and I'm hit in the face with a blast of warm, humid air.

There are three students in the pool. Two are splashing each other and messing about and a lone swimmer is ploughing back and forth doing lengths. There's no one in the lifeguard's chair, no one sitting on the benches that run along the wall. The only people in the room are me, the kids in the pool and

Mouse and Mason, standing with their arms crossed over their chests on the other side of the room, at the deep end.

'No running!' Mason shouts as I sprint towards them. I ignore him. Across the field Dr Rothwell and Jeff Kinsey are approaching the treatment unit. I don't have much time.

'Drew!' Mouse says, turning as I round the pool and speed towards her. 'What on earth are you –'

I glance at the huge clock on the opposite wall of the pool then shove her, full force, in the back. Then, before Mason can react, I push him too. They both tip forwards, arms circling wildly as they fight to regain their balance then pitch head first into the water. Mouse screams, a split second before she hits the surface then she's gone. Mason doesn't shout. He sinks like a stone.

The first one to break the surface is Mouse, arms flailing, mouth open, gasping for air. Her terrified eyes latch onto mine for a split second then she's gone, swallowed by the pool. On the other side of the room the students have stopped playing. They're standing up in the water, staring at me, mouths agape.

'What happened?' a rangy, brown-haired boy shouts.

'Should I get help?' screams a small girl with short, black hair.

I shake my head. 'Everything's under control.'

But everything is *not* under control. Whilst Mouse is thrashing about in the water, breaking the surface every couple of seconds to gasp for air, Mason is still underwater. Mouse's frantic splashing has churned up the water so much I can no longer see the murky green blur of Mason's overalls at the bottom of the pool. Why hasn't he come up for air? He's scared of water but he knows how to swim. Unless – fear grips my stomach – unless he knocked himself out when he fell in or he's swallowed so much water he's passed out.

On the other side of the pool the second hand of the clock is ticking interminably slow. They've both been in the water for twenty seconds now. I can only hold my breath for forty-five seconds and that's if I'm completely relaxed. Every bone in my body is telling me to jump in the water NOW and rescue them both, but if I do it too soon their conditioning won't be reversed. But if I leave it too long they'll both drown . . .

Twenty-one.

Twenty-two.

Twenty-three.

Twenty –

Mouse, her hair spread across the pool like dark seaweed, bobs to the surface. She tips her chin and opens her mouth to breathe but she's tired and disorientated and gulps down water instead. She coughs – a short, sharp sound like a dog bark – and then disappears back beneath the water, floating down, down, down, her arms and legs splayed and unmoving.

I can't wait a second longer.

SPLASH!

I dive head first into the water. It's colder than I thought and my chest constricts as I swim deeper and deeper. My eyes sting as I search the chlorinated water for my brother and best friend. At first all I see are the tiles, grimy and pale, and then I see him, curled up on his side on the bottom of the pool, his eyes closed. I grab hold of his arm, scull until my feet are near the floor and then bend my knees and push against the tiles. I lurch upwards but Mason is so heavy I don't get anywhere near the surface. I spin around in the water and hook my arm around his shoulder, across his chest and under his other arm and kick with my legs. Progress is slow. Each time I kick, I rise a little higher in the water then sink back down again. My lungs start to burn as I get closer and closer to the surface of the water and then – SMACK – I'm thumped in the side of the head. The force of the kick sends me reeling to one side and Mason slips from my arm and drifts back towards the bottom of the pool. Above me, I can see Mouse, arms and legs flailing, heading towards the side. Someone has thrown her a lifebuoy and she's been pulled in. I kick with all my strength, gasp for air as my head breaks through the water, and then back down I go. *Please*, I beg as I grab hold of Mason for the second time, *please don't die. I'd never forgive myself.*

*

Finally, *finally*, I manage to pull Mason to the side of the pool. Two of the students who were messing about in the shallow end are standing on the edge, staring down at me, their eyes wide with fear, a lifebuoy at their feet. Mouse is sitting up against the far wall, beneath a red fire alarm box, a towel over her shoulders, her face in her knees. The female student is sitting beside her, stroking her back.

Mason, still unconscious, lies limply beneath my arm. 'Help me!' I scream up at the boys.

'OK, OK.' The dark-haired boy leaps into action. He crouches down and reaches for Mason's left arm, gesturing for the other boy to do the same. When I'm one hundred per cent sure that they've got a good hold of him I let go and duck out of the way. I watch, clinging onto the handrail, as they haul him out of the water. His slips and slides onto the wet tiles like a large fish being landed in a boat. For several seconds he lies unmoving on the side of the pool, then he suddenly gasps. The sound reverberates off the walls.

'Mason!' I try to lift myself up and out of the water but all the strength in my arms has gone and one of the boys has to take my hand and yank me out.

'Mason?' I crawl towards him and touch a hand to his cold cheek. 'Mason? Are you Ok? Can you hear me?'

His eyes remain closed, tiny droplets of water glistening on the ends of his dark eyelashes. His green overall looks black, wrapped around his body like a shroud. I reach for his left hand and roll him over into the recovery position.

'Joe, go and get help,' the boy with dark hair barks.

'No.' I hold up a hand. 'No, not yet.'

'What?' He stares at me in astonishment. 'But he's –'

'He's breathing.' I press a hand to Mason's chest. It rises and falls under my palm. 'He's going to wake up.'

'He looks unconscious to me.'

'HE'LL WAKE UP.' I shout so loudly both boys start.

'Mason!' I shake my brother's shoulder. 'Mason, open your eyes!'

Please, I beg silently. *Please open your eyes.*

'Drew.' I jump as someone touches my shoulder.

'Drew,' Mouse says quietly. 'Is he OK?'

'I don't know, he was on the bottom for a . . .' I break off, unsettled by the way she's looking at me. There's so much compassion in her eyes. So much warmth. Fear and confusion too. Oh my God. She's back to normal. But that doesn't matter if I can't get Mason to wake up. If he's hurt or brain-damaged I'll never forgive myself. I'll never . . .

'He's opened his eyes!' one of the boys squawks. 'Look! Look, he's opened his eyes.'

My brother blinks rapidly several times then his whole body jolts as he raises his arms and lashes out. One fist hits the boy standing over him. The other smacks against my cheekbone and I nearly topple straight back into the pool.

'Mason!' I wrap my hands around his wrists, struggling to restrain him. 'Mason, it's OK. It's Drew. Mason, it's Drew. You're going to be OK.'

He continues to wriggle and squirm, his eyes wide and terrified, then slowly, slowly the frantic expression on his face fades and his body goes limp.

'Drew?' His voice is little more than a whisper.

'Yes.' I lean closer. 'Yes, it's me. It's OK, Mason. You fell in the pool but you're OK. You're OK now.'

He shakes his head. 'I'm . . . I'm . . . I'm really confused . . . where . . . what . . .'

He's coming round from the reverse conditioning, I can see the fear and confusion I felt when it happened to me reflected in his eyes.

'How is he even alive?' I hear one of the boys gasp. 'I thought he was dead for sure.'

'Diver's reflex,' the girl who was with Mouse says from behind me. 'Didn't you learn about it in biology? If your face hits cold water you automatically hold your breath and your heart rate slows down. Babies have –'

'Woah, woah. He's getting up.'

They all take a step back as my brother shifts onto his

knees then, reaching out a hand for me to take, yanks himself up onto his feet.

'Mason, no.' I clutch hold of him as he sways slightly. 'You need to sit back down.'

'No, Drew, I'm –' We all snap round at the sound of a door slamming shut.

Standing on the other side of the pool, staring straight at me with a look of pure anger, is Stuart.

Chapter Forty-Two

'Drew?' Mouse nudges up against me. 'What's going on? Why is he staring at you like that?'

'Long story.' Keeping one hand on Mason's shoulder, I angle her away from the gawping students and hiss in her ear. 'We need to get out. Now.'

'He's . . .' Her eyes widen in fear and I glance over my shoulder. Stuart is marching along the length of the pool, shoulders back, chin up like he means business. I scan the room, looking for something, anything, to slow his progress. There's a net on a long stick but it's on the wall near the door. The lifeguard chair is bolted to the floor. Other than that the only other things in the room are a couple of damp towels and some buoyancy aids. Unless . . . I turn sharply and, pushing Mason towards Mouse, leap towards the wall that Mouse was leaning against. I jab two fingers against the small glass panel in the centre of the red box. Nothing happens. The glass stays intact. I jab at it, harder. There's a small clicking sound, the glass indents and the button presses. An ear-splitting wail immediately fills the air as the fire alarm goes off. I spin round to see Stuart rounding the edge of the pool, his face red with fury, his arms pumping the air as he runs.

'Push him in!' I scream to the three students who are staring at me with a mixture of astonishment and respect. 'Now! We're getting out of here!'

For one horrible moment I don't think they've heard me above the screech of the fire alarm, but then the taller boy turns and, in one swift movement, he sticks out his foot and pushes Stuart into the pool.

'Quick! This way!' As Stuart flounders around in the pool, I grab Mason's hand and pull him after me. He's completely disorientated and trips several times as we head for the door. Mouse and the three students speed after us. As we approach the door, I peel to the right and reach for the net.

'What are you doing?' Mouse squeals. 'He's getting out of the pool. We need to go!'

'We need to smash the lock. So he can't get back out.'

'I'll do that.' The smaller boy – Joe – reaches for the net. 'Just get the door open and I'll follow you out when I've done it.'

He doesn't need to ask me twice. I let go of the pole, wrench the staff pass from around my neck and press it against the lock. The door springs open and we hurry through it.

'Mouse!' I shout, as we run down the corridor, past the cinema and the canteen. 'Can you get Israel out of the san? It's over there!'

She follows the line of my outstretched hand and nods.

'You guys,' I shout to the two students, 'stay with Mouse. She's got a pass too. She'll get you out of here.'

'Where are you going?' Mouse shouts, as I loop Mason's arm over my shoulders and half lollop, half jog past the isolation rooms.

'To get our dad!'

I stop running as we approach the door to the entrance hall and press my pass to the door. I push it open a tiny crack and listen.

'Our dad?' Mason whispers. 'Our dad's here?'

I press a finger to my lips to shush him. If we're going to stand any chance of finding Dad we need to get into the entrance hall and up the stairs without anyone seeing us. As soon as Stuart drags himself out of the pool he'll do whatever he can to alert Mrs H. and Dr Rothwell. That's if they don't already know.

The fire alarm is so loud it blocks out every other sound. I'm going to have to check that the coast is clear. I hold up a finger to Mason, warning him not to move or breathe, then push on the door, opening it an inch. My heart's beating so hard in my chest I feel sick.

All I can see through the gap is the closed door to the library. I push on the door a bit harder, bracing myself to run, but the entrance hall is empty. Mrs H.'s and Dr Rothwell's doors are both ajar, as though they left in a hurry.

'Quick,' I signal to Mason to follow me. 'We need to run.'

*

I take the steps two at a time, using the bannister to wrench myself upwards. By the time we reach the second floor we're both gasping and Mason is deathly pale.

I touch his arm. 'Are you OK?'

He nods stoically, too out of breath to speak, and gestures

at the lock next to the staff quarters door. He doesn't need to ask me twice. I touch my pass against it then push on the door. A long corridor opens out before me. There are at least ten or eleven doors to our left, all of them closed, and a smooth wall to our right. When I saw the silhouette in the window, watching me jog around the running track and again when I was dragged to the treatment unit, it was somewhere near the middle of the building. I gesture for Mason to follow me then knock on the fifth door.

'Dad!' I shout. 'Dad, are you in there?'

There are keyholes in each door and no locking units. We can't get in unless Dad lets us.

'Dad?' I wait for a couple of seconds then move onto the next door.

'Dad!' I pound on the wood with both fists. 'It's Drew and Mason!'

Nothing. I look up and down the corridor, half expecting an angry friend to burst out of one of the doors but they all remain closed. The fire alarm is still wailing. If anyone's after us we won't be able to hear them thudding up the stairs. We can't get caught now. Not when we're so close to finding Dad.

'Mason!' I shout. 'Help me!'

He leaps forward and bangs on door number seven. I overtake him and bang on door number eight. When door number seven remains closed, Mason heads for door number nine and pounds his fist and feet against it. His face is pinched with tension. Where the hell is Dad? Dr Rothwell told me he was up here.

I bang on door number ten as Mason bangs on door number eleven, then we run back up the corridor and smash our fists against the first four doors. Where is he? Where's Dad? My eyes prick with tears as I thump on door five again. There's no way he could ignore the noise we're making. He's not in any of these rooms. Doctor Rothwell must have lied to me.

'Where is he?' Mason shouts over the din of the fire alarm.

I shake my head. 'I don't know.'

'You said he was up here, Drew.'

'I know . . . but . . . but . . .' I look desperately up and down the corridor. Mouse, Israel and the other three will be waiting for us in the entrance hall, if they haven't already escaped. The longer we stay up here the more chance there is of us getting caught, but I can't leave without finding Dad. Eight years. That's how long he's been missing. I can't go back home, torturing myself that it's him each time the doorbell rings or running into the living room when I get home from school just in case he's sitting on the sofa, waiting for me. He's not dead. I know he's not dead. Dr Rothwell knows where he is but he's not here, he's not bloody here.

I pound my fists into the door as eight years of loss, grief and sorrow explode out of me.

'Drew!' Mason grabs me round the waist and tries to pull me away. 'Drew, stop it! Your knuckles are bleeding. Drew!'

He might be stronger than me normally but he's no match for the rage I feel inside and I don't budge an inch as I continue to punch the door, blind to the blood that streaks the pale wood.

'Dad!' I scream. 'Dad!'

'He's not here!' Mason shouts in my ear. 'He's not here. We need to go.'

Using all his strength, he hauls me away from the door and

frogmarches me towards the stairs. I try to put up a fight, to wriggle out of his grip, but all the fight has gone out of me and I'm as weak as a kitten. Dad's not here. He's not here. He's never coming home.

I twist in Mason's arms as he carries me through the doorway, and look back at the corridor.

'Mason!' His name catches in my throat. 'A door. A door's opened.'

My brother looks over his shoulder. 'They're still shut, Drew.'

'No.' I pull against him. 'No, they're not. Door five just opened a crack. I can see it.'

'Drew, it's not –'

I duck down and out of his arms and sprint down the corridor.

'Drew!' he shouts, running after me. 'You have to stop this you. You have to –' A gasp steals the words from his mouth and he stops running.

Standing in the doorway of the fifth bedroom is a tall man with dark hair, peppered with grey, with thick black eyebrows, a straggly beard and wide, staring blue eyes. He's dressed in a navy blue suit, white shirt and grey tie and he's wearing a single, shiny black shoe on his left foot. Beneath the other trouser leg there's a curve of black steel.

'Dad?' The word is a whisper.

He turns his head to look from me to Mason. A tiny frown appears between his brows but, otherwise, his expression is completely blank.

'Dad,' I say again, louder this time. 'Dad, it's me. Drew. And Mason.'

I am trembling from head to foot and I feel so light-headed I have to steady myself on the wall. I can't believe it's really him. That he's standing right in front of me. I want to touch him but I'm scared that, if I do, he'll disappear.

'Dad!' Mason says. 'Dad, say something!'

The frown between Dad's eyebrows deepens. He looks confused and as disorientated as I feel. He's either drugged, brain-damaged or brainwashed.

'Dad.' I slowly reach out a hand, terrified that if I move too suddenly he'll bolt back into his room and lock the door. My fingers graze one of his frayed jacket cuffs. 'Dad, you need to come with us.'

He turns his head slowly to look at me then starts, as though seeing me for the first time. 'Who are you?'

'I'm Drew. Drew Finch. I'm your daughter. This is Mason, your son.'

'No.' He shakes his head and takes a step backwards into his room, his eyes wide and uncomprehending. 'My children are small.'

'We're teenagers now,' Mason says, leaping forwards and reaching for Dad's hand. Dad snatches it away as though stung and the pain on my brother's face is more than I can bear.

'You're my children?' Dad looks back at me. His eyes are a void, empty and uncomprehending, but then something seems to spark in the dark pupils and I see a flash of the man I love. 'You're . . .' He reaches out a hand and, for a heartbreaking second I think he's going to touch my cheek, but then his hand falls away again. 'I remember you. I saw you in . . .' He clutches the side of his head and winces as though he's in pain. 'I tried to help you. I was in the CCTV room and . . . Aaarggh.' He doubles over, his arms wrapped around his head.

'Dad! What's the matter?' I hook an arm across his bent back and squeeze him tightly. He recoils at my embrace and drops to his knees, still nursing his head, his teeth gritted against the pain.

Mason tugs on my arm. 'Drew, we need to get him out of here. Quickly!'

'I know, I know!'

I crouch down beside my dad, who is still whimpering with pain. 'Dad, we need to leave.'

He shakes his head and, using his desk for support, pulls himself back onto his feet.

'We need to get out of here!'

'Leave? No, I like it here. And I must finish my work.' He gestures at the piles of books, research papers and notepads filled with his big, looping handwriting. When he looks back at me, his eyes have dulled again. He's looking at me as though I'm a stranger.

'What's that noise?' He grimaces and looks up at the ceiling, as though hearing the fire alarm for the first time. 'I don't like that noise. I can't concentrate with that racket going on.'

'We can make it stop,' I shout. I reach for his hand then think the better of it. 'But you need to come with us first. Dr Rothwell wants to see you.'

'Dr Rothwell?' His spine straightens as he pulls himself up to his full six feet. He's suddenly alert and interested. 'Did you say Dr Rothwell?'

'Yes,' Mason shouts from behind me. 'He wants to see you. We're taking you to see him.'

'Will I need my notes?' He reaches for a green notebook.

'No, no. Just you. Come on, Dad, I mean, Dr Finch. Please hurry. He needs to see you urgently.'

*

Dad takes the stairs so slowly I could scream. I know he can move faster than this, despite his artificial leg, but he doesn't feel the same sense of urgency as us. As far as he's concerned, he's going for a nice little chat with 'his boss' Dr Rothwell and I have to cajole him into hurrying. When we reach the bottom of the second set of stairs, I hold out an arm, signalling him to stop, then peer around the stairwell and into the entrance hall.

Lacey and Jude are standing against the front door, feet splayed wide, hands behind their backs.

Chapter Forty-Three

'Going somewhere?' Lacey smirks, as I step from the stairs onto the polished wooden floor of the entrance hall.

'This is to do with you, isn't it?' Jude says, waving a hand around as the fire alarm echoes off the wood-clad walls. 'We knew it was.'

'We can take them,' Mason hisses, as we slowly walk towards them. 'You grab Lacey, I'll deal with Jude.'

'That's not going to be necessary.' I glance to my left, to check on Dad. But he's not by my side. He's wandered off and is standing outside Dr Rothwell's open office door looking puzzled.

'Who's that?' Jude asks, looking.

Lacey sneers as she looks him up and down, taking in his worn suit, straggly beard and messy hair. As her gaze reaches his feet, her jaw drops and she stares at me, wide eyed.

'Is that your dad? I thought you said he was dead.'

'I never said that.'

'Yes you did, you liar.'

I ignore her. 'What are you doing here?'

She tilts her head to one side and smiles tightly. 'I could ask you the same question.'

'Just move, Lacey.'

'Oh, look at you,' she says in her sneering sing-song voice, 'thinking you're some kind of hard ass because you locked someone in her room and then set off the fire alarm.' She nudges Jude, who laughs.

'Give us the pass, Andrew,' Jude says, holding out her hand. 'If you're leaving we're leaving too.'

'I'm not giving you anything.'

She glares up at me, nostrils flaring, lips pulled tightly over her teeth. 'Give us the pass or we'll radio Dr Rothwell and tell him that you, your skanky brother and that tramp you call your dad –'

Mason lurches forward. 'What did you just call my dad?'

'Mason!' I grab his arm. 'No.'

Jude's a weaselly excuse for a human being but I won't let my brother touch her. We won't sink to her level. I've done that before and I won't do it again.

'Radio Dr Rothwell?' I say. 'You haven't got a . . .'

Lacey moves one of her hands from behind her back. She waggles a black radio in front of my face then whips it back behind her.

'Mouse isn't the only thief round here,' Jude says. 'We found it in a drawer in Mrs H.'s office.'

'How did you get out of the rec room?' I ask. 'All the doors are locked.'

'When the fire alarm went off one of the new friends propped the doors to the library and the entrance hall open. She didn't bother closing them when Abi told her that we needed to assemble on the running track out the back. Everyone was so hysterical it was easy to double back. Anyway –' she feigns a yawn and holds out a hand '– give me the pass.'

'No, I don't trust you.'

'That makes two of us. Give it to me or I'll take it off you.'

'I won't let you.'

'Oh yeah.' She casts a scornful look at Mason. 'You and whose army?'

'This army.'

I whip round at the sound of Mouse's voice and there they are, Mouse, Israel and the three students, filing out of the door that leads to the isolation rooms. They must have been hiding behind the door this whole time, watching and waiting. I'm so pleased to see them I could scream with joy, instead I turn back to Lacey and Jude.

'Get out of my way.'

'We'll just come after you,' Jude whines, as she steps away from the door. 'You can't stop us.'

'They can't stop you from doing *what*?' a shrill female voice says and any joy I feel instantly turns to dread. Mrs H. and Dr Rothwell are standing in the door to the library, holding a radio in each hand.

'Nobody move,' Dr Rothwell says. He scans the room, jolting as his gaze rests on Dad, still standing obediently outside his office. 'David, what are you doing here?'

'I was told that you wanted to speak to me.'

'And who told you that, I wonder?' His dark eyes fix on me.

'Dr Rothwell . . .' Lacey skirts around me and heads towards the library door. 'Dr Rothwell, I can explain –'

'We both can,' Jude says, moving away from Mason and heading towards Mrs H. 'It's not what it looks like. We were actually trying to –'

'Stay where you are!' Dr Rothwell barks.

We don't move a muscle, but Lacey and Jude continue to stalk across the entrance hall.

'I'm warning, you girls,' Dr Rothwell says, 'stop walking and stand still.'

'We need to tell you something,' Lacey says, but she's interrupted by a sharp screech from Mrs H.

'Listen to Dr Rothwell!'

She's scared, I realize with surprise. Instead of congregating outside like good little sheep we've broken away from the pack. She's not in control any more. Dr Rothwell looks worried too.

Jude and Lacey exchange a look of irritation and hasten their pace. Mrs H. and Dr Rothwell aren't used to losing control but the girls aren't used to being ignored. As they get closer, the fire alarm stops as quickly as it started and a strange eerie silence fills the large hall.

'We can explain everything,' Lacey says, holding out the radio to Dr Rothwell. 'It's not what it looks –'

Dr Rothwell raises his arm and presses what I thought was a radio against the side of Lacey's neck. There is a flash of blue and a crackling sound then her hands drop, her head tips back, her mouth opens and she screams. A second later, she drops to the floor.

'What the –' Jude stops dead and stares at her friend in horror. 'You tasered her,' she says, open-mouthed as she looks at Doctor Rothwell. 'I can't believe you –'

This time it's Mrs H. who raises her taser. With Jude's attention focused on Dr Rothwell there's no time for her to react or move out of the way and she too jolts, screams and then crumples to the floor.

No one says a word. The only sounds are low groans from Lacey and Jude as they squirm on the floorboards.

Dr Rothwell regards them dispassionately then sighs. 'Mrs H., can you radio the nurse. She needs to take these two to the san.' He looks across at the rest of us. 'You lot, head in that direction.' He nods his head towards the door that leads to the isolation rooms.

No one moves.

'Go!' Dr Rothwell shouts, brandishing his taser. 'Now!'

The male students exchange a look, shrug and shuffle across the floorboards, heads hung low.

'And you two.' Dr Rothwell points to Mouse and the female student who are clutching each other like they'll never let go. 'They made me do that,' Dr Rothwell says, gesturing towards Jude and Lacey. 'They were coming for me. I had no choice but to defend myself.'

The girl looks at Mouse. 'I'll go if you go.'

Mouse shakes her head. 'I'm not going anywhere.'

'Neither am I,' I say.

'Count me out,' Israel says.

'And me,' Mason adds.

I brace myself, waiting for the inevitable attack but, instead of brandishing his taser, Dr Rothwell gathers it into his hand, holds out his arm and points at Dad.

'David!'

Dad turns away from the open office door. He smiles as he sees Dr Rothwell's face.

'What are you going to do to him?' I shout.

'I'm going to give him a taser,' Dr Rothwell says. 'And you're going to watch as he holds it to his own neck and presses the button. Maybe when you realize how futile this ridiculous escape attempt is you'll all DO AS YOU'RE BLOODY TOLD!'

'David!' He crooks his finger. 'Come over here. I'd like you to give yourself a little shock, purely for scientific purposes, of course.'

'No!' Mason leaps away from me and speeds across the hall towards Dr Rothwell. He launches himself at the older man, fists flying, but Dr Rothwell's too quick for him, he lunges to his left then, with one swift movement, chops his hand against Mason's windpipe. My brother's hands fly to his throat, his legs give way beneath him and he drops to his knees. He makes a barking sound like a seal as he clutches his throat desperately trying to breathe.

Mrs H. raises her radio to just below her chin. 'Hello, is that Sally? We've got two students in the hallway who need medication attention. They've both had small electric shocks. Over.'

She lowers the radio and gazes across the room, smiling as her eyes meet mine. 'Sorry, did I say two? I actually meant three.'

'No!' I scream as she crouches beside Mason and presses the taser against the back of his neck.

I move quickly, but not as quickly as Mrs H. She springs back up as I launch myself at her and throws out an arm. I feel a sharp pain in my cheek as her rings scrape across my skin. The force of the blow knocks me off balance and I fall, smacking my face against a small side table before I hit the ground. My top lip feels warm and damp and when I touch my nose my fingers are covered in blood.

'Come along, David,' Dr Rothwell says, walking towards

my dad. 'The nurse will clear up the mess. Let's get you back upstairs to your room. We've got some important work to do tomorrow.'

'No, Dad!' I shout as he stares at the headmaster. He looks confused, disorientated and unsteady on his feet. 'Dad, don't go with him.'

'Run, Dad!' Mason screams. 'Please, please run.'

But our dad doesn't run. He takes a step towards Dr Rothwell, his face soft and trusting, his eyes glassy and fixed.

'That's it,' Dr Rothwell says. 'Take it nice and easy, David. I know it's been upsetting, everything that's happened today, but we can have a little chat tomorrow and make sure you forget all about it.'

'I would appreciate that,' Dad says as he takes another step towards the headmaster. 'Today has been a little . . . How did you phrase it? Upsetting.'

One second the two men are a metre apart, the next my dad jumps forward, his right arm raised, fist clenched. His right fist smashes against Dr Rothwell's cheekbone. Before he can react, Dad hits him again, an uppercut to the chin with his left hand. The radio and taser fly from Dr Rothwell's hands as he lurches backwards. Smack! Dad hits him again. And again. Dr Rothwell stumbles to his left, then his right, then his legs seems to give way beneath him and he tumbles to the floor, narrowly missing Lacey who is curled up on her side. Mrs H., her hands pressed to her mouth in horror, retreats into the doorway of the library.

'Mason! Drew!' Dad hurries over to us, reaches out his hands and hauls us to our feet. 'Come on, we need to go!'

'We need to take them too.' I gesture towards Mouse and

Israel, who are still standing beside the front door, frozen with fear.

'Of course.' Dad's eyes meet mine and I feel as though my heart is going to explode through my chest. It's him. It's really him. I don't why he's not brainwashed and I don't really care. I've got my dad back.

'Oh no you don't.'

Something cold presses against the back of my neck. I reach up a hand to see what it is but my hand is swatted away.

'Don't move,' Mrs H. hisses, as she presses the taser against my skin. 'And don't do anything stupid.'

Dad stiffens but he does what Mrs H. says. He doesn't move a muscle. Neither does Mason. I want them to do something but neither of them wants to be responsible for me getting hurt.

'Mrs H. to all support staff. Please come to the entrance hall immediately. *Immediately*. Lock the students outside. Do you understand? Over.'

I hear the crackle of a radio.

'This is Kyle. I'm on my way. Over.'

Out of the corner of my eye, I spot Mouse ducking down beside Dr Rothwell. She looks as though she's tying her shoelace.

'Megan, get up!' Mrs H. barks. 'Get up and stand still.'

Mouse slowly rises to her feet. She lowers her chin to her chest and her eyes to the floor. 'I need a hug,' she says quietly.

'What?' Mrs H. snaps.

'A hug.' She looks up and stares straight at our housemistress. 'I really need one.'

'Shut up. Stop talking. And don't move.' Mrs H.'s voice is

raspy with fear. There's just one of her and six of us – eight if you count the two boys standing beside the door to the isolation room – and she knows it. The moment reinforcements arrive she'll feel stronger and more in control again. We've got minutes, seconds maybe, until they arrive.

'Please give me a hug, Mrs H.,' Mouse says again. 'You give such good hugs. They make me feel really happy and secure.'

'Don't move!' Mrs H. shouts as Megan steps over Dr Rothwell and around Jude and Lacey. Her hands are knotted behind her back. 'Don't come an inch closer.'

'Please. Just a little one. I'll be as good as gold afterwards.'

'Go away!' The taser quivers against the back of my neck as Megan draws closer. 'I'll hurt her, Megan, and you don't want that, do you?'

Mouse shrugs. 'I don't care what you do to Drew. I just want my hug. Didn't you say you'd always be available for hugs? You don't want to break your promise do you, Mrs H.?'

One second Mouse looks mournful with her hands knotted behind her back, the next her arms are wide and there's the most magnificent grin on her face. It reaches from one ear to the other.

'Hug me, Mrs H.,' she says, as she throws her arms around our housemistress. 'Just hug me.'

There's a horrible crackling sound, just behind my head, and, for one horrible second, I think Mrs H. has gone through with her promise to taser me. But the scream that follows it isn't mine. Nor is the blonde, blue-eyed body that hits the floor.

'Go!' Dad shouts, pushing me towards the door. 'Go! Go!'

Chapter Forty-Four

'What now?' Israel asks, as we pour down the steps of Norton House. 'Do we just run?'

'Why run when you can drive?' Mouse says, dangling a set of car keys from her fingers.

I stare at her in astonishment. 'What the . . . ?'

She winks. 'Dr Rothwell's pocket. I grabbed them when I picked up the taser.'

She chucks the keys at my dad who catches them with one swift swipe of his hand through the air.

'Don't just stand there gawping at each other,' he says, jerking a thumb in the direction of a shiny red Range Rover. 'Get in!'

We bundle into the car, stepping on each other's feet and elbowing each other in our desperation to get in. Through the wide open doorway, I can see Dr Rothwell reaching for a radio as he picks himself up off the floor. Mrs H. is on her hands and knees, trying to get up.

'Wait! Wait!' Jude and Lacey spill out of the door and speed down the steps, their faces ashen. Their arms waving.

'Go!' I scream at Dad. 'Go, go!'

He glances over his shoulder. There are eight of us and only seven seats. Mason, Israel and Mouse are in the row behind and the three students are squished together into the two seats at the back. Even if we wanted to fit anyone else in there's no space.

'Please Dad,' I scream, as Lacey and Jude sprint across the gravel driveway towards us. 'Please just go!'

I don't need to ask him twice. He turns the key in the ignition and presses his foot flat to the floor. The huge car leaps forward but Lacey and Jude have already caught up with us. Lacey reaches for the driver side door but, before her fingers can make contact, Dad yanks the steering wheel to the left and we're away, tyres crunching on the gravel, engine roaring. As we speed down the long, tree-lined driveway I glance into the rear-view mirror, half expecting to see another car chasing after us but there's no one behind us.

'No,' Dad breathes and I twist back around. We've reached the metal gates at the end of the driveway. They're shut.

'Check the glovebox,' he says as he dips a hand into the driver's side door compartments. 'He might have some kind of electronic key.'

I unclick the glovebox and reach a hand inside. There's a map, a car manual, various bits of paperwork and some hard-boiled sweets but no key. I unclip my seat belt and feel under my seat. Nothing there apart from an empty can of Coke and a manky apple core. Nothing in the door compartments either.

'Anything?' I look hopefully at Dad.

He shakes his head.

'Mouse?' I twist round in my seat. 'You went through his pockets, didn't you? Dr Rothwell's? Did you find anything else apart from his car keys?'

She shakes her head. 'Nothing worth stealing.'

'Are they on the key chain?' I ask Dad.

Again he shakes his head. I can't believe it. We can't have come all this way only to get stuck here. The key has to be in the car somewhere. It just has to. I rifle through the drinks holder next to the gear stick and stick my fingers into every other little nook and cranny I can find. As I do, Dad flips down the visor and I hear the clunk of something falling into his lap.

'Say your prayers,' he says, as he holds a key fob at arm's length, points it at the gates, and then presses a black button.

Everyone in the car holds their breath.

And then the gates creak open.

*

I can't stop staring at my dad. Whilst Mouse, Mason and Israel have all fallen asleep and the students are talking quietly in the back, I'm terrified that if I take my eyes off my father for one second he'll vanish in a puff of smoke or I'll wake up and find myself lying on my uncomfortable bunk in Norton House.

'Dad,' I say softly.

'Yes, Drew.' He keeps his eyes on the road but the corners of his mouth edge up into a warm smile.

'This is going to sound weird . . .'

He laughs. 'No weirder than the last hour or two.'

'Can I . . . can I . . . touch your face?'

He gives me a puzzled look then raises his eyebrows.

'I told you it was weird.'

'It's not weird at all, Drew. You need to check that I'm real, don't you?'

'Mmm.' I bite down on my lip to stop myself from crying. It doesn't work and tears roll down my cheeks.

'It's OK, sweetheart.' He takes his hand off the gear stick and covers mine. He squeezes it tightly. 'It's OK. I'm not going anywhere. I can promise you that.'

'What happened? Why did you leave?'

'I never left you.' He looks at me sharply. 'I was taken.'

'By Dr Rothwell?'

He snorts softly. 'Not just him.'

I listen as he tells me how, ten years earlier, the Department of Education had brought together him, Tony, Dr Rothwell and various other psychologists to investigate solutions to help stem the number of children who were permanently excluded from school.

'That was a different Government,' he says, 'from the one we have now. They genuinely wanted to help those kids but the new lot . . .' He shakes his head. 'I'm assuming they're still in power. I didn't dream that, did I?'

'No,' I say. 'Unfortunately.'

'I can't say I'm surprised. Disappointed, yes, but not surprised. Anyway, when they got into power, they became interested in the project me, Tony and Phil were working on. They told us they didn't want a "special snowflake" solution – you know, a caring, nurturing approach – they wanted something more radical, cheaper, more immediate and guaranteed to work. They said they wanted us to come up with a way to make excluded kids useful members of society rather than dropouts, drug addicts and criminals.'

'I'm none of those,' Israel murmurs from behind us.

'I know you're not,' Dad says, glancing over his shoulder. 'I didn't agree with any of those statements and I made it perfectly clear that I thought the approach we'd developed was a good one. Not Phil though, he proposed a . . .' he makes quotation marks in the air with the fingers of his left hand ' . . . *radical and effective solution.* He suggested that we should look at the Korean and Cold War brainwashing techniques. I was horrified. Prisoners were brutalized using those techniques. There was no way I was going to agree to develop a treatment to use on teenagers. But the Home Secretary –'

'Jeff Kinsey?'

'No, his predecessor, Nigel Johnson. He said he'd sanction it, but only if we kept it on the down low. If the press found out, he'd deny all knowledge. By this point Tony was quite high in the academies feeding chain but he wasn't in charge. He told Nigel that if he pulled a few strings and arranged for him to become head he'd support the proposal. Not only that he'd source the kids for the first wave of treatment.'

I slap a hand over my mouth but it doesn't muffle my horrified gasp.

'I know.' Dad gives me a sideways look. 'Shocking, isn't it? I always sensed there was something dodgy about him but I didn't know the half of it.'

Oh God. He doesn't know. He's got no idea that Mum's married to Tony Coleman. That he's mine and Mason's stepdad. I need to tell him, but how? I twist round in my seat but Mason is still asleep.

Dad sighs heavily. 'Anyway. I told them they'd go ahead with the treatment over my dead body. I said I'd go to the press and blow the whistle but I didn't even make it as far as our house. When I went to the car park I was grabbed and thrown into the back of a van. They took me to an isolated house somewhere, I don't know, I didn't see much and then they –'

'They brainwashed you.'

'Yes.' He nods. 'They experimented on me. I was the first person to go through the treatment, but brainwashing only really works if it's continually reinforced and I was left to my own devices for a long time. Phil Rothwell was so convinced that my treatment was permanent that he let me wander freely through Norton House. I saw you and Mason but I thought you were apparitions, ghosts of a different life that didn't really exist. You'd appear but, as soon as I tried to work out who you were, you'd disappear. I felt as though I was getting a glimpse through a window into the real world, only for the curtain to snap shut whenever I looked too hard. I thought I was going mad. I nearly told Phil about the hallucinations but something deep inside me warned me not to. When I saw you and Mason being attacked by Rothwell and Hatch I felt so afraid. My children were being hurt and there was nothing I could do about it. It was my worst nightmare come true. Then something inside me snapped. It was like the curtains had been ripped of the wall and I was . . . I was me again.'

'You were de-conditioned.'

He gives me a surprised look. 'How do you know that term?'

I laugh softly. 'We've got a lot of catching up to do. Was it you who turned off the CCTV the first time me and Mouse tried to escape?'

'Yeah. It was. The friends were used to me wandering about, asking them questions and watching what they were doing. I was in the CCTV room with Destiny when I saw you on one of the screens. I recognized you. You'd changed so much but I knew you were my daughter.' He squeezes my hand. 'I could tell you were up to no good, I could see it in your face. Exactly the same expression you'd have if you were going to steal one of Mason's toys. Then, when the fight kicked off –'

'My fight?' Israel interjects.

'Yes. When that kicked off and Destiny was radioed to provide backup, I saw you and that one –' he jerks a thumb back towards Mouse '– hanging round by the door. I knew what you were going to do and turned off the CCTV. But by the time I'd walked back out the door, I'd forgotten who you were.'

'Dad, did you know someone called Dr Rebecca Cobey?'

His brow furrows as he stares through the windscreen at the rain-washed motorway that stretches into the distance. 'Yes, I think I did. Quite tall, dark hair, young. Younger than me anyway. Why?'

I don't answer. Instead I stare out of the window as the grey-green-brown countryside flashes past us. I should feel safe, being in the car with Dad and the others, already hundreds of miles from Norton House, but the tight feeling in the pit of my stomach is still there. It's so big, all *this*. Rebecca Cobey was murdered for trying to escape. The Home Secretary knows about it. The Minister for Education knows about it. The Prime Minister might even know it. What chance have we – a 'mad' psychologist and eight excluded kids – got of exposing the truth?

Chapter Forty-Five

Dad puts an arm around my shoulders and pulls me close. His does the same with Mason, standing on the other side of him and we shelter under the warmth of his thick grey overcoat as the wind whips our hair onto our cheeks and the Chancellor of the University of London delivers his speech in his deep baritone voice. I close my eyes and rewind time. I'm seven years old. It's Christmas Day and I've just opened two of my presents – a Nutcracker Barbie and a *Who Wants to Be a Millionaire* board game. Mason's opened two of his – a WWF real sounds arena and a *Thunderbirds* playset. The carpet is covered with discarded wrapping paper. The living room smells of chocolate, pine needles and coffee. Mum and Dad are sitting on the sofa, bleary-eyed, nursing their hot drinks but they're smiling. They don't take their eyes off us as Mason and I reach for the next present on our pile and rip off the wrapping paper. This is my world, these four walls, these three people. Nothing can hurt me. I am safe. But then the door to the hallway opens and Mrs H. and Dr Rothwell charge into the living room. They raise their right hands and point their tasers around the room. One by one, Mum, Dad and Mason disappear.

'Drew?' Mum touches my gloved hand as my eyes fly open.

'Are you OK, sweetheart? You were making a weird panting noise.'

'I'm OK,' I lie. I've barely slept since we got home. I wake up several times a night, convinced that I'm back at Norton House.

'We'll take you to see someone just as soon as this is over.' She glances up at Dad. 'Won't we, David?'

He nods gravely. 'They're all going to need some help after what they've been through.'

Dad drove all the way from Northumberland to London, only stopping to get petrol (Mouse had also lifted Dr Rothwell's wallet, it turned out). When we arrived in London, he parked outside a huge, red-brick gated building and shepherded us to the intercom.

'My name is Dr David Finch, he said. 'Myself, and these children were illegally abducted and subjected to practices outlawed by the United Nations Convention against Torture.'

After a pause, the gate swung open and Dad led us up four stone steps to a huge, black door.

'We're safe here,' he said. 'I promise.'

Things happened very quickly after that. We were interviewed in turn, by a kindly looking woman in a red suit and a man with oversized spectacles, then were told that we'd be spending the night in a secure hotel with a guard at each end of the corridor. If I was worried before, I was terrified when I was told that. I shared a room with Mouse and the female student, Yolanda. Mason and Israel shared a room, so did the other two boys, Alfie and Joe.

The next morning, we were shipped back to the red building in a van with blacked-out windows and told to wait in a boring, green-walled room that looked like some kind of gentlemen's club. Our parents had been contacted, we were told, and would be arriving to collect us. I had heart palpitations when I was told that – how would Dad react when Tony turned up with Mum? But Tony didn't turn up with Mum. She came alone, and he wasn't mentioned once the whole way home. No one really spoke. Mum drove but, whenever she stopped at a red light, she stared at Dad. I couldn't tell from the expression on her face whether she was happy to see him, annoyed with him or, like I was, extremely weirded out.

Dad didn't come back to the house. Mum dropped him off at a hotel in town. When he got out he hugged me and Mason and said he'd see us soon. I immediately burst into tears. I was terrified that, if we drove off, I'd never see him again. But I did. He came round the next day and he and Mum sat side by side on the sofa, close but not touching, and answered every question that Mason and I threw at them:

Where was Tony?

Arrested and in police custody.

What had happened to Jeff Kinsey?

Arrested and in police custody.

Dr Rothwell and Mrs H.?

The same.

The other kids at Norton House?

Returned to their parents.

The friends?

Arrested and in police custody. The orderlies too.

What was going to happen to the kids who'd already been brainwashed?

Dad said he was developing a treatment to reverse their conditioning.

And Norton House?

Closed and cordoned off from the public, pending a police investigation.

That was a month ago. Tony and Jeff Kinsey were released on bail after twenty-four hours. Pending further investigations, apparently, but Tony hasn't come back to our house. I peered out of my bedroom window when he turned up in a taxi to get some of his stuff. I couldn't see more than the top of Mum's head as she shoved a suitcase and a couple of bin bags at him but I saw how quickly she turned away when he tried to touch her arm. And I heard her crying after the front door slammed shut. Dad hasn't moved back in either. He's staying with some friends while he and Mum get to know each other again. I'm not a kid. I didn't expect them to fall into each other's arms after so many years apart, but I desperately want them to get back together. Mum's been talking about moving somewhere new. There are too many bad memories in Bristol, she says. I just hope she wants to bring Dad with us. Dr Rothwell and the Government stole eight years of our lives. I won't let them steal our future too.

Now, I hear a soft snuffling noise from behind me and slip out from under Dad's arm. Israel is doing his best to console Mouse but she looks as though her heart is breaking.

'Mouse!' I throw my arms around her and hold her tight. 'It's OK. Everything's going to be OK.'

'It's just so sad,' she says between sobs. 'She shouldn't have died. She was trying to do the right thing.'

Dr Cobey was the first therapist Mouse was assigned when

she arrived at Norton House. Unlike Mason, Mouse didn't open up to her. She didn't know what a decent, kind, woman she was and how appalled she was when she discovered what was going on in the treatment unit.

'In a couple of minutes,' the Chancellor says, 'we will unveil the plaque that will commemorate the life and work of Dr Rebecca Cobey but first, I'd like to invite Mason Finch to the stage.'

The huge crowd of people filling the small green park in the heart of the university grounds turn expectantly. The arrest of the Home Secretary was splashed across the front page of every newspaper in the country and, despite Mum and Dad's best efforts, mine and Mason's photos also appeared within the black and white pages. We can't go anywhere without people pointing and staring. That's another reason Mum wants us to move somewhere smaller. She knows how difficult it will be if we go back to our old schools. Then there's Lacey. Unlike the rest of us, who've been really careful about who we speak to, she – or her mum – have been pedalling her story to any media outlet that will give her the time of day. You'd think Lacey was the one who'd been given electric shocks and tortured, rather than someone who spent most of her days lying on beanbags gossiping. I haven't heard a thing about Jude and I'd rather it stayed that way.

Dad gives Mason's shoulder a squeeze and Mum gives him a kiss then my brother is off, shoulders back, walking through the crowd that parts in his wake.

'You OK?' Zed (I'll never be able to call her Evie) steps from behind Mouse and touches me on the arm. She never met Dr Cobey but she wanted to be here too, she said, to support us and pay homage to the woman whose bravery helped bring down the RRA. Charlie's standing beside her, back in his skate uniform. It took half a dozen sessions with Dad before his brainwashing was reversed but he's pretty much back to his old self now, according to Zed.

'Yeah,' I say. 'But Mason's bricking it. He must have read his speech half a dozen times on the train up here.'

'Drew.' Mum nudges me. 'He's on the stage.'

My brother looks so grown up, standing in front of a lectern, an enormous photo of Dr Cobey propped up on an easel to his right. It's the same photo I saw on her LinkedIn page. Mason clears his throat then looks down at his notes.

'My name is Mason Finch,' he says in a strong, confident voice, looking out at the audience. Only the piece of paper, fluttering in his hands, betrays his nerves. 'And Dr Rebecca Cobey saved my life . . .'

Out of the corner of my eye, I sense movement in the bushes at the edge of the park, and turn my head. There's a flash, so bright it makes me blink, and then it's gone.

'Bloody paps,' my dad grumbles. 'This is a private service. You'd think they'd respect Dr Cobey's memory but no, not if it means making a few quid –'

Mum nudges him and he falls silent.

'Dr Rebecca Cobey was a gentle woman,' Mason continues from the stage. 'Kind, warm and understanding. When everyone else seemed to have given up on me, Dr Cobey listened to me without judgement. Without knowing it, she reunited my family. A family I thought was forever broken. Through Rebecca Cobey's bravery she reunited me with the father I thought was dead.' He looks up again. 'I love you, Dad.'

There's another flash from the bushes but, this time, I see two circular shapes glint before the light becomes so bright I have to cover my eyes. That isn't a pap. It's someone with binoculars. And they're trained on us. I turn and glance up at the sky. The sun is covered by a cloud. They can't have been binoculars, reflecting the light back at me.

'You all right?' Mouse says.

I want to lie and tell her that I'm fine but I'm done with lying. It used to make me feel safe, hiding behind different aliases, pretending to be someone else, but finally I've realized that this lot won't judge me if I tell them how I feel. They know who I really am and they still want to be my friends. They've seen me at my best and my worst but they're still here, supporting me, because they care.

'I . . . er . . .' I look from Mouse to Israel to Zed to Charlie, then open my arms wide to gather them close and lower my voice. 'I thought I saw someone in the bushes, just now, watching us. Tell me I'm just being paranoid.'

'Um . . .' Mouse raises her eyebrows.

'Actually, Drew . . .' Israel says.

Zed and Charlie share a look. 'We saw him too.'

'Drew.' Dad taps me on the shoulder. 'Stop talking. Mason's about to mention about you.'

Me? Mason let Mum and Dad read his speech but he refused to let me read it. I assumed he was scared I'd criticize something he'd written.

'Listen.' Dad loops his arm around my shoulders and twists me back to face the stage. Mum squeezes my right hand. Her eyes are red and puffy and there are white streaks in her foundation.

'You Ok?' I ask her.

'I'm just . . . Mason's been saying the loveliest things.' She jerks her head towards the stage, indicating that we need to stop talking.

'I know we're here to celebrate the life and work of Dr Rebecca Cobey,' Mason says, his voice booming out of the speakers on either side of the stage, 'but I couldn't make this speech without mentioning another brave, courageous woman – my sister, Drew Finch. When Dr Cobey risked her life to pass my message to my sister, she had no way of knowing whether Drew would do anything about it. I haven't always been the best brother in the world –' he looks straight at me '– and if it had been the other way round I probably would have shrugged my shoulders and ignored the note. But not Drew. She put her own life in danger to save mine. She is brave. She is fearless. And I am so, so proud to call her my sister. Drew, and Doctor Cobey, the kids at Norton House salute you. Together, you saved us and I, and dozens of others, will never, ever be able to thank you enough.' His voice breaks on the word 'enough' and he drops his head, fighting back emotion. The crowd seems to hold its collective breath, waiting to see what he does next, then one person starts to clap. Then another and another and another until the whole park is clapping and cheering, smiling and crying. Mason raises his head, nods in embarrassment, then sprints off the stage and disappears back into the crowd.

'Drew Finch,' Dad says, tightening his grip on my shoulder and looking me straight in the eye, 'I have never been more proud of you and your brother than I am today.' He glances over the top of my head, at Mum. 'We've never been more proud. Have we, love?'

'Never.' As Mum starts to cry again, Mason fights his way through the crowd of back-slappers and well-wishers.

'Come here.' Dad opens his arms wide and pulls Mason into his chest. He pulls me in too, and Mum, so we're all bundled up together. My family. Finally, back together. This is all I ever wanted and I'm so happy I could cry but I'm scared too. Scared that something terrible is going to happen that will destroy my happiness.

'Drew,' Dad says. 'Drew, look at me.'

I turn my head to look at him. My dad, my amazing, resilient dad. And my mum, her tear-stained face, so full of love. And Mason with his stupid floppy fringe and mischievous eyes.

'It's OK, Drew,' Dad says. 'You can relax now. You don't have to protect us any more. There's nothing to fear. Sweetheart, it's over. Finished. Done.'

Acknowledgements

Huge thanks to my editor Anna Baggaley for her enthusiasm, excitement and hard work. *The Treatment* is a story I've wanted to tell for a long time and it's thanks to Anna and the team at HarperCollins HQ that Drew, Mouse and Mason have finally come to life within the pages of this book.

Thanks too to my amazing agent Madeleine Milburn for being so enthusiastic when I pitched the original idea to her – 'Prison Break meets One Flew Over the Cuckoo's Nest but for teens' – and for supporting and encouraging me as I wrote the first draft in the tiny snatches of time between my adult psychological thrillers. I'm also hugely grateful to Hayley Steed, Alice Sutherland-Hawes and Giles Milburn for all their hard work.

Thank you to Dr Jez Phillips - my go-to man for all things psychological. Despite being hugely busy he took the time to answer my questions about conditioning, reverse conditioning and brainwashing. Thanks to Dr Mark Moss for all his help.

I'd also like to thank my partner Chris Hall for patiently answering my questions about how Academies are run, how OFSTED works and other questions to do with the education system in the UK. As *The Treatment* is set in the near future I had to take a few liberties with the facts in order to make the story more dramatic so blame me for any inaccuracies, not him!

Big love to my family – Reg and Jenny Taylor, Bec Taylor, Lou Foley, David Taylor, Sophie Taylor (you'll have to read this book now I've dedicated it to you!), Rose Taylor and Sami Eaton and the boys. Also, Ana Hall, James Loach, Angela Aspell, Nick Aspell, Steve Hall, Guin Hall and Great Nan. And to my extended family – there are too many of you to mention but I appreciate all your support.

Kate, Rowan, Miranda, Tamsyn, Julie – I love you all.

Writing two books in one year was tough – I had very little downtime – and I need to send more love Chris's way for being so incredibly supportive and patient and for taking our son out and about on adventures at the weekend so I could grab a few extra hours. Seth, I love the fact you've started writing little stories of your own in your notebook before you go to bed. I'm so proud of you. You mean the world to me and I love you with all my heart.

Finally, I'd like to thank everyone who's bought a copy of this book. I hope you enjoyed it. Do get in touch on social media to let me know what you think and if you'd like to join the free CL Taylor Book Club you'll receive exclusive news, reviews, access to members-only giveaways and a free 9,000 word story, *The Lodger* just for signing up.

http://www.callytaylor.co.uk/cltaylorbookclub.html

Facebook: http://www.facebook.com/CallyTaylorAuthor
Twitter: http://www.twitter.com/CallyTaylor
Instagram: http://www.instagram.com/CLTaylorAuthor
Website: http://www.cltaylorauthor.com

HQ Young Adult
One Place. Many Stories

YOUNG
ADULT

The home of fun, contemporary
and meaningful Young Adult fiction.

Follow us online

 @HQYoungAdult

 @HQYoungAdult

 HQYoungAdult

 HQMusic